W9-BKF-873

What I Saw in California

What I Saw in California

Edwin Bryant

WHAT I SAW IN CALIFORNIA

Published in the United States by IndyPublish.com
Boston, Massachusetts

Published in July 2007

ISBN 1-4353-2450-1 (hardcover)
ISBN 1-4353-2441-2 (paperback)

To which is annexed, an Appendix

Containing official documents and letters authenticating the accounts of the quantities of gold found, with its actual value ascertained by chemical assay.

Also late communications containing accounts of the highest interest and importance from the gold districts.

With a Map.

1849

"All which I saw, and part of which I was."
—Dryden.

CHAPTER I.

For the general information of the reader, it will be proper to give a brief geographical sketch of California, and some account of its political and social institutions, as they have heretofore existed.

The district of country known geographically as Upper California is bounded on the north by Oregon, the forty-second degree of north latitude being the boundary line between the two territories; on the east by the Rocky Mountains and the Sierra de los Mimbres, a continuation of the same range; on the south by Sonora and Old or Lower California, and on the west by the Pacific Ocean. Its extent from north to south is about 700 miles, and from east to west from 600 to 800 miles, with an area of about 400,000 square miles. A small portion only of this extensive territory is fertile or inhabitable by civilized man, and this portion consists chiefly in the strip of country along the Pacific Ocean, about 700 miles in length, and from 100 to 150 in breadth, bounded on the east by the Sierra Nevada, and on the west by the Pacific. In speaking of Upper California this strip of country is what is generally referred to.

The largest river of Upper California is the Colorado or Red, which has a course of about 1000 miles, and empties into the Gulf of California in latitude about 32 degrees north. But little is known of the region through which this stream flows. The report of trappers, however, is that the river is canoned between high mountains and precipices a large portion of its course, and that its banks and the country generally through which it flows are arid, sandy, and barren. Green and Grand Rivers are its principal upper tributaries, both of which rise in the Rocky Mountains, and within the territories of the United States. The Gila is its lowest and largest branch, emptying into the Colorado, just above its mouth. Sevier and Virgin Rivers are also tributaries of the Colorado. Mary's River rises near latitude 42 degrees north, and has a course of about 400 miles, when its waters sink in the sands of the desert. This river is not laid down on any map which I have seen. The Sacramento and San Joaquin Rivers have each a course of from 300 to 400 miles, the first flowing from the north and the last from the south, and both emptying into the Bay of St. Francisco at the same point. They water the large and fertile valley lying between the Sierra Nevada and the coast range of mountains. I subjoin a description of the valley and river San Joaquin, from the pen of a gentleman (Dr. Marsh) who has explored the river from its source to its mouth.

"This noble valley is the first undoubtedly in California, and one of the most magnificent in the world. It is about 500 miles long, with an-average width of about fifty miles. It is bounded on the east by the great Snowy Mountains, and on the west by the low range, which in many places dwindles into insignificant hills, and has its northern terminus at the Strait of Carquines, on the Bay of San Francisco, and its southern near the Colorado River.

"The river of San Joaquin flows through the middle of the valley for about half of its extent, and thence diverges towards the eastern mountain, in which it has its source. About sixty miles further south is the northern end of the Buena Vista Lake, which is about one hundred miles long, and from ten to twenty wide. Still farther south, and near the western side of the valley, is another and much smaller lake.

"The great lake receives about a dozen tributaries on its eastern side, which all rise in the great range of the Snowy Mountains. Some of these streams flow through broad and fertile valleys within the mountain's range, and, from thence emerging, irrigate the plains of the great valley for the distance of twenty or thirty miles. The largest of these rivers is called by the Spanish inhabitants the river Reyes, and falls into the lake near its northern end; it is a well-timbered stream, and flows through a country of great fertility and beauty. The tributaries of the San Joaquin are all on the east side.

"On ascending the stream we first meet with the Stanislaus, a clear rapid mountain stream, some forty or fifty yards wide, with a considerable depth of water in its lower portion. The Mormons have commenced a settlement, called New Hope, and built some two or three houses near the mouth.

"There are considerable bodies of fertile land along the river, and the higher plains afford good pasturage.

"Ten miles higher up is the river of the Tawalomes; it is about the size of the Stanislaus, which it greatly resembles, except that the soil is somewhat better, and that it particularly abounds with salmon.

"Some thirty miles farther comes in the Merced, much the largest of the tributaries of the San Joaquin. The lands along and between the tributaries of the San Joaquin and the lake of Buena Vista form a fine pastoral region, with a good proportion of arable land, and a very inviting field for emigration. The whole of this region has been but imperfectly explored; enough, however, is known to make it certain that it is one of the most desirable regions on the continent.

"In the valleys of the rivers which come down from the great Snowy Mountains are vast bodies of pine, and red-wood, or cedar timber, and the streams afford water power to any desirable amount.

"The whole country east of the San Joaquin, and the water communication which connects it with the lakes, is considered, by the best judges, to be particularly adapted to the culture of the vine, which must necessarily become one of the principal agricultural resources of California."

The Salinas River empties into the Pacific, about twelve miles above Monterey. Bear River empties into the Great Salt Lake. The other streams of California are all small. In addition to the Great Salt Lake and the Utah Lake there are numerous small lakes in the Sierra Nevada. The San Joaquin is connected with Tule Lake, or Lake Buena Vista, a sheet of water about eighty miles in length and fifteen in breadth. A lake, not laid down in any map, and known as the Laguna among the Californians, is situated about sixty miles north of the Bay of San Francisco. It is between forty and sixty miles in length. The valleys in its vicinity are highly fertile, and romantically beautiful. In the vicinity of this lake there is a mountain of pure sulphur. There are also soda springs, and a great variety of other mineral waters, and minerals.

The principal mountains west of the eastern boundary of California (the Rocky Mountains) are the Bear River, Wahsatch, Utah, the Sierra Nevada, and the Coast range. The Wahsatch Mountains form the eastern rim of the "great interior basin." There are numerous ranges in this desert basin, all of which run north and south, and are separated from each other by spacious and barren valleys and plains. The Sierra Nevada range is of greater elevation than the Rocky Mountains. The summits of the most elevated peaks are covered with perpetual snow. This and the coast range run nearly parallel with the shore of the Pacific. The first is from 100 to 200 miles from the Pacific, and the last from forty to sixty miles. The valley between them is the most fertile portion of California.

Upper California was discovered in 1548, by Cabrillo, a Spanish navigator. In 1578, the northern portion of it was visited by Sir Francis Drake, who called it New Albion. It was first colonized by the Spaniards, in 1768, and formed a province of Mexico until after the revolution in that country. There have been numerous revolutions and civil wars in California within the last twenty years; but up to the conquest of the country by the United States in 1846, Mexican authority has generally been exercised over it.

The following description of the political and social condition of Upper California in 1822 is extracted and translated from a Spanish writer of that date. I have thought that the extract would not be uninteresting:—

"Government.—Upper California, on account of its small population, not being able to become a state of the great Mexican republic, takes the character of territory, the government of which is under the charge of a commandant-general, who exercises the charge of a superior political chief, whose attributes depend entirely upon the president of the republic and the general congress. But, to amplify the legislation of its centre, it has a deputation made up of seven vocals, the half of these individuals being removed every two years. The superior political chief presides at their sessions. The inhabitants of the territory are divided amongst the presidios, missions, and towns.

"Presidios.—The necessity of protecting the apostolic predication was the obligatory reason for forming the presidios, which were established according to circumstances. That of San Diego was the first; Santa Barbara, Monterey, and San Francisco were built afterwards. The form of all of them is nearly the same, and this is a square, containing about two hundred yards in each front, formed of a weak wall made of mud-bricks. Its height may be four yards in the interior of the square, and built on to the same wall. In its entire circumference are a chapel, storehouses, and houses for the commandant, officers, and troops, having at the entrance of the presidio quarters for a corps-de-garde.

"These buildings in the presidios, at the first idea, appear to have been sufficient, the only object having been for a defence against a surprise from the gentiles, or wild Indians in the immediate vicinity. But this cause having ceased, I believe they ought to be demolished, as they are daily threatening a complete ruin, and, from the very limited spaces of habitation, must be very incommodious to those who inhabit them. As to the exterior of the presidios, several private individuals have built some very decent houses, and, having evinced great emulation in this branch of business, I have no doubt but in a short time we shall see very considerable towns in California.

"At the distance of one, or at the most two miles from the presidio, and near to the anchoring-ground, is a fort, which has a few pieces of artillery of small calibre. The situation of most of them is very advantageous for the defence of the port, though the form of the walls, esplanades, and other imperfections which may be seen, make them very insignificant.

"The battalion of each presidio is made up of eighty or more horse soldiers, called cuera; besides these, it has a number of auxiliary troops and a detachment of artillery. The commandant of each presidio is the captain of its respective company, and besides the intervention, military and political, he has charge of all things relating to the marine department.

"Missions.—The missions contained in the territory are twenty-one. They were built at different epochs: that of San Diego, being the first, was built in 1769; its distance from the presidio of the same name is two leagues. The rest were built successively, according to circumstances and necessity. The last one was founded in the year 1822, under the name of San Francisco Dolores, and is the most northern of all.

"The edifices in some of those missions are more extensive than in others, but in form they are all nearly equal. They are all fabricated of mud-bricks, and the divisions are according to necessity. In all of them may be found commodious habitations for the ministers, storehouses to keep their goods in, proportional granaries, offices for soap-makers, weavers, blacksmiths, and large parterres, and horse and cattle pens, independent apartments for Indian youths of each sex, and all such offices as were necessary at the time of its institution. Contiguous to and communicating with the former is a church, forming a part of the edifices of each mission; they are all very proportionable, and are adorned with profusion.

"The Indians reside about two hundred yards distant from the above-mentioned edifice. This place is called the rancheria. Most of the missions are made up of very reduced quarters, built with mud-bricks, forming streets, while in others the Indians have been allowed to follow their primitive customs; their dwellings being a sort of huts, in a conical shape, which at the most do not exceed four yards in diameter, and the top of the cone may be elevated three yards. They are built of rough sticks, covered with bulrushes or grass, in such a manner as to completely protect the inhabitants from all the inclemencies of the weather. In my opinion, these rancherias are the most adequate to the natural uncleanliness of the Indians, as the families often renew them, burning the old ones, and immediately building others with the greatest facility. Opposite the rancherias, and near to the mission, is to be found a small garrison, with proportionate rooms, for a corporal and five soldiers with their families. This small garrison is quite sufficient to prevent any attempt of the Indians from taking effect, there having been some examples made, which causes the Indians to respect this small force. One of these pickets in a mission has a double object; besides keeping the Indians in subjection, they run post with a monthly correspondence, or with any extraordinaries that may be necessary for government.

"All the missions in this California are under the charge of religious men of the order of San Francisco. At the present time their number is twenty-seven, most of them of an advanced age. Each mission has one of these fathers for its administrator, and he holds absolute authority. The tilling of the ground, the gathering of the harvest, the slaughtering of cattle, the weaving, and everything that concerns the mission, is under the direction of the fathers, without any other person interfering in any way whatever, so that, if any one mission has the good fortune to be superintended by an industrious and discreet padre, the Indians disfrute in abundance all the real necessaries of life; at the same time the nakedness and misery of any one mission are a palpable proof of the inactivity of its director. The missions extend their possessions from one extremity of the territory to the other, and have made the limits of one mission from those of another. Though they do not require all this land for their agriculture and the maintenance of their stock, they have appropriated the whole; always strongly opposing any individual who may wish to settle himself or his family on any piece of land between them. But it is to be hoped that the new system of illustration, and the necessity of augmenting private properly, and the people of reason, will cause the government to take such adequate measures as will conciliate the interests of all. Amongst all the missions there are from twenty-one to twenty-two thousand Catholic Indians; but each mission has not an equal or a proportionate part in its congregation. Some have three or four thousand, whilst others have scarcely four hundred; and at this difference may be computed the riches of the missions in proportion. Besides the number of Indians already spoken of, each mission has a considerable number of gentiles, who live chiefly on farms annexed to the missions. The number of these is undetermined.

"The Indians are naturally filthy and careless, and their understanding is very limited. In the small arts they are not deficient in ideas of imitation but they never will be inventors. Their true character is that of being revengeful and timid, consequently they are very much addicted to treachery. They have no knowledge of benefits received, and ingratitude is common amongst them. The education they receive in their infancy is not the proper one to develope their reason, and, if it were, I do not believe them capable of any good impression. All these Indians, whether from the continual use of the sweat-house, or from their filthiness, or the little ventilation in their habitations, are weak and unvigorous; spasms and rheumatics, to which they are so much subject, are the consequences of their customs. But what most injures them, and prevents propagation, is the venereal disease, which most of them have very strongly, clearly proving that their humours are analogous to receiving the impressions of this contagion. From this reason may be deduced the enormous differences between the births and deaths, which, without doubt, is one-tenth per year in favour of the latter; but the missionaries do all in their power to prevent this, with respect to the catechumens situated near them.

"The general productions of the missions are, the breed of the larger class of cattle, and sheep, horses, wheat, maize or Indian corn, beans, peas, and other vegetables; though the productions of the missions situated more to the southward are more extensive, these producing the grape and olive in abundance. Of all these articles of production, the most lucrative is the large cattle, their hides and tallow affording an active commerce with foreign vessels on this coast. This being the only means the inhabitants, missionaries, or private individuals have of supplying their actual necessities, for this reason they give this branch all the impulse they possibly can, and on it generally place all their attention.

"It is now six years since they began to gather in hides and tallow for commerce. Formerly they merely took care of as many or as much as they required for their own private use, and the rest was thrown away as useless; but at this time the actual number of hides sold annually on board of foreign vessels amounts to thirty or forty thousand, and about the same amount of arrobas (twenty-five pounds) of tallow; and, in pursuing their present method, there is no doubt but in three or four years the amount of the exportation of each of these articles will be doubled. Flax, linen, wine, olive-oil, grain, and other agricultural productions, would be very extensive if there were stimulants to excite industry; but, this not being the case, there is just grain enough sown and reaped for the consumption of the inhabitants in the territory.

"The towns contained in this district are three; the most populous being that of Angeles, which has about twelve hundred souls; that of St. Joseph's of Guadaloupe may contain six hundred, and the village of Branciforte two hundred; they are all formed imperfectly and without order, each person having built his own house on the spot he thought most convenient for himself. The first of these pueblos is governed by its corresponding body of magistrates, composed of an alcalde or judge, four regidores or municipal officers, a syndic, and secretary; the second, of an alcalde, two regidores, a syndic, and secretary; and the third, on account of the smallness of its population, is subject to the commandancia of Monterey.

"The inhabitants of the towns are white, and, to distinguish them from the Indians, are vulgarly called people of reason. The number of these contained in the territory may be nearly five thousand. These families are divided amongst the pueblos and presidios. They are nearly all the descendants of a small number of individuals who came from the Mexican country, some as settlers, others in the service of the army, and accompanied by their wives. In the limited space of little more than fifty years the present generation has been formed.

"The whites are in general robust, healthy, and well made. Some of them are occupied in breeding and raising cattle, and cultivating small quantities of wheat and beans; but for want of sufficient land, for which they cannot obtain a rightful ownership, their labours are very limited. Others dedicate themselves to the service of arms. All the presidial companies are composed of the natives of the country, but the most of them are entirely indolent, it being very rare for any individual to strive to augment his fortune. Dancing, horse-riding, and gambling occupy all their time. The arts are entirely unknown, and I am doubtful if there is one individual who exercises any trade; very few who understand the first rudiments of letters, and the other sciences are unknown amongst them.

"The fecundity of the people of reason is extreme. It is very rare to find a married couple with less than five or six children, while there are hundreds who have from twelve to fifteen. Very few of them die in their youth, and in reaching the age of puberty are sure to see their grand-children. The age of eighty and one hundred has always been common in this climate; most infirmities are unknown here, and the freshness and robustness of the people show the beneficial influence of the climate; the women in particular have always the roses stamped on their cheeks. This beautiful species is without doubt the most active and laborious, all their vigilance in duties of the house, the cleanliness of their children, and attention to their husbands, dedicating all their leisure moments to some kind of occupation that may be useful towards their maintenance. Their clothing is always clean and decent, nakedness being entirely unknown in either sex.

"Ports and Commerce.—There are four ports, principal bays, in this territory, which take the names of the corresponding presidios. The best guarded is that of San Diego. That of San Francisco has many advantages. Santa Barbara is but middling in the best part of the season; at other times always bad. Besides the above-mentioned places, vessels sometimes anchor at Santa Cruz, San Luis Obispo, El Refugio, San Pedro, and San Juan, that they may obtain the productions of the missions nearest these last-mentioned places; but from an order sent by the minister of war, and circulated by the commandante-general, we are given to understand that no foreign vessel is permitted to anchor at any of these places, Monterey only excepted, notwithstanding the commandante-general has allowed the first three principal ports to remain open provisionally. Were it not so, there would undoubtedly be an end to all commerce with California, as I will quickly show.

"The only motive that induces foreign vessels to visit this coast is for the hides and tallow which they barter for in the territory. It is well known, that at any of these parts there is no possibility of realizing any money, for here it does not circulate. The goods imported by foreign vessels are intended to facilitate the purchase of the aforesaid articles, well knowing that the missions have no interest in money, but rather such goods as are necessary for the Indians, so that several persons who have brought goods to sell for nothing but money have not been able to sell them. It will appear very extraordinary that money should not be appreciated in a country where its value is so well known; but the reason may be easily perceived by attending to the circumstances of the territory.

"The quantity of hides gathered yearly is about thirty or forty thousand; and the arrobas of tallow, with very little difference, will be about the same. Averaging the price of each article at two dollars, we shall see that the intrinsic value in annual circulation in California is 140,000 dollars. This sum, divided between twenty-one missions, will give each one 6666 dollars. Supposing the only production of the country converted into money, with what would the Indians be clothed, and by what means would they be able to cover a thousand other necessaries? Money is useful in amplifying speculations; but in California, as yet, there are no speculations, and it productions are barely sufficient for the absolute necessary consumption. The same comparison may be made with respect to private individuals, who are able to gather a few hides and a few arrobas of tallow, these being in small quantities."

CHAPTER II.

Slaughtering of a bullock
Fossil oyster-shells
Skeleton of a whale on a high mountain
Arrive at mission of San Jose
Ruinous and desolate appearance of the mission
Pedlars
Landlady
Filth
Gardens of the mission
Fruit orchards
Empty warehouses and workshops
Foul lodgings.

September 13th.—We commenced to-day our journey from New Helvetia to San Francisco. Our party consisted, including myself, of Colonel Russell, Dr. McKee of Monterey, Mr. Pickett, a traveller in the country, recently from Oregon, and an Indian servant, who had been furnished us by Captain Sutter. Starting about 3 o'clock P.M., we travelled in a south course over a flat plain until sunset, and encamped near a small lake on the rancho of Mr. Murphy, near the Coscumne River, a tributary of the Sacramento, which heads near the foot of the Sierra Nevada. The stream is small, but the bottom-lands are extensive and rich. Mr. Murphy has been settled in California about two years, and, with his wife and several children, has resided at this place sixteen months, during which time he has erected a comfortable dwelling-house, and other necessary buildings and conveniences. His wheat crop was abundant this year; and he presented us with as much milk and fresh butter as we desired. The grass on the upland plain over which we have travelled is brown and crisp from the annual drought. In the low bottom it is still green. Distance 18 miles.

September 14.—We crossed the Coscumne River about a mile from our camp, and travelled over a level plain covered with luxuriant grass, and timbered with the evergreen oak, until three o'clock, when we crossed the Mickelemes River, another tributary of the Sacramento, and encamped on its southern bank in a beautiful grove of live oaks. The Mickelemes, where we crossed it, is considerably larger than the Coscumnes. The soil of the bottom appears to be very rich, and produces the finest qualities of grasses. The grass on the upland is also abundant, but at this time it is brown and dead. We passed through large tracts of wild oats during the day; the stalks are generally from three to five feet in length.

Our Indian servant, or vaquero, feigned sickness this morning, and we discharged him. As soon as he obtained his discharge, he was entirely relieved from the excru-

ciating agonies under which he had affected to be suffering for several hours.
Eating his breakfast, and mounting his horse, he galloped off in the direction of
the fort. We overtook this afternoon an English sailor, named Jack, who was travelling towards Monterey; and we employed him as cook and hostler for the
remainder of the journey.

A variety of autumnal flowers, generally of a brilliant yellow, are in bloom along
the beautiful and romantic bunks of the rivulet. Distance 25 miles.

September 15.—Our horses were frightened last night by bears, and this morning, with the exception of those which were picketed, had strayed so far that we
did not recover them until ten o'clock. Our route has continued over a flat plain,
generally covered with luxuriant grass, wild oats, and a variety of sparkling flowers. The soil is composed of a rich argillaceous loam. Large tracts of the land are
evidently subject to annual inundations. About noon we reached a small lake surrounded by tule. There being no trail for our guidance, we experienced some difficulty in shaping our course so as to strike the San Joaquin River at the usual
fording place. Our man Jack, by some neglect or mistake of his own, lost sight of
us, and we were compelled to proceed without him. This afternoon we saw several large droves of antelope and deer. Game of all kinds appears to be very abundant in this rich valley. Passing through large tracts of tule, we reached the San
Joaquin River at dark, and encamped on the eastern bank. Here we immediately
made large fires, and discharged pistols as signals to our man Jack, but he did not
come into camp. Distance 35 miles.

September 16.—Jack came into camp while we were breakfasting, leading his
tired horse. He had bivouacked on the plain, and, fearful that his horse would
break loose if he tied him, he held the animal by the bridle all night.

The ford of the San Joaquin is about forty or fifty miles from its mouth. At this
season the water is at its lowest stage. The stream at the ford is probably one hundred yards in breadth, and our animals crossed it without much difficulty, the
water reaching about midway of their bodies. Oak and small willows are the principal growth of wood skirting the river. Soon after we crossed the San Joaquin this
morning we met two men, couriers, bearing despatches from Commodore
Stockton, the governor and commander-in-chief in California, to Sutter's Fort.
Entering upon the broad plain, we passed, in about three miles, a small lake, the
water of which was so much impregnated with alkali as to be undrinkable. The
grass is brown and crisp, but the seed upon it is evidence that it had fully matured
before the drought affected it. The plain is furrowed with numerous deep trails,
made by the droves of wild horses, elk, deer, and antelope, which roam over and

graze upon it. The hunting sportsman can here enjoy his favourite pleasure to its fullest extent.

Having determined to deviate from our direct course, in order to visit the rancho of Dr. Marsh, we parted from Messrs. McKee and Pickett about noon. We passed during the afternoon several tule marshes, with which the plain of the San Joaquin is dotted. At a distance, the tule of these marshes presents the appearance of immense fields of ripened corn. The marshes are now nearly dry, and to shorten our journey we crossed several of them without difficulty. A month earlier, this would not have been practicable. I have but little doubt that these marshes would make fine rice plantations, and perhaps, if properly drained, they might produce the sugar-cane.

While pursuing our journey we frequently saw large droves of wild horses and elk grazing quietly upon the plain. No spectacle of moving life can present a more animated and beautiful appearance than a herd of wild horses. They were divided into droves of some one or two hundred. When they noticed us, attracted by curiosity to discover what we were, they would start and run almost with the fleetness of the wind in the direction towards us. But, arriving within a distance of two hundred yards, they would suddenly halt, and after bowing their necks into graceful curves, and looking steadily at us a few moments, with loud snortings they would wheel about and bound away with the same lightning speed. These evolutions they would repeat several times, until, having satisfied their curiosity, they would bid us a final adieu, and disappear behind the undulations of the plain.

The herds of elk were much more numerous. Some of them numbered at least two thousand, and with their immense antlers presented, when running, a very singular and picturesque appearance. We approached some of these herds within fifty yards before they took the alarm. Beef in California is so abundant, and of so fine a quality, that game is but little hunted, and not much prized, hence the elk, deer, and even antelope are comparatively very tame, and rarely run from the traveller, unless he rides very near them. Some of these elk are as large as a medium-sized Mexican mule.

We arrived at the rancho of Dr. Marsh about 5 o'clock P.M., greatly fatigued with the day's ride. The residence of Dr. M. is romantically situated, near the foot of one of the most elevated mountains in the range separating the valley of the San Joaquin from the plain surrounding the Bay of San Francisco. It is called "Mount Diablo," and may be seen in clear weather a great distance. The dwelling of Dr. M. is a small one-story house, rudely constructed of adobes, and divided into two or three apartments. The flooring is of earth, like the walls. A table or two, and some benches and a bed, are all the furniture it contains. Such are the privations to which those who settle in new countries must submit. Dr. M. is a native of New England, a graduate of Harvard University, and a gentleman of fine natural abilities and extensive scientific and literary acquirements. He emigrated to California some seven or eight years since, after having travelled through most of the Mexican States. He speaks the Spanish language fluently and correctly, and his accurate knowledge of Mexican institutions, laws, and customs was fully displayed in his conversation in regard to them. He obtained the grant of land upon which he now resides, some ten or twelve miles square, four or fire years ago; and although he has been constantly harassed by the wild Indians, who have several times stolen all his horses, and sometimes numbers of his cattle, he has succeeded in permanently establishing himself. The present number of cattle on his rancho is about two thousand, and the increase of the present year he estimates at five hundred.

I noticed near the house a vegetable garden, with the usual variety of vegetables. In another inclosure was the commencement of an extensive vineyard, the fruit of which (now ripe) exceeds in delicacy of flavour any grapes which I have ever tasted. This grape is not indigenous, but was introduced by the padres, when they first established themselves in the country. The soil and climate of California have probably improved it. Many of the clusters are eight and ten inches in length, and weigh several pounds. The fruit is of medium size, and in colour a dark purple. The rind is very thin, and when broken the pulp dissolves in the mouth immediately. Although Dr. M. has just commenced his vineyard, he has made several casks of wine this year, which is now in a stale of fermentation. I tasted here, for the first time, aguardiente, or brandy distilled from the Californian grape. Its flavour is not unpleasant, and age, I do not doubt, would render it equal to the brandies of France. Large quantities of wine and aguardiente are made from the extensive vineyards farther south. Dr. M. informed me that his lands had produced a hundredfold of wheat without irrigation. This yield seems almost incredible; but, if we can believe the statements of men of unimpeached veracity, there have been numerous instances of reproduction of wheat in California equalling and even exceeding this.

Some time in July, a vessel arrived at San Francisco from New York, which had been chartered and freighted principally by a party of Mormon emigrants, numbering between two and three hundred, women and children included. These Mormons are about making a settlement for agricultural purposes on the San Joaquin River, above the rancho of Dr. Marsh. Two of the women and one of the men are now here, waiting for the return of the main party, which has gone up the river to explore and select a suitable site for the settlement. The women are young, neatly dressed, and one of them may be called good-looking. Captain Gant, formerly of the U.S. Army, in very bad health, is also residing here. He has crossed the Rocky Mountains eight times, and, in various trapping excursions, has explored nearly every river between the settlements of the United States and the Pacific Ocean.

The house of Dr. Marsh being fully occupied, we made our beds in a shed, a short distance from it. Suspended from one of the poles forming the frame of this shed was a portion of the carcass of a recently slaughtered beef. The meat was very fat, the muscular portions of it presenting that marbled appearance, produced by a mixture of the fat and lean, so agreeable to the sight and palate of the epicure. The horned cattle of California, which I have thus far seen, are the largest and the handsomest in shape which I ever saw. There is certainly no breed in the United States equalling them in size. They, as well as the horses, subsist entirely on the indigenous grasses, at all seasons of the year; and such are the nutritious qualities of the herbage, that the former are always in condition for slaughtering, and the latter have as much flesh upon them as is desirable, unless (which is often the case) they are kept up at hard work and denied the privilege of eating, or are broken down by hard riding. The varieties of grass are very numerous, and nearly all of them are heavily seeded when ripe, and are equal, if not superior, as food for animals, to corn and oats. The horses are not as large as the breeds of the United States, but in point of symmetrical proportions and in capacity for endurance they are fully equal to our best breeds. The distance we have travelled to-day I estimate at thirty-five miles.

September 17.—The temperature of the mornings is most agreeable, and every other phenomenon accompanying it is correspondingly delightful to the senses. Our breakfast consisted of warm bread, made of unbolted flour, stewed beef, seasoned with chile colorado, a species of red pepper, and frijoles, a dark-coloured bean, with coffee. After breakfast I walked with Dr. Marsh to the summit of a conical hill, about a mile distant from his house, from which the view of the plain on the north, south, and east, and the more broken and mountainous country on the west, is very extensive and picturesque. The hills and the plain are ornamented with the evergreen oak, sometimes in clumps or groves, at others standing solitary. On the summits, and in the gorges of the mountains, the cedar, pine, and fir display their tall symmetrical shapes; and the San Joaquin, at a distance of about ten miles, is belted by a dense forest of oak, sycamore, and smaller timber and shrubbery. The herds of cattle are scattered over the plain,—some of them grazing upon the brown but nutritious grass; others sheltering themselves from the sun under the wide-spreading branches of the oaks. The tout ensemble of the landscape is charming.

Leaving Dr. Marsh's about three o'clock P.M., we travelled fifteen miles, over a rolling and well-watered country, covered generally with wild oats, and arrived at the residence of Mr. Robert Livermore just before dark. We were most kindly and hospitably received, and entertained by Mr. L. and his interesting family. After our mules and baggage had been cared for, we were introduced to the principal room in the house, which consisted of a number of small adobe buildings, erected apparently at different times, and connected together. Here we found chairs, and, for the first time in California, saw a side-board set out with glass tumblers and chinaware. A decanter of aguardiente, a bowl of loaf sugar, and a pitcher of cold water from the spring, were set before us, and, being duly honoured, had a most reviving influence upon our spirits as well as our corporeal energies. Suspended from the walls of the room were numerous coarse engravings, highly coloured with green, blue, and crimson paints, representing the Virgin Mary, and many of the saints. These engravings are held in great veneration by the devout Catholics of this country. In the corners of the room were two comfortable-looking beds, with clean white sheets and pillow-cases, a sight with which my eyes have not been greeted for many months.

The table was soon set out, and covered with a linen cloth of snowy whiteness, upon which were placed dishes of stewed beef, seasoned with chile Colorado, frijoles, and a plentiful supply of tortillas, with an excellent cup of tea, to the merits of which we did ample justice. Never were men blessed with better appetites than we are at the present time.

Mr. Livermore has been a resident of California nearly thirty years, and, having married into one of the wealthy families of the country, is the proprietor of some of the best lands for tillage and grazing. An arroyo, or small rivulet fed by springs, runs through his rancho, in such a course that, if expedient, he could, without much expense, irrigate one or two thousand acres. Irrigation in this part of California, however, seems to be entirely unnecessary for the production of wheat or any of the small grains. To produce maize, potatoes, and garden vegetables, irrigation is indispensable. Mr. Livermore has on his rancho about 3500 head of cattle. His horses, during the late disturbances, have nearly all been driven off or stolen by the Indians. I saw in his corral a flock of sheep numbering several hundred. They are of good size, and the mutton is said to be of an excellent quality, but the wool is coarse. It is, however, well adapted to the only manufacture of wool that is carried on in the country,—coarse blankets and serapes. But little attention is paid to hogs here, although the breeds are as fine as I have ever seen elsewhere. Beef being so abundant, and of a quality so superior, pork is not prized by the native Californians.

The Senora L. is the first Hispano-American lady I have seen since arriving in the country. She was dressed in a white cambric robe, loosely banded round the waist, and without ornament of any kind, except several rings on her small delicate fingers. Her complexion is that of a dark brunette, but lighter and more clear than the skin of most Californian women. The dark lustrous eye, the long black and glossy hair, the natural ease, grace, and vivacity of manners and conversation, characteristic of Spanish ladies, were fully displayed by her from the moment of our introduction. The children, especially two or three little senoritas, were very beautiful, and manifested a remarkable degree of sprightliness and intelligence. One of them presented me with a small basket wrought from a species of tough grass, and ornamented with the plumage of birds of a variety of brilliant colours. It was a beautiful specimen of Indian ingenuity.

Retiring to bed about ten o'clock, I enjoyed, the first time for four months, the luxury of clean sheets, with a mattress and a soft pillow. My enjoyment, however, was not unmixed with regret, for I noticed that several members of the family, to accommodate us with lodgings in the house, slept in the piazza outside. To have objected to sleeping in the house, however, would have been considered discourteous and offensive.

September 18.—Early this morning a bullock was brought up and slaughtered in front of the house. The process of slaughtering a beef is as follows: a vaquero, mounted on a trained horse, and provided with a lasso, proceeds to the place where the herd is grazing. Selecting an animal, he soon secures it by throwing the noose of the lasso over the horns, and fastening the other end around the pommel of the saddle. During the first struggles of the animal for liberty, which usually are very violent, the vaquero sits firmly in his seat, and keeps his horse in such a position that the fury and strength of the beast are wasted without producing any other result than his own exhaustion. The animal, soon ascertaining that he cannot release himself from the rope, submits to be pulled along to the place of execution. Arriving here, the vaquero winds the lasso round the legs of the doomed beast, and throws him to the ground, where he lies perfectly helpless and motionless. Dismounting from his horse, he then takes from his leggin the butcher-knife that he always carries with him, and sticks the animal in the throat. He soon bleeds to death, when, in an incredibly short space of time for such a performance, the carcass is flayed and quartered, and the meat is either roasting before the fire or simmering in the stew-pan. The lassoing and slaughter of a bullock is one of the most exciting sports of the Californians; and the daring horsemanship and dexterous use of the lariat usually displayed on these occasions are worthy of admiration. I could not but notice the Golgotha-like aspect of the grounds surrounding the house. The bones of cattle were thickly strewn in all directions, showing a terrible slaughter of the four-footed tribe and a prodigious consumption of flesh.

A carretada of fossil oyster—shells was shown to me by Mr. Livermore, which had been hauled for the purpose of being manufactured into lime. Some of these shells were eight inches in length, and of corresponding breadth and thickness. They were dug from a hill two or three miles distant, which is composed almost entirely of this fossil. Several bones belonging to the skeleton of a whale, discovered by Mr. L. on the summit of one of the highest elevations in the vicinity of his residence, were shown to me. The skeleton when discovered was nearly perfect and entirely exposed, and its elevation above the level of the sea between one and two thousand feet. How the huge aquatic monster, of which this skeleton is the remains, managed to make his dry bed on the summit of an elevated mountain, more experienced geologists than myself will hereafter determine. I have an opinion on the subject, however; but it is so contrary in some respects to the received geological theories, that I will not now hazard it.

Leaving Mr. Livermore's about nine o'clock A.M., we travelled three or four miles over a level plain, upon which immense herds of cattle were grazing. When we approached, they fled from us with as much alarm as herds of deer and elk. From this plain we entered a hilly country, covered to the summits of the elevations with wild oats and tufts or hunches of a species of grass, which remains green through the whole season. Cattle were scattered through these hills, and more sumptuous grazing they could not desire. Small streams of water, fed by springs, flow through the hollows and ravines, which, as well as the hill-sides, are timbered with the evergreen oak and a variety of smaller trees. About two o'clock, P.M., we crossed an arroyo which runs through a narrow gorge of the hills, and struck an artificial wagon-road, excavated and embanked so as to afford a passage for wheeled vehicles along the steep hill-side. A little farther on we crossed a very rudely constructed bridge. These are the first signs of road-making I have seen in the country. Emerging from the hills, the southern arm of the Bay of San Francisco came in view, separated from us by a broad and fertile plain, some ten or twelve miles in width, sloping gradually down to the shore of the bay, and watered by several small creeks and estuaries.

We soon entered through a narrow street the mission of San Jose, or St. Joseph. Passing the squares of one-story adobe buildings once inhabited by thousands of busy Indians, but now deserted, roofless, and crumbling into ruins, we reached the plaza in front of the church, and the massive two-story edifices occupied by the padres during the flourishing epoch of the establishment. These were in good repair; but the doors and windows, with the exception of one, were closed, and nothing of moving life was visible except a donkey or two, standing near a fountain which gushed its waters into a capacious stone trough. Dismounting from our mules, we entered the open door, and here we found two Frenchmen dressed in sailor costume, with a quantity of coarse shirts, pantaloons, stockings, and other small articles, together with aguardiente, which they designed retailing to such of the natives in the vicinity as chose to become their customers. They were itinerant merchants, or pedlars, and had opened their wares here for a day or two only, or so long as they could find purchasers.

Having determined to remain here the residue of the day and the night, we inquired of the Frenchmen if there was any family in the place that could furnish us with food. They directed us to a house on the opposite side of the plaza, to which we immediately repaired. The senora, a dark-skinned and rather shrivelled and filthy specimen of the fair sex, but with a black, sparkling, and intelligent eye, met us at the door of the miserable hovel, and invited us in. In one corner of this wretched and foul abode was a pile of raw hides, and in another a heap of wheat. The only furniture it contained were two small benches, or stools, one of which, being higher than the other, appeared to have been constructed for a table. We informed the senora that we were travellers, and wished refreshment and lodgings for the night. "Esta bueno, senores, esta bueno," was her reply; and she immediately left us, and, opening the door of the kitchen, commenced the preparation of our dinner. The interior of the kitchen, of which I had a good view through the door, was more revolting in its filthiness than the room in which we were seated. In a short time, so industrious was our hostess, our dinner, consisting of two plates of jerked beef, stewed, and seasoned with chile colorado, a plate of tortillas, and a bowl of coffee, was set out upon the most elevated stool. There were no knives, forks, or spoons, on the table. Our amiable landlady apologized for this deficiency of table-furniture, saying that she was "muy pobre" (very poor), and possessed none of these table implements. "Fingers were made before forks," and in our recent travels we had learned to use them as substitutes, so that we found no difficulty in conveying the meat from the plates to our mouths.

Belonging to the mission are two gardens, inclosed by high adobe walls. After dinner we visited one of these. The area of the inclosure contains fifteen or twenty acres of ground, the whole of which was planted with fruit trees and grape-vines. There are about six hundred pear trees, and a large number of apple and peach trees, all bearing fruit in great abundance and in full perfection. The quality of the pears is excellent, but the apples and peaches are indifferent. The grapes have been gathered, as I suppose, for I saw none upon the vines, which appeared healthy and vigorous. The gardens are irrigated with very little trouble, from large springs which flow from the hills a short distance above them. Numerous aqueducts, formerly conveying and distributing water over an extensive tract of land surrounding the mission, are still visible, but as the land is not now cultivated, they at present contain no water.

The mission buildings cover fifty acres of ground, perhaps more, and are all constructed of adobes with tile roofs. Those houses or barracks which were occupied by the Indian families are built in compact squares, one story in height. They are generally partitioned into two rooms, one fronting on the street, the other upon a court or corral in the rear. The main buildings of the mission are two stories in height, with wide corridors in front and rear. The walls are massive, and, if protected from the winter rains, will stand for ages. But if exposed to the storms by the decay of the projecting roofs, or by leaks in the main roof, they will soon crumble, or sink into shapeless heaps of mud. I passed through extensive warehouses and immense rooms, once occupied for the manufacture of woollen blankets and other articles, with the rude machinery still standing in them, but unemployed. Filth and desolation have taken the place of cleanliness and busy life. The granary was very capacious, and its dimensions were an evidence of the exuberant fertility of the soil, when properly cultivated under the superintendence of the padres. The calaboose is a miserable dark room of two apartments, one with a small loop-hole in the wall, the other a dungeon without light or ventilation. The stocks, and several other inventions for the punishment of offenders, are still standing in this prison. I requested permission to examine the interior of the church, but it was locked up, and no person in the mission was in possession of the key. Its length I should suppose is from one hundred to one hundred and twenty feet, and its breadth between thirty and forty, with small exterior pretensions to architectural ornament or symmetry of proportions.

Returning from our rambles about the mission, we found that our landlady had been reinforced by an elderly woman, whom she introduced as "mi madre," and two or three Indian muchachas, or girls, clad in a costume not differing much from that of our mother Eve. The latter were obese in their figures, and the mingled perspiration and filth standing upon their skins were any thing but agreeable to the eye. The two senoras, with these handmaids near them, were sitting in front of the house, busily engaged in executing some needlework.

Supper being prepared and discussed, our landlady informed us that she had a husband, who was absent, but would return in the course of the night, and, if he found strange men in the house, he would be much offended with her. She had therefore directed her muchachas to sweep out one of the deserted and half-ruined rooms on the opposite square, to which we could remove our baggage, and in which we could lodge during the night; and as soon as the necessary preparations were made, we retired to our dismal apartment. The "compound of villanous smells" which saluted our nostrils when we entered our dormitory for the night augured unfavourably for repose. The place had evidently been the abode of horses, cattle, pigs, and foul vermin of every description. But with the aid of a dark-coloured tallow-candle, which gave just light enough to display the murkiness and filth surrounding us, we spread our beds in the cleanest places, and laid down to rest. Distance travelled, 18 miles.

CHAPTER III.

Fast riding
Cruel treatment of horses
Arrive at the mission of San Francisco
A poor but hospitable family
Arrive at the town of San Francisco
W.A. Leidesdorff, Esq., American vice-consul
First view of the bay of San Francisco
Muchachos and Muchachas
Capt. Montgomery
U.S. sloop-of-war, Portsmouth
Town of San Francisco; its situation, appearance, population
Commerce of California
Extortion of the government and traders.

September 19.—Several Californians came into the mission during the night or early this morning; among them the husband of our hostess, who was very kind and cordial in his greetings.

While our man Jack was saddling and packing the mules, they gathered around us to the number of a dozen or more, and were desirous of trading their horses for articles of clothing; articles which many of them appeared to stand greatly in need of, but which we had not to part from. Their pertinacity exceeded the bounds of civility, as I thought; but I was not in a good humour, for the fleas, bugs, and other vermin, which infested our miserable lodgings, had caused me a sleepless night, by goring my body until the blood oozed from the skin in countless places. These ruinous missions are prolific generators, and the nurseries of vermin of all kinds, as the hapless traveller who tarries in them a few hours will learn to his sorrow. When these bloodthirsty assailants once make a lodgment in the clothing or bedding of the unfortunate victim of their attacks, such are their courage and perseverance, that they never capitulate. "Blood or death" is their motto;—the war against them, to be successful, must be a war of extermination.

Poor as our hostess was, she nevertheless was reluctant to receive any compensation for her hospitality. We, however, insisted upon her receiving a dollar from each of us (dos pesos), which she finally accepted; and after shaking us cordially by the hand she bade us an affectionate adios, and we proceeded on our journey.

From the Mission of San Jose to the Pueblo of San Jose, the distance is fifteen miles, for the most part over a level and highly fertile plain, producing a variety of indigenous grasses, among which I noticed several species of clover and mustard, large tracts of which we rode through, the stalks varying from six to ten feet in height. The plain is watered by several arroyos, skirted with timber, generally the evergreen oak.

We met this morning a Californian carreta, or travelling-cart, freighted with women and children, bound on a pleasure excursion. The carreta is the rudest specimen of the wheeled vehicle I have seen. The wheels are transverse sections of a log, and are usually about 2-1/2 feet in diameter, and varying in thickness from the centre to the rim. These wheels are coupled together by an axletree, into which a tongue is inserted. On the axletree and tongue rests a frame, constructed of square pieces of timber, six or eight feet in length, and four or five in breadth, into which are inserted a number of stakes about, four feet in length. This frame-work being covered and floored with raw hides, the carriage is complete. The car-reta which we met was drawn by two yokes of oxen, driven by an Indian vaque-ro, mounted on a horse. In the rear were two caballeros, riding fine spirited hors-es, with gaudy trappings. They were dressed in steeple-crowned glazed sombreros, serapes of fiery colours, velvet (cotton) calzoneros, white cambric calzoncillos, and leggins and shoes of undressed leather. Their spurs were of immense size.

The party halted as soon as we met them, the men touching their heavy som-breros, and uttering the usual salutation of the morning, "Buenos dios, senores," and shaking hands with us very cordially. The same salutation was repeated by all the senoras and senoritas in the carreta. In dress and personal appearance the women of this party were much inferior to the men. Their skins were dark, sal-low, and shrivelled; and their costume, a loose gown and reboso, were made of very common materials. The children, however, were all handsome, with sparkling eyes and ruddy complexions. Women and children were seated, a la Turque, on the bottom of the carreta, there being no raised seats in the vehicle.

We arrived at the Pueblo do San Jose about twelve o'clock. There being no hotels in California, we were much at a loss where to apply for refreshments and lodg-ings for the night. Soon, however, we were met by Captain Fisher, a native of Massachusetts, but a resident of this country for twenty years or more, who invit-ed us to his house. We were most civilly received by Senora F., who, although she did not speak English, seemed to understand it very well. She is a native of the southern Pacific coast of Mexico, and a lady of fine manners and personal appear-ance. Her oldest daughter, about thirteen years of age, is very beautiful. An excel-lent dinner was soon set out, with a variety of the native wines of California and other liquors. We could not have felt ourselves more happy and more at home, even at our own firesides and in the midst of our own families.

The Pueblo de San Jose is a village containing some six or eight hundred inhabi-tants. It is situated in what is called the "Pueblo Valley," about fifteen miles south of the southern shore of the Bay of San Francisco. Through a navigable creek, vessels of considerable burden can approach the town within a distance of five or six miles. The embarcadero, or landing, I think, is six miles from the Pueblo. The fertile plain between this and the town, at certain seasons of the year, is sometimes inundated. The "Pueblo Valley," which is eighty or one hundred miles in length, varying from ten to twenty in breadth, is well watered by the Rio Santa Clara and numerous arroyos, and is one of the most fertile and picturesque plains in California. For pastoral charms, fertility of soil, variety of productions, and delicious voluptuousness of climate and scenery, it cannot be surpassed. This valley, if properly cultivated, would alone produce breadstuffs enough to supply millions of population. The buildings of the Pueblo, with few exceptions, are constructed of adobes, and none of them have even the smallest pretensions to architectural taste or beauty. The church, which is situated near the centre of the town, exteriorly resembles a huge Dutch barn. The streets are irregular, every man having erected his house in a position most convenient to him. Aqueducts convey water from the Santa Clara River to all parts of the town. In the main plaza hundreds, perhaps thousands, of squirrels, whose abodes are under ground, have their residences. They are of a brownish colour, and about the size of our common gray squirrel. Emerging from their subterraneous abodes, they skip and leap about over the plaza without the least concern, no one molesting them.

The population of the place is composed chiefly of native Californian land-proprietors. Their ranchos are in the valley, but their residences and gardens are in the town. We visited this afternoon the garden of Señor Don Antonio Sugnol. He received us with much politeness, and conducted us through his garden. Apples, pears, peaches, figs, oranges, and grapes, with other fruits which I do not now recollect, were growing and ripening. The grape-vines were bowed to the ground with the luxuriance arid weight of the yield; and more delicious fruit I never tasted. From the garden we crossed over to a flouring-mill recently erected by a son-in-law of Don Antonio, a Frenchman by birth. The mill is a creditable enterprise to the proprietor, and he will coin money from its operations.

The Pueblo de San Jose is one of the oldest settlements in Alta California. Captain Fisher pointed out to me a house built of adobes, which has been standing between 80 and 90 years, and no house in the place appeared to be more substantial or in better repair. A garrison, composed of marines from the United States' ships, and volunteers enlisted from the American settlers in the country, is now stationed here. The post is under the command of Purser Watmough, of the United States sloop-of-war Portsmouth, commanded by Captain Montgomery. During the evening I visited several public places (bar-rooms), where I saw men and women engaged promiscuously at the game of monte. Gambling is a universal vice in California. All classes and both sexes participate in its excitements to some extent. The games, however, while I was present, were conducted with great propriety and decorum so far as the native Californians were concerned. The loud swearing and other turbulent demonstrations generally proceeded from the unsuccessful foreigners. I could not but observe the contrast between the two races in this respect. The one bore their losses with stoical composure and indifference; the other announced each unsuccessful bet with profane imprecations and maledictions. Excitement prompted the hazards of the former, avarice the latter.

September 20.—The morning was cloudy and cool; but the clouds broke away about nine o'clock, and the sun shone from a vapourless sky, as usual. We met, at the Pueblo, Mr. Grove Cook, a native of Gerrard county, Ky., but for many years a resident of California. He is the proprietor of a rancho in the vicinity. We determined to leave our mules in charge of Mr. Cook's vaquero, and proceed to San Francisco on hired horses. The distance from the Pueblo de San Jose to San Francisco is called sixty miles. The time occupied in performing the journey, on Californian horses at Californian speed, is generally six or seven hours. Procuring horses for the journey, and leaving our baggage, with the exception of a change of clothing, we left the Pueblo about eleven o'clock A.M.

The mission of Santa Clara is situated about two and a half miles from the town. A broad alameda, shaded by stately trees (elms and willows), planted by the padres, extends nearly the entire distance, forming a most beautiful drive or walk for equestrians or pedestrians. The motive of the padres in planting this avenue was to afford the devout senoras and senoritas a shade from the sun, when walking from the Pueblo to the church at the mission to attend mass. A few minutes over the smooth level road, at the rapid speed of our fresh Californian horses, brought us to the mission, where we halted to make our observations. This mission is not so extensive in its buildings as that of San Jose, but the houses are generally in better repair. They are constructed of adobes; the church was open, and, entering the interior, I found the walls hung with coarse paintings and engravings of the saints, etc., etc. The chancel decorated with numerous images, and symbolical ornaments used by the priests in their worship. Gold-paper, and tinsel, in barbaric taste, are plastered without stint upon nearly every object that meets the eye, so that, when on festive occasions the church is lighted, it must present a very glittering appearance.

The rich lands surrounding the mission are entirely neglected. I did not notice a foot of ground under cultivation, except the garden inclosure, which contained a variety of fruits and plants of the temperate and tropical climates. From want of care these are fast decaying. Some excellent pears were furnished us by Mrs. Bennett, an American lady, of Amazonian proportions, who, with her family of sons, has taken up her residence in one of the buildings of the mission. The picture of decay and ruin presented by this once flourishing establishment, surrounded by a country so fertile and scenery so enchanting, is a most melancholy spectacle to the passing traveller, and speaks a language of loud condemnation against the government.

Proceeding on our journey, we travelled fifteen miles over a flat plain, timbered with groves and parks of evergreen oaks, and covered with a great variety of grasses, wild oats, and mustard. So rank is the growth of mustard in many places, that it is with difficulty that a horse can penetrate through it. Numerous birds flitted from tree to tree, making the groves musical with their harmonious notes. The black-tailed deer bounded frequently across our path, and the lurking and stealthy coyotes were continually in view. We halted at a small cabin, with a corral near it, in order to breathe our horses, and refresh ourselves. Captain Fisher had kindly filled a small sack with bread, cheese, roasted beef, and a small jug of excellent schiedam. Entering the cabin, the interior of which was cleanly, we found a solitary woman, young, neatly dressed, and displaying many personal charms. With the characteristic ease and grace of a Spanish woman, she gave the usual salutation for the hour of the day, "Buenas tardes, senores caballeros;" to which we responded by a suitable salutation. We requested of our hostess some water, which she furnished us immediately, in an earthen bowl. Opening our sack of provisions, we spread them upon the table, and invited the senora to partake of them with us, which invitation she accepted without the slightest hesitation, and with much good-nature, vivacity, and even thankfulness for our politeness. There are no women in the world for whose manners nature has done so much, and for whom art and education, in this respect, have done so little, as these Hispano-American females on the coast of the Pacific. In their deportment towards strangers they are queens, when, in costume, they are peasants. None of them, according to our tastes, can be called beautiful; but what they want in complexion and regularity of feature is fully supplied by their kindliness, the soul and sympathy which beam from their dark eyes, and their grace and warmth of manners and expression.

While enjoying the pic-nic with our agreeable hostess, a caballada was driven into the corral by two vaqueros, and two gentlemen soon after came into the house. They were Messrs. Lightson and Murphy, from the Pueblo, bound for San Francisco, and had stopped to change their horses. We immediately made ready to accompany them, and were soon on the road again, travelling at racehorse speed; these gentlemen having furnished us with a change of horses, in order that we might be able to keep up with them.

To account for the fast travelling in California on horseback, it is necessary to explain the mode by which it is accomplished. A gentleman who starts upon a journey of one hundred miles, and wishes to perform the trip in a day, will take with him ten fresh horses and a vaquero. The eight loose horses are placed under the charge of the vaquero, and are driven in front, at the rate of ten or twelve miles an hour, according to the speed that is required for the journey. At the end of twenty miles, the horses which have been rode are discharged and turned into the caballada, and horses which have not been rode, but driven along without weight, are saddled and mounted and rode at the same speed, and so on to the end of the journey. If a horse gives out from inability to proceed at this gait, he is left on the road. The owner's brand is on him, and, if of any value, he can be recovered without difficulty. But in California no one thinks of stopping on the road, on account of the loss of a horse, or his inability to travel at the rate of ten or twelve miles an hour. Horseflesh is cheap, and the animal must go as long as he can, and when he cannot travel longer he is left, and another horse is substituted.

Twenty-five miles, at a rapid gait over a level and fertile plain, brought us to the rancho of Don Francisco Sanchez, where we halted to change horses. Breathing our animals a short time, we resumed our journey, and reached the mission of San Francisco Dolores, three miles from the town of San Francisco, just after sunset. Between the mission and the town the road is very sandy, and we determined to remain here for the night, corraling the loose animals, and picketing those we rode. It was some time, however, before we could find a house to lodge in. The foreign occupants of the mission buildings, to whom we applied for accommodations for the night, gave us no satisfaction. After several applications, we were at last accommodated by an old and very poor Californian Spaniard, who inhabited a small house in one of the ruinous squares, formerly occupied by the operative Indians. All that he had (and it was but little) was at our disposal. A more miserable supper I never sat down to; but the spirit of genuine hospitality in which it was given imparted to the poor viands a flavour that rendered the entertainment almost sumptuous—in my imagination. A cup of water cheerfully given to the weary and thirsty traveller, by him who has no more to part with, is worth a cask of wine grudgingly bestowed by the stingy or the ostentatious churl. Notwithstanding we preferred sleeping on our own blankets, these poor people would not suffer us to do it, but spread their own pallets on the earth floor of their miserable hut, and insisted so strongly upon our occupying them, that we could not refuse.

September 21.—We rose at daylight. The morning was clear, and our horses were shivering with the cold. The mission of San Francisco is situated at the northern terminus of the fertile plain over which we travelled yesterday, and at the foot, on the eastern side, of the coast range of mountains. These mountains are of considerable elevation. The shore of the Bay of San Francisco is about two miles distant from the mission. An arroyo waters the mission lands, and empties into the bay. The church of the mission, and the main buildings contiguous, are in tolerable repair. In the latter, several Mormon families, which arrived in the ship Brooklyn from New York, are quartered. As in the other missions I have passed through, the Indian quarters are crumbling into shapeless heaps of mud.

Our aged host, notwithstanding he is a pious Catholic, and considers us as heretics and heathens, gave us his benediction in a very impressive manner when we were about to start. Mounting our horses at sunrise, we travelled three miles over low ridges of sand-hills, with sufficient soil, however, to produce a thick growth of scrubby evergreen oak, and brambles of hawthorn, wild currant and gooseberry bushes, rose bushes, briers, etc. We reached the residence of Wm. A. Leidesdorff, Esq., late American vice-consul at San Francisco, when the sun was about an hour high. The morning was calm and beautiful. Not a ripple disturbed the placid and glassy surface of the magnificent bay and harbour, upon which rested at anchor thirty large vessels, consisting of whalemen, merchantmen, and the U.S. sloop-of-war Portsmouth, Captain Montgomery. Besides these, there were numerous small craft, giving to the harbour a commercial air, of which some of the large cities on the Atlantic coast would feel vain. The bay, from the town of San Francisco due east, is about twelve miles in breadth. An elevated range of hills bounds the view on the opposite side. These slope gradually down, and between them and the shore there is a broad and fertile plain, which is called the Contra Costa. There are several small islands in the bay, but they do not present a fertile appearance to the eye.

We were received with every mark of respectful attention and cordial hospitality by Mr. Leidesdorff. Mr. L. is a native of Denmark; was for some years a resident of the United States; but subsequently the captain of a merchant vessel, and has been established at this place as a merchant some five or six years. The house in which he resides, now under the process of completion, is the largest private building in the town. Being shown to a well-furnished room, we changed our travel-soiled clothing for a more civilized costume, by which time breakfast was announced, and we were ushered into a large dining-hall. In the centre stood a table, upon which was spread a substantial breakfast of stewed and fried beef, fried onions, and potatoes, bread, butter, and coffee. Our appetites were very sharp, and we did full justice to the merits of the fare before us. The servants waiting upon the table were an Indian muchachito and muchachita, about ten or twelve years of age. They had not been long from their wild rancherias, and knew but little of civilized life. Our host, however, who speaks, I believe, nearly every living language, whether of Christian, barbarian, or savage nations, seemed determined to impress upon their dull intellects the forms and customs of civilization. He scolded them with great vivacity, sometimes in their own tongue, sometimes in French, Spanish, Portuguese, Danish, German, and English, in accordance with the language in which he was thinking at the moment. It seemed to me that the little fat Indians were more confused than enlightened by his emphatic instructions. At the table, besides ourselves and host, was Lieutenant W.A. Bartlett, of the U.S. sloop-of-war Portsmouth, now acting as Alcalde of the town and district of San Francisco.

The Portsmouth, Commander Montgomery, is the only United States vessel of war now lying in the harbour. She is regarded as the finest vessel of her class belonging to our navy. By invitation of Lieutenant Bartlett, I went on board of her between ten and eleven o'clock. The crew and officers were assembled on deck to attend Divine service. They were all dressed with great neatness, and seemed to listen with deep attention to the Episcopal service and a sermon, which were read by Commander Montgomery, who is a member of the church.

In the afternoon I walked to the summit of one of the elevated hills in the vicinity of the town, from which I had a view of the entrance to the bay of San Francisco and of the Pacific Ocean. A thick fog hung over the ocean outside of the bay. The deep roar of the eternally restless waves, as they broke one after another upon the beach, or dashed against the rock-bound shore, could be heard with great distinctness, although some five or six miles distant. The entrance from the ocean into the bay is about a mile and half in breadth. The waters of the bay appear to have forced a passage through the elevated ridge of hills next to the shore of the Pacific. These rise abruptly on either side of the entrance. The water at the entrance and inside is of sufficient depth to admit the largest ship that was ever constructed; and so completely land-locked and protected from the winds is the harbour, that vessels can ride at anchor in perfect safety in all kinds of weather. The capacity of the harbour is sufficient for the accommodation of all the navies of the world.

The town of San Francisco is situated on the south side of the entrance, fronting on the bay, and about six miles from the ocean. The flow and ebb of the tide are sufficient to bring a vessel to the anchorage in front of the town and carry it outside, without the aid of wind, or even against an unfavourable wind. A more approachable harbour, or one of greater security, is unknown to navigators. The permanent population of the town is at this time between one and two hundred,[1] and is composed almost exclusively of foreigners. There are but two or three native Californian families in the place. The transient population, and at present it is quite numerous, consists of the garrison of marines stationed here, and the officers and crews attached to the merchant and whale ships lying in the harbour. The houses, with a few exceptions, are small adobes and frames, constructed without regard to architectural taste, convenience, or comfort. Very few of them have either chimneys or fire-places. The inhabitants contrive to live the year round without fires, except for cooking. The position of San Francisco for commerce is, without doubt, superior to any other port on the Pacific coast of North America. The country contiguous and contributory to it cannot be surpassed in fertility, healthfulness of climate, and beauty of scenery. It is capable of producing whatever is necessary to the sustenance of man, and many of the luxuries of tropical climates, not taking into the account the mineral wealth of the surrounding hills and mountains, which there is reason to believe is very great. This place is, doubtless, destined to become one of the largest and most opulent commercial cities in the world, and under American authority it will rise with astonishing rapidity. The principal merchants now established here are Messrs. Leidesdorff, Grimes and Davis, and Frank Ward, a young gentleman recently from New York. These houses carry on an extensive and profitable commerce with the interior, the Sandwich Islands, Oregon, and the southern coast of the Pacific. The produce of Oregon for exportation is flour, lumber, salmon, and cheese; of the Sandwich Islands, sugar, coffee, and preserved tropical fruits.

California, until recently, has had no commerce, in the broad signification of the term. A few commercial houses of Boston and New York have monopolized all the trade on this coast for a number of years. These houses have sent out ships freighted with cargoes of dry goods and a variety of knick-knacks saleable in the country. The ships are fitted up for the retail sale of these articles, and trade from port to port, vending their wares on board to the rancheros at prices that would be astonishing at home. For instance, the price of common brown cotton cloth is one dollar per yard, and other articles in this and even greater proportion of advance upon home prices. They receive in payment for their wares, hides and tallow. The price of a dry hide is ordinarily one dollar and fifty cents. The price of tallow I do not know. When the ship has disposed of her cargo, she is loaded with hides, and returns to Boston, where the hides bring about four or five dollars, according to the fluctuations of the market. Immense fortunes have been made by this trade; and between the government of Mexico and the traders on the coast California has been literally skinned, annually, for the last thirty years. Of natural wealth the population of California possess a superabundance, and are immensely rich; still, such have been the extortionate prices that they have been compelled to pay for their commonest artificial luxuries and wearing-apparel, that generally they are but indifferently provided with the ordinary necessaries of civilized life. For a suit of clothes, which in New York or Boston would cost seven-ty-five dollars, the Californian has been compelled to pay five times that sum in hides at one dollar and fifty cents; so that a caballero, to clothe himself genteelly, has been obliged, as often as he renewed his dress, to sacrifice about two hundred of the cattle on his rancho. No people, whether males or females, are more fond of display; no people have paid more dearly to gratify this vanity; and yet no civ-ilized people I have seen are so deficient in what they most covet.

[1] This was in September, 1846. In June, 1847, when I left San Francisco, on my return to the United States, the population had   increased to about twelve hundred, and houses were rising in all   directions.

CHAPTER IV.

From the 21st of September to the 13th of October I remained at San Francisco. The weather during this period was uniformly clear. The climate of San Francisco is peculiar and local, from its position. During the summer and autumnal months, the wind on this coast blows from the west and northwest, directly from the ocean. The mornings here are usually calm and pleasantly warm. About twelve o'clock M., the wind blows strong from the ocean, through the entrance of the bay, rendering the temperature cool enough for woollen clothing in midsummer. About sunset the wind dies away, and the evenings and nights are comparatively calm. In the winter months the wind blows in soft and gentle breezes from the south-east, and the temperature is agreeable, the thermometer rarely sinking below 50 deg. When the winds blow from the ocean, it never rains; when they blow from the land, as they do during the winter and spring months, the weather is showery, and resembles that of the month of May in the same latitude on the Atlantic coast. The coolness of the climate and briskness of the air above described are confined to particular positions on the coast, and the description in this respect is not applicable to the interior of the country, nor even to other localities immediately on the coast.

On the 21st, by invitation of Captain Montgomery, I dined on board of the sloop-of-war Portsmouth. The party, including myself, consisted of Colonel Russell, Mr. Jacob, Lieutenant Bartlett, and a son of Captain M. There are few if any officers in our navy more highly and universally esteemed, for their moral qualities and professional merits, than Captain M. He is a sincere Christian, a brave officer, and an accomplished gentleman. Under the orders of Commodore Sloat, he first raised the American flag in San Francisco. We spent the afternoon most agreeably, and the refined hospitality, courteous manners, and intelligent and interesting conversation of our host made us regret the rapidly fleeting moments. The wines on the table were the produce of the vine of California, and, having attained age, were of an excellent quality in substance and flavour.

I attended a supper-party given this evening by Mr. Frank Ward. The party was composed of citizens of the town, and officers of the navy and the merchant and whale ships in the harbour. In such a company as was here assembled, it was very difficult for me to realize that I was many thousand miles from, home, in a strange and foreign country. All the faces about me were American, and there was nothing in scene or sentiment to remind the guests of their remoteness from their native shores. Indeed, it seems to be a settled opinion, that California is henceforth to compose a part of the United States, and every American who is now here considers himself as treading upon his own soil, as much as if he were in one of the old thirteen revolutionary states. Song, sentiment, story, and wit heightened the enjoyments of the excellent entertainment of our host, and the jovial party did not separate until a late hour of the night. The guests, as may be supposed, were composed chiefly of gentlemen who had, from their pursuits, travelled over most of the world—had seen developments of human character under every variety of circumstance, and observed society, civilized, barbarous, and savage, in all its phases. Their conversation, therefore, when around the convivial board, possessed an unhackneyed freshness and raciness highly entertaining and instructive.

On the 27th of September, the U.S. frigate Congress, Captain Livingston, bearing the broad pennant of Commodore Stockton, and the U.S. frigate Savannah,

Captain Mervine, anchored in the harbour, having sailed from Monterey a day or two previously. The arrival of these large men-of-war produced an increase of the bustle in the small town. Blue coats and bright buttons (the naval uniform) became the prevailing costume at the billiard-rooms and other public places, and the plain dress of a private citizen might be regarded as a badge of distinction.

On the 1st of October a courier arrived from the south with intelligence that the Californians at Los Angeles had organized a force and rebelled against the authority of the Americans—that they had also captured an American merchant-vessel lying at San Pedro, the port of the city of Angels, about thirty miles distant, and robbed it of a quantity of merchandise and specie. Whether this latter report was or was not true, I do not know—the former was correct. The frigate Savannah sailed for Los Angeles immediately.

Among those American naval officers whose agreeable acquaintance I made at San Francisco, was Mr. James F. Schenck, first-lieutenant of the frigate Congress, brother of the distinguished member of congress from Ohio of that name,—a native of Dayton, Ohio,—a gentleman of intelligence, keen wit, and a most accomplished officer. The officers of our navy are our representatives in foreign countries, and they are generally such representatives as their constituents have reason to feel proud of. Their chivalry, patriotism, gentlemanlike deportment, and professional skill cannot be too much admired and applauded by their countrymen. I shall ever feel grateful to the naval officers of the Pacific squadron for their numerous civilities during my sojourn on the Pacific coast.

Among the novelties presented while at San Francisco was a trial by jury—the second tribunal of this kind which had been organized in California. The trial took place before Judge Bartlett, and the litigants were two Mormons. Counsel was employed on both sides. Some of the forms of American judicial proceedings were observed, and many of the legal technicalities and nice flaws, so often urged in common-law courts, were here argued by the learned counsel of the parties, with a vehemence of language and gesticulation with which I thought the legal learning and acumen displayed did not correspond. The proceedings were a mixture, made up of common law, equity, and a sprinkling of military despotism—which last ingredient the court was compelled to employ, when entangled in the intricate meshes woven by the counsel for the litigants, in order to extricate itself. The jury, after the case was referred to them, were what is called "hung;" they could not agree, and the matters in issue, therefore, remained exactly where they were before the proceedings were commenced.

I attended one evening a fandango given by Mr. Ridley, an English gentleman, whose wife is a Californian lady. Several of the senoras and senoritas from the ran-

chos of the vicinity were present. The Californian ladies dance with much ease
and grace. The waltz appears to be a favourite with them. Smoking is not pro-
hibited in these assemblies, nor is it confined to the gentlemen. The cigarita is
freely used by the senoras and senoritas, and they puff it with much gusto while
threading the mazes of the cotillion or swinging in the waltz.

I had the pleasure of being introduced, at the residence of Mr. Leidesdorff, to two
young ladies, sisters and belles in Alta California. They are members of an old and
numerous family on the Contra Costa. Their names are singular indeed, for, if I
heard them correctly, one of them was called Donna Maria Jesus, and the other
Donna Maria Conception. They were interesting and graceful young ladies, with
regular features, symmetrical figures, and their dark eyes flashed with all the intelligence and passion characteristic of Spanish women.

Among the gentlemen with whom I met soon after my arrival at San Francisco,
and whoso acquaintance I afterwards cultivated, were Mr. E. Grimes and Mr. N.
Spear, both natives of Massachusetts, but residents of this coast and of the Pacific
Islands, for many years. They may be called the patriarchs of American pioneers
on the Pacific. After forming an acquaintance with Mr. G., if any one were to say
to me that   "Old Grimes is dead, that good old man,"

I should not hesitate to contradict him with emphasis; for he is still living, and
possesses all the charities and virtues which can adorn human nature, with some
of the eccentricities of his name-sake in the song. By leading a life of peril and
adventure on the Pacific Ocean for fifty years he has accumulated a large fortune,
and is a man now proverbial for his integrity, candour, and charities. Both of these
gentlemen have been largely engaged in the local commerce of the Pacific. Mr. S.,
some twenty-five or thirty years ago, colonized one of the Cannibal Islands, and
remained upon it with the colony for nearly two years. The attempt to introduce
agriculture into the island was a failure, and the enterprise was afterwards abandoned.

On the evening of the third of October, it having been announced that
Commodore Stockton would land on the fifth, a public meeting of the citizens
was called by the alcalde, for the purpose of adopting suitable arrangements for
his reception, in his civic capacity as governor. The meeting was convened in the
plaza (Portsmouth Square). Colonel Russell was appointed chairman, and on
motion of E. Bryant a committee was appointed to make all necessary and suitable arrangements for the reception of his excellency, Governor Stockton. The following account of this pageant I extract from the "California" newspaper of
October 24th, 1846.

"Agreeable to public notice, a large number of the citizens of San Francisco and vicinity assembled in Portsmouth Square for the purpose of meeting his excellency Robert F. Stockton, to welcome his arrival, and offer him the hospitalities of the city. At ten o'clock, a procession was formed, led by the Chief Marshal of the day, supported on either hand by two aids, followed by an excellent band of music—a military escort, under command of Captain J. Zeilen, U.S.M.C.—Captain John B. Montgomery and suite—Magistracy of the District, and the Orator of the day—Foreign Consuls—Captain John Paty, Senior Captain of the Hawanian Navy—Lieutenant-Commanding Ruducoff, Russian Navy, and Lieutenant-Commanding Bonnett, French Navy. The procession was closed by the Committee of Arrangements, captains of ships in port, and a long line of citizens.

"General Mariano Guadaloupe Vallejo, with several others who had held office under the late government, took their appropriate place in the line.

"The procession moved in fine style down Portsmouth Street to the landing, and formed a line in Water Street. The Governor-General landed from his barge, and was met on the wharf by Captain John B. Montgomery, U.S.N., Judge W.A. Bartlett, and Marshal of the day (Frank Ward), who conducted him to the front of the line, and presented him to the procession, through the orator of the day, Colonel Russell, who addressed the commodore."

When the governor and commander-in-chief had closed his reply, the procession moved through the principal streets, and halted in front of Captain Leidesdorff's residence, where the governor and suite entered, and was presented to a number of ladies, who welcomed him to the shores of California. After which a large portion of the procession accompanied the governor, on horseback, to the mission of San Francisco Dolores, several miles in the country, and returned to an excellent collation prepared by the committee of arrangements, at the house of Captain Leidesdorff. After the cloth was removed, the usual number of regular toasts, prepared by the committee of arrangements, and numerous volunteer sentiments by the members of the company, were drunk with many demonstrations of enthusiasm, and several speeches were made. In response to a complimentary toast, Commodore Stockton made an eloquent address of an hour's length. The toasts given in English were translated into Spanish, and those given in Spanish were translated into English. A ball in honour of the occasion was given by the committee of arrangements in the evening, which was attended by all the ladies, native and foreign, in the town and vicinity, the naval officers attached to the three ships of war, and the captains of the merchant vessels lying in the harbour. So seductive were the festivities of the day and the pleasures of the dance, that they were not closed until a late hour of the night, or rather until an early hour in the morning.

Among the numerous vessels of many nations at anchor in the harbour is a Russian brig from Sitca, the central port of the Russian-American Fur Company, on the northwestern coast of this continent. She is commanded by Lieutenant Ruducoff of the Russian navy, and is here to be freighted with wheat to supply that settlement with breadstuff. Sitca is situated in a high northern latitude, and has a population of some four or five thousand inhabitants. A large portion of these, I conjecture, are christianized natives or Indians. Many of the crew of this vessel are the aborigines of the country to which she belongs, and from which she last sailed. I noticed, however, from an inscription, that the brig was built at Newburyport, Massachusetts, showing that the autocrat of all the Russias is tributary, to some extent, to the free Yankees of New England for his naval equipment. On the 11th of October, by invitation of Lieutenant Ruducoff, in company of Mr. Jacob and Captain Leidesdorff, I dined on board this vessel. The Russian customs are in some respects peculiar. Soon after we reached the vessel and were shown into the cabin, a lunch was served up. This consisted of a variety of dried and smoked fish, pickled fish-roe, and other hyperborean pickles, the nature of which, whether animal or vegetable, I could not determine. Various wines and liquors accompanied this lunch, the discussion of which lasted until an Indian servant, a native of the north-pole, or thereabouts, announced dinner. We were then shown into a handsomely furnished dining-cabin, where the table was spread. The dinner consisted of several courses, some of which were peculiarly Russian or Sitcan, and I regret that my culinary knowledge is not equal to the task of describing them, for the benefit of epicures of a more southern region than the place of their invention. They were certainly very delightful to the palate. The afternoon glided away most agreeably.

On the 12th of October, Captain Fremont, with a number of volunteers destined for the south, to co-operate with Commodore Stockton in the suppression of the reported rebellion at Los Angeles, arrived at San Francisco from the Sacramento. I had previously offered my services, and Mr. Jacob had done the same, to Commodore Stockton, as volunteers in this expedition, if they were necessary or desirable. They were now repeated. Although travellers in the country, we were American citizens, and we felt under obligation to assist in defending the flag of our country wherever it had been planted by proper authority. At this time we were given to understand that a larger force than was already organised was not considered necessary for the expedition.

CHAPTER V.

October 13.—This morning the United States frigate Congress, Commodore Stockton, and the merchant-ship Sterling, employed to transport the volunteers under the command of Captain Fremont (one hundred and eighty in number), sailed for the south. The destination of these vessels was understood to be San Pedro or San Diego. While those vessels were leaving the harbour, accompanied by Mr. Jacob, I took passage for Sonoma in a cutter belonging to the sloop-of-war Portsmouth. Sonoma is situated on the northern side of the Bay of San Francisco, about 15 miles from the shore, and about 45 miles from the town of San Francisco. Sonoma creek is navigable for vessels of considerable burden to within four miles of the town.

Among the passengers in the boat were Mr. Ide, who acted so conspicuous a part in what is called the "Bear Revolution," and Messrs. Nash and Grigsby, who were likewise prominent in this movement. The boat was manned by six sailors and a cockswain. We passed Yerba Buena, Bird, and several other small islands in the bay. Some of these are white, as if covered with snow, from the deposit upon them of bird-manure. Tens of thousands of wild geese, ducks, gulls, and other water-fowls, were perched upon them, or sporting in the waters of the bay, making a prodigious cackling and clatter with their voices and wings. By the aid of oars and sails we reached the mouth of Sonoma creek about 9 o'clock at night, where we landed and encamped on the low marsh which borders the bay on this side. The marshes contiguous to the Bay of San Francisco are extensive, and with little trouble I believe they could be reclaimed and transformed into valuable and productive rice plantations. Having made our supper on raw salt pork and bread generously furnished by the sailors, as soon as we landed, we spread our blankets on the damp and rank vegetation and slept soundly until morning.

October 14.—Wind and tide being favourable, at daylight we proceeded up the serpentine creek, which winds through a flat and fertile plain, sometimes marshy, at others more elevated and dry, to the embarcadero, ten or twelve miles from the bay. We landed here between nine and ten o'clock, A.M. All the passengers, except ourselves, proceeded immediately to the town. By them we sent for a cart to transport our saddles, bridles, blankets, and other baggage, which we had brought with us. While some of the sailors were preparing breakfast, others, with their muskets, shot wild geese, with which the plain was covered. An excellent breakfast was prepared in a short time by our sailor companions, of which we partook with them. No benevolent old gentleman provides more bountifully for his servants than "Uncle Sam." These sailors, from the regular rations served out to them from their ship, gave an excellent breakfast, of bread, butter, coffee, tea, fresh beefsteaks, fried salt pork, cheese, pickles, and a variety of other delicacies, to which we had been unaccustomed for several months, and which cannot be obtained at present in this country. They all said that their rations were more than ample in quantity, and excellent in quality, and that no government was so generous in supplying its sailors as the government of the United States. They appeared to be happy, and contented with their condition and service, and animated with a patriotic pride for the honour of their country, and the flag under which they sailed. The open frankness and honest patriotism of these single-heart-ed and weather-beaten tars gave a spice and flavour to our entertainment which I shall not soon forget.

From the embarcadero we walked, under the influence of the rays of an almost broiling sun, four miles to the town of Sonoma. The plain, which lies between the landing and Sonoma, is timbered sparsely with evergreen oaks. The luxuriant grass is now brown and crisp. The hills surrounding this beautiful valley or plain are gentle, sloping, highly picturesque, and covered to their tops with wild oats. Reaching Sonoma, we procured lodgings in a large and half-finished adobe house, erected by Don Salvador Vallejo, but now occupied by Mr. Griffith, an American emigrant, originally from North Carolina. Sonoma is one of the old mission establishments of California; but there is now scarcely a mission building stand-ing, most of them having fallen into shapeless masses of mud; and a few years will prostrate the roofless walls which are now standing. The principal houses in the place are the residences of Gen. Don Mariano Guadaloupe Vallejo; his brother-in-law, Mr. J.P. Leese, an American; and his brother, Don Salvador Vallejo. The quartel, a barn-like adobe house, faces the public square. The town presents a most dull and ruinous appearance; but the country surrounding it is exuberantly fertile, and romantically picturesque, and Sonoma, under American authority, and with an American population, will very soon become a secondary commer-cial point, and a delightful residence. Most of the buildings are erected around a plaza, about two hundred yards square. The only ornaments in this square are numerous skulls and dislocated skeletons of slaughtered beeves, with which hideous remains the ground is strewn. Cold and warm springs gush from the hills near the town, and supply, at all seasons, a sufficiency of water to irrigate any required extent of ground on the plain below. I noticed outside of the square sev-eral groves of peach and other fruit trees, and vineyards, which were planted here by the padres; but the walls and fences that once surrounded them are now fall-en, or have been consumed for fuel; and they are exposed to the mercies of the immense herds of cattle which roam over and graze upon the plain.

October 15.—I do not like to trouble the reader with a frequent reference to the myriads of fleas and other vermin which infest the rancherias and old mission establishments in California; but, if any sinning soul ever suffered the punish-ments of purgatory before leaving its tenement of clay, those torments were endured by myself last night. When I rose from my blankets this morning, after a sleepless night, I do not think there was an inch square of my body that did not exhibit the inflammation consequent upon a puncture by a flea, or some other equally rabid and poisonous insect. Small-pox, erysipelas, measles, and scarlet-fever combined, could not have imparted to my skin a more inflamed and san-

guineous appearance. The multitudes of these insects, however, have been generated by Indian filthiness. They do not disturb the inmates of those casas where
cleanliness prevails.

Having letters of introduction to General Vallejo and Mr. Leese, I delivered them
this morning. General Vallejo is a native Californian, and a gentleman of intelligence and taste far superior to most of his countrymen. The interior of his house
presented a different appearance from any house occupied by native Californians
which I have entered since I have been in the country. Every apartment, even the
main entrance-hall and corridors, were scrupulously clean, and presented an air
of comfort which I have not elsewhere seen in California. The parlour was furnished with handsome chairs, sofas, mirrors, and tables, of mahogany framework,
and a fine piano, the first I have seen in the country. Several paintings and some
superior engravings ornamented the walls. Senora Vallejo is a lady of charming
personal appearance, and possesses in the highest degree that natural grace, ease,
and warmth of manner which render Spanish ladies so attractive and fascinating
to the stranger. The children, some five or six in number, were all beautiful and
interesting. General V. is, I believe, strongly desirous that the United States shall
retain and annex California. He is thoroughly disgusted with Mexican sway,
which is fast sending his country backwards, instead of forwards, in the scale of
civilization, and for years he has been desirous of the change which has now taken
place.

In the afternoon we visited the house of Mr. Leese, which is also furnished in
American style. Mr. L. is the proprietor of a vineyard in the vicinity of the town,
and we were regaled upon grapes as luscious, I dare say, as the forbidden fruit that
provoked the first transgression. Nothing of the fruit kind can exceed the delicious richness and flavour, of the California grape.

This evening Thomas O. Larkin, Esq., late United States Consul for California,
arrived here, having left San Francisco on the same morning that we did, travelling by land. Mr. L. resides in Monterey, but I had the pleasure of an introduction to him at San Francisco several days previously to my leaving that place. Mr.
L. is a native of Boston, and has been a resident in California for about fifteen
years, during which time he has amassed a large fortune, and from the changes
now taking place he is rapidly increasing it. He will probably be the first American
millionnaire of California.

October 17.—The last two mornings have been cloudy and cool. The rainy season, it is thought by the weather-wise in this climate, will set in earlier this year
than usual. The periodical rains ordinarily commence about the middle of

November. It is now a month earlier, and the meteorological phenomena portend "falling weather." The rains during the winter, in California, are not continuous, as is generally supposed. It sometimes rains during an entire day, without cessation, but most generally the weather is showery, with intervals of bright sunshine and a delightful temperature. The first rains of the year fall usually in November, and the last about the middle of May. As soon as the ground becomes moistened, the grass, and other hardy vegetation, springs up, and by the middle of December the landscape is arrayed in a robe of fresh verdure. The grasses grow through the entire winter, and most of them mature by the first of May. The season for sowing wheat commences as soon as the ground is sufficiently softened by moisture to admit of ploughing, and continues until March or April.

We had made preparations this morning to visit a rancho, belonging to General Vallejo, in company with the general and Mr. Larkin. This rancho contains about eleven leagues of land, bordering upon a portion of the Bay of San Francisco, twenty-five or thirty miles distant from Sonoma. Just as we were about mounting our horses, however, a courier arrived from San Francisco with despatches from Captain Montgomery, addressed to Lieutenant Revere, the military commandant at this post, giving such intelligence in regard to the insurrection at the south, that we determined to return to San Francisco forthwith. Procuring horses, and accompanied by Mr. Larkin, we left Sonoma about two o'clock in the afternoon, riding at the usual California speed. After leaving Sonoma plain we crossed a ridge of hills, and entered the fertile and picturesque valley of Petaluma creek, which empties into the bay. General Vallejo has an extensive rancho in this valley, upon which he has recently erected, at great expense, a very large house. Architecture, however, in this country is in its infancy. The money expended in erecting this house, which presents to the eye no tasteful architectural attractions, would, in the United States, have raised a palace of symmetrical proportions, and adorned it with every requisite ornament. Large herds of cattle were grazing in this valley.

From Petaluma valley we crossed a high rolling country, and reached the mission of San Rafael (forty-five miles) between seven and eight o'clock in the evening. San Rafael is situated two or three miles from the shore of the bay, and commands an extensive view of the bay and its islands. The mission buildings are generally in the same ruinous condition I have before described. We put up at the house of a Mr. Murphy, a scholastic Irish bachelor, who has been a resident of California for a number of years. His casa, when we arrived, was closed, and it was with some difficulty that we could gain admission. When, however, the occupant of the house had ascertained, from one of the loopholes of the building, who we were, the doors were soon unbarred and we were admitted, but not without many sallies of Irish wit, sometimes good-natured, and sometimes keenly caustic and ironical. We found a table spread with cold mutton and cold beef upon it. A cup of coffee was soon prepared by the Indian muchachos and muchachas, and our host brought out some scheidam and aguardiente. A draught or two of these liquids seemed to correct the acidity of his humour, and he entertained us with his jokes and conversation several hours.

October 18.—From San Rafael to Sausolito, opposite San Francisco on the north side of the entrance to the bay, it is five leagues (fifteen miles), generally over elevated hills and through deep hollows, the ascents and descents being frequently steep and laborious to our animals. Starting at half-past seven o'clock, we reached the residence of Captain Richardson, the proprietor of Sausolito, about nine o'clock in the morning. In travelling this distance we passed some temporary houses, erected by American emigrants on the mission lands, and the rancho of Mrs. Reed, a widow. We immediately hired a whale-boat from one of the ships, lying here, at two dollars for each passenger, and between ten and eleven o'clock we landed in San Francisco.

I met, soon after my arrival, Mr. Lippincott, heretofore mentioned, who accompanied us a portion of the distance over the mountains; and Mr. Hastings, who, with Mr. Hudspeth, conducted a party of the emigrants from fort Bridger by the new route, via the south end of the Salt Lake, to Mary's River. From Mr. Lippincott I learned the particulars of an engagement between a party of the emigrants (Captain West's company) and the Indians on Mary's River, which resulted, as has before been stated, in the death of Mr. Sallee and a dangerous arrow wound to Mr. L. He had now, however, recovered from the effects of the wound. The emigrants, who accompanied Messrs. Hastings and Hudspeth, or followed their trail, had all reached the valley of the Sacramento without any material loss or disaster.

I remained at San Francisco from the 18th to the 22d of October. The weather during this time was sufficiently cool to render fires necessary to comfort in the houses; but fireplaces or stoves are luxuries which but few of the San Franciscans have any knowledge of, except in their kitchens. This deficiency, however, will soon be remedied. American settlers here will not build houses without chimneys. They would as soon plan a house without a door, or with the entrance upon its roof, in imitation of the architecture of the Pueblo Indians of New Mexico.

CHAPTER VI.

October 22.—Having determined to make a trip to Nueva Helvetia by water, for the purpose of examining more particularly the upper portion of the bay and the Sacramento river, in conjunction with Mr. Larkin, we chartered a small open sail-boat for the excursion. The charter, to avoid disputes, was regularly drawn and signed, with all conditions specified. The price to be paid for a certain number of passengers was thirty-two dollars, and demurrage at the rate of twenty-five cents per hour for all delays ordered by the charter-party, on the trip upwards to Nueva Helvetia. The boat was to be ready at the most convenient landing at seven o'clock this morning, but when I called at the place appointed, with our baggage, the boat was not there. In an hour or two the skipper was found, but refused to comply with his contract. We immediately laid our grievance before the alcalde, who, after reading the papers and hearing the statements on both sides, ordered the skipper to perform what he had agreed to perform, to which decision he reluctantly assented. In order to facilitate matters, I paid the costs of the action myself, although the successful litigant in the suit.

We left San Francisco about two o'clock P.M., and, crossing the mouth of the bay, boarded a Mexican schooner, a prize captured by the U.S. sloop-of-war Cyane, Captain Dupont, which had entered the bay this morning and anchored in front of Sausolito. The prize is commanded by Lieutenant Renshaw, a gallant officer of our navy. Our object in boarding the schooner was to learn the latest news, but she did not bring much. We met on board the schooner Lieutenant Hunter of the Portsmouth, a chivalrous officer, and Lieutenant Ruducoff, commanding the Russian brig previously mentioned, whose vessel, preparatory to sailing, was taking in water at Sausolito. Accepting of his pressing invitation, we visited the brig, and took a parting glass of wine with her gallant and gentlemanly commander.

About five o'clock P.M., we proceeded on our voyage. At eight o'clock a dense fog hung over the bay, and, the ebb-tide being adverse to our progress, we were compelled to find a landing for our small and frail craft. This was not an easy matter, in the almost impenetrable darkness. As good-luck would have it, however, after we had groped about for some time, a light was discovered by our skipper. He rowed the boat towards it, but grounded. Hauling off, he made another attempt with better success, reaching within hailing distance of the shore. The light proceeded from a camp-fire of three Kanacka (Sandwich island) runaway sailors. As soon as they ascertained who we were and what we wanted, they stripped themselves naked, and, wading through the mud and water to the boat, took us on their shoulders, and carried us high and dry to the land. The boat, being thus lightened of her burden, was rowed farther up, and landed.

The natives of the Sandwich islands (Kanackas, as they are called) are, without doubt, the most expert watermen in the world. Their performances in swimming and diving are so extraordinary, that they may almost be considered amphibious in their natures and instincts. Water appears to be as much their natural element as the land. They have straight black hair, good features, and an amiable and intelligent expression of countenance. Their complexion resembles that of a bright mulatto; and, in symmetrical proportions and muscular developments, they will advantageously compare with any race of men I have seen. The crews of many of the whale and merchant ships on this coast are partly composed of Kanackas, and they are justly esteemed as most valuable sailors.

October 23.—The damp raw weather, auguring the near approach of the autumnal rains, continues. A drizzling mist fell on us during the night, and the clouds were not dissipated when we resumed our voyage this morning. Passing through the straits of San Pablo and San Pedro, we entered a division of the bay called the bay of San Pablo. Wind and tide being in our favour, we crossed this sheet of water, and afterwards entered and passed through the Straits of Carquinez. At these straits the waters of the bay are compressed within the breadth of a mile, for the distance of about two leagues. On the southern side the shore is hilly, and canoned in some places. The northern shore is gentle, the hills and table-land sloping gradually down to the water. We landed at the bend of the Straits of Carquinez, and spent several hours in examining the country and soundings on the northern side. There is no timber here. The soil is covered with a growth of grass and white oats. The bend of the Straits of Carquinez, on the northern side, has been thought to be a favourable position for a commercial town. It has some advantages and some disadvantages, which it would be tedious for me now to detail.

[Subsequently to this my first visit here, a town of extensive dimensions has been laid off by Gen. Vallejo and Mr. Semple, the proprietors, under the name of "Francisca." It fronts for two or three miles on the "Soeson," the upper division of the Bay of San Francisco, and the Straits of Carquinez. A ferry has also been established, which crosses regularly from shore to shore, conveying travellers over the bay. I crossed, myself and horses, here in June, 1847, when on my return to the United States. Lots had then been offered to settlers on favourable conditions, and preparations, I understand, were making for the erection of a number of houses.]

About sunset we resumed our voyage. The Wind having lulled, we attempted to stem the adverse tide by the use of oars, but the ebb of the tide was stronger than the propelling force of our oars. Soon, in spite of all our exertions, we found ourselves drifting rapidly backwards, and, after two or three hours of hard labour in the dark, we were at last so fortunate as to effect a landing in a cove on the southern side of the straits, having retrograded several miles. In the cove there is a small sandy beach, upon which the waves have drifted, and deposited a large quantity of oat-straw, and feathers shed by the millions of water-fowls which sport upon the bay. On this downy deposit furnished by nature we spread our blankets, and slept soundly.

October 24.—We proceeded on our voyage at daylight, coasting along the southern shore of the Soeson. About nine o'clock we landed on a marshy plain, and cooked breakfast. A range of mountains bounds this plain, the base of which is

several miles from the shore of the bay. These mountains, although of considerable elevation, exhibit signs of fertility to their summits. On the plain, numerous
herds of wild cattle were grazing. About two o'clock, P.M., we entered the mouth
of the Sacramento. The Sacramento and San Joaquin Rivers empty into the Bay
of San Francisco at the same point, about sixty miles from the Pacific, and by
numerous mouths or sloughs as they are here called. These sloughs wind through
an immense timbered swamp, and constitute a terraqueous labyrinth of such
intricacy, that unskilful and inexperienced navigators have been lost for many
days in it, and some, I have been told, have perished, never finding their way out.
A range of low sloping hills approach the Sacramento a short distance above its
mouth, on the left-hand side as you ascend, and run parallel with the stream several miles. The banks of the river, and several large islands which we passed during the day, are timbered with sycamore, oak, and a variety of smaller trees and
shrubbery. Numerous grape-vines, climbing over the trees, and loaded down with
a small and very acid fruit, give to the forest a tangled appearance. The islands of
the Sacramento are all low, and subject to overflow in the spring of the year. The
soil of the river bottom, including the islands, is covered with rank vegetation, a
certain evidence of its fertility. The water, at this season, is perfectly limpid, and,
although the tide ebbs and flows more than a hundred miles above the mouth of
the river, it is fresh and sweet. The channel of the Sacramento is remarkably free
from snags and other obstructions to navigation. A more beautiful and placid
stream of water I never saw.

At twelve o'clock at night, the ebb-tide being so strong that we found ourselves
drifting backwards, with some difficulty we effected a landing on one of the
islands, clearing a way through the tangled brush and vines with our hatchets and
knives. Lighting a fire, we bivouacked until daylight.

October 25.—Continuing our voyage, we landed, about nine o'clock, A.M., at an
Indian rancheria, situated on the bank of the river. An old Indian, his wife, and
two or three children, were all the present occupants of this rancheria. The
woman was the most miserable and emaciated object I ever beheld. She was probably a victim of the "sweat-house." Surrounding the rancheria were two or three
acres of ground, planted with maize, beans, and melons. Purchasing a quantity of
water and musk-melons, we re-embarked and pursued our voyage. As we ascended the stream, the banks became more elevated, the country on both sides opening into vast savannas, dotted occasionally with parks of evergreen oak.

The tide turning against us again about eleven or twelve o'clock, we landed at an
encampment of Walla-Walla Indians, a portion of the party previously referred to,
and reported to have visited California for hostile purposes. Among them was a

Delaware Indian, known as "Delaware Tom," who speaks English as fluently as any Anglo-Saxon, and is a most gallant and honourable Indian. Several of the party, a majority of whom were women and children, were sick with chills and fever. The men were engaged in hunting and jerking deer and elk meat. Throwing our hooks, baited with fresh meat, into the river, we soon drew out small fish enough for dinner.

The specimens of Walla-Wallas at this encampment are far superior to the Indians of California in features, figure, and intelligence. Their complexion is much lighter, and their features more regular, expressive, and pleasing. Men and women were clothed in dressed skins. The men were armed with rifles.

At sunset we put our little craft in motion again, and at one o'clock at night landed near the cabin of a German emigrant named Schwartz, six miles below the embarcadero of New Helvetia. The cabin is about twenty feet in length by twelve in breadth, constructed of a light rude frame, shingled with tule. After gaining admission, we found a fire blazing in the centre of the dwelling on the earth-floor, and suspended over us were as many salmon, taken from the Sacramento, as could be placed in position to imbibe the preservative qualities of the smoke.

Our host, Mr. Schwartz, is one of those eccentric human phenomena rarely met with, who, wandering from their own nation into foreign countries, forget their own language without acquiring any other. He speaks a tongue (language it cannot be called) peculiar to himself, and scarcely intelligible. It is a mixture, in about equal parts, of German, English, French, Spanish, and rancheria Indian, a compounded polyglot or lingual pi—each syllable of a word sometimes being derived from a different language. Stretching ourselves on the benches surrounding the fire, so as to avoid the drippings from the pendent salmon, we slept until morning.

October 26.—Mr. Schwartz provided us with a breakfast of fried salmon and some fresh milk. Coffee, sugar, and bread we brought with us, so that we enjoyed a luxurious repast.

Near the house was a shed containing some forty or fifty barrels of pickled salmon, but the fish, from their having been badly put up, were spoiled. Mr. Schwartz attempted to explain the particular causes of this, but I could not understand him. The salmon are taken with seines dragged across the channel of the river by Indians in canoes. On the bank of the river the Indians were eating their breakfast, which consisted of a large fresh salmon, roasted in the ashes or embers, and a kettle of atole, made of acorn-meal. The salmon was four or five feet in length, and, when taken out of the fire and cut open, presented a most tempting appearance. The Indians were all nearly naked, and most of them, having been wading in the water at daylight to set their seines, were shivering with the cold whilst greedily devouring their morning meal.

We reached the embarcadero of New Helvetia about eleven o'clock, A.M., and, finding there a wagon, we placed our baggage in it, and walked to the fort, about two and a half miles.

CHAPTER VII.

Disastrous news from the south
Return of Colonel Fremont to Monterey
Call for volunteers
Volunteer our services
Leave New Helvetia
Swimming the Sacramento
First fall of rain
Beautiful and romantic valley
Precipitous mountains
Deserted house
Arable land of California
Fattening qualities of the acorn
Lost in the Coast Mountains
Strange Indians
Indian women gathering grass-seed for bread
Indian guide
Laguna
Rough dialogue
Hunters' camp
"Old Greenwood"
Grisly bear meat
Greenwood's account of himself
His opinion of the Indians and Spaniards
Retrace our steps
Severe storm

Nappa valley
Arrive at Sonoma
More rain
Arrive at San Francisco
Return to New Helvetia.

I remained at the fort from the 27th to the 30th of October. On the 28th, Mr. Reed, whom I have before mentioned as belonging to the rear emigrating party, arrived here. He left his party on Mary's River, and in company with one man crossed the desert and the mountains. He was several days without provisions, and, when he arrived at Johnson's, was so much emaciated and exhausted by fatigue and famine, that he could scarcely walk. His object was to procure provisions immediately, and to transport them with pack-mules over the mountains for the relief of the suffering emigrants behind. He had lost all of his cattle, and had been compelled to cache two of his wagons and most of his property. Captain Sutter generously furnished the requisite quantity of mules and horses, with Indian vaqueros, and jerked meat and flour. This is the second expedition for the relief of the emigrants he has fitted out since our arrival in the country. Ex-governor Boggs and family reached Sutter's Fort to-day.

On the evening of the 28th, a courier arrived with letters from Colonel Fremont, now at Monterey. The substance of the intelligence received by the courier was, that a large force of Californians (varying, according to different reports, from five to fifteen hundred strong) had met the marines and sailors, four hundred strong, under the command of Captain Mervine, of the U.S. frigate Savannah, who had landed at San Pedro for the purpose of marching to Los Angeles, and had driven Captain Mervine and his force back to the ship, with the loss, in killed, of six men. That the towns of Angeles and Santa Barbara had been taken by the insurgents, and the American garrisons there had either been captured or had made their escape by retreating. What had become of them was unknown.[2] Colonel Fremont, who I before mentioned had sailed with a party of one hundred and eighty volunteers from San Francisco to San Pedro, or San Diego, for the purpose of co-operating with Commodore Stockton, after having been some time at sea, had put into Monterey and landed his men, and his purpose now was to increase his force and mount them, and to proceed by land for Los Angeles.

[2] The garrison under Captain Gillespie, at Los Angeles, capitulated.   The garrison at Santa Barbara, under Lieutenant Talbot, marched   out in defiance of the enemy, and after suffering many hardships   arrived in safety at Monterey.

On the receipt of this intelligence, I immediately drew up a paper, which was signed by myself, Messrs Reed, Jacob, Lippincott, and Grayson, offering our services as volunteers, and our exertions to raise a force of emigrants and Indians which would be a sufficient reinforcement to Colonel Fremont. This paper was addressed to Mr. Kern, the commandant of Fort Sacramento, and required his sanction. The next morning (29th) he accepted of our proposal, and the labour of raising the volunteers and of procuring the necessary clothing and supplies for them and the Indians was apportioned.

It commenced raining on the night of the twenty-eighth, and the rain fell heavily and steadily until twelve o'clock, P.M., on the twenty-ninth. This is the first fall of rain since March last. About one o'clock, P.M., the clouds cleared away and the weather and temperature were delightful.

About twelve o'clock, on the 30th, accompanied by Mr. Grayson, I left New Helvetia. We crossed the Sacramento at the embarcadero, swimming our horses, and passing ourselves over in a small canoe. The method of swimming horses over so broad a stream as the Sacramento is as follows. A light canoe or "dug-out" is manned by three persons, one at the bow one at the stern and one in the centre; those at the bow and stern have paddles, and propel and steer the craft. The man in the centre holds the horses one on each side, keeping their heads out of water. When the horses are first forced into the deep water, they struggle prodigiously, and sometimes upset the canoe; but, when the canoe gets fairly under way, they cease their resistance, but snort loudly at every breath to clear their mouths and nostrils of the water.

Proceeding ten miles over a level plain, we overtook a company of emigrants bound for Nappa valley, and encamped with them for the night on Puta creek, a tributary of the Sacramento. Five of the seven or eight men belonging to the company enrolled their names as volunteers. The grass on the western side of the Sacramento is very rank and of an excellent quality.

It commenced raining about two o'clock on the morning of the 31st, and continued to rain and mist all day. We crossed from Puta to Cache creek, reaching the residence of Mr. Gordon (25 miles) about three o'clock P.M. Here we enrolled several additional emigrants in our list of volunteers, and then travelled fifteen miles up the creek to a small log-house, occupied temporarily by some of the younger members of the family of Mr. Gordon, who emigrated from Jackson county, Mo., this year, and by Mrs. Grayson. Here we remained during the night, glad to find a shelter and a fire, for we were drenched to our skins.

On the morning of the 1st of November the sun shone out warm and pleasant. The birds were singing, chattering, and flitting from tree to tree, through the romantic and picturesque valley where we had slept during the night. The scenery and its adjuncts were so charming and enticing that I recommenced my travels with reluctance. No scenery can be more beautiful than that of the small valleys of California. Ascending the range of elevated mountains which border the Cache creek, we had a most extensive view of the broad plain of the Sacramento, stretching with islands and bells of limber far away to the south as the eye could penetrate. The gorges and summits of these mountains are timbered with largo pines, firs, and cedars, with a smaller growth of magnolias, manzanitas, hawthorns, etc., etc. Travelling several miles over a level plateau, we descended into a beautiful valley, richly carpeted with grass and timbered with evergreen oak. Proceeding across this three or four miles, we rose another range of mountains, and, travelling a league along the summit ridge, we descended through a crevice in a sleep rocky precipice, just sufficient in breadth to admit the passage of our animals. Our horses were frequently compelled to slide or leap down nearly perpendicular rocks or stairs, until we finally, just after sunset, reached the bottom of the mountain, and found ourselves in another level and most fertile and picturesque valley.

We knew that in this valley, of considerable extent, there was a house known as "Barnett's," where we expected to find quarters for the night. There were numerous trails of cattle, horses, deer, and other wild animals, crossing each other in every direction through the live oak-timber. We followed on the largest of the cattle trails until it became so blind that we could not see it. Taking another, we did the same, and the result was the same; another and another with no better success. We then shouted so loud that our voices were echoed and re-echoed by the surrounding mountains, hoping, if there were any inhabitants in the valley, that they would respond to us. There was no response—all was silent when the sound of our voices died away in the gorges and ravines; and at ten o'clock at night we encamped under the wide-spreading branches of an oak, having travelled about 40 miles. Striking a fire and heaping upon it a large quantity of wood, which blazed brightly, displaying the Gothic shapes of the surrounding oaks, we picketed our animals, spread our blankets, and slept soundly.

It rained several hours during the night, and in the morning a dense fog filled the valley. Saddling our animals, we searched along the foot of the next range of mountains for a trail, but could find none. Returning to our camp, we proceeded up the valley, and struck a trail, by following which two miles, we came to the house (Barnett's). The door was ajar, and entering the dwelling we found it tenantless. The hearth was cold, and the ashes in the jambs of the large fire-place were baked. In the corners of the building there were some frames, upon which beds had been once spread. The house evidently had been abandoned by its former occupants for some time. The prolific mothers of several families of the swinish species, with their squealing progenies, gathered around us, in full expectation, doubtless, of the dispensation of an extra ration, which we had not to give. Having eaten nothing but a crust of bread for 24 hours, the inclination of our appetites was strong to draw upon them for a ration; but for old acquaintance' sake, and because they were the foreshadowing of the "manifest destiny," they were permitted to pass without molestation. There were two or three small inclosures near the house, where corn and wheat had been planted and harvested this year; but none of the product of the harvest could be found in the empty house, or on the place. Dismounting from our horses at a limpid spring-branch near the house, we slaked our thirst, and made our hydropathical breakfast from its cool and delicious water.

Although the trail of the valley did not run in our course, still, under the expectation that it would soon take another direction, we followed it, passing over a fertile soil, sufficiently timbered and watered by several small streams. The quantity of arable land in California, I believe, is much greater than has generally been supposed from the accounts of the country given by travellers who have visited only the parts on the Pacific, and some few of the missions. Most of the mountain valleys between the Sierra Nevada and the coast are exuberantly fertile, and finely watered, and will produce crops of all kinds, while the hills are covered with oats and grass of the most nutritious qualities, for the sustenance of cattle, horses, and hogs. The acorns which fall from the oaks are, of themselves, a rich annual product for the fattening of hogs; and during the period of transition (four or five weeks after the rains commence falling) from the dry grass to the fresh growth, horses, mules, and even horned cattle mostly subsist and fatten upon these large and oleaginous nuts.

We left the valley in a warm and genial sunshine, about 11 o'clock, and commenced ascending another high mountain, timbered as those I have previously described. When we reached the summit, we were enveloped in clouds, and the rain was falling copiously, and a wintry blast drove the cold element to our skins. Crossing this mountain three or four miles, we descended its sleep sides, and entered another beautiful and romantic hollow, divided as it were into various apartments by short ranges of low conical hills, covered to their summits with grass and wild oats. The grass and other vegetation on the level bottom are very rank, indicating a soil of the most prolific qualities. In winding through this valley, we met four Indians on foot, armed with long bows, and arrows of corresponding weight and length, weapons that I have not previously seen among the Indians. Their complexions were lighter than those of the rancheria Indians of California. They evidently belonged to some more northern tribe. We stopped them to make inquiries, but they seemed to know nothing of the country, nor could we learn from them from whence they came or where they were going. They were clothed in dressed skins, and two of them were highly rouged.

Ascending and descending gradually over some low hills, we entered another circular valley, through which flows a stream, the waters of which, judging from its channel, at certain seasons are broad and deep. The ground, from the rains that have recently fallen and are now falling, is very soft, and we had difficulty in urging our tired animals across this valley. We soon discovered fresh cattle signs, and afterwards a large herd grazing near the stream. Farther on, we saw five old and miserably emaciated Indian women, gathering grass-seed for bread. This process is performed with two baskets, one shaped like a round shield, and the other having a basin and handle. With the shield the lop of the grass is brushed, and the seed by the motion is thrown into the deep basket held in the other hand. The five women appeared at a distance like so many mowers cutting down the grass of a meadow. These women could give us no satisfaction in response to inquiries, but pointed over the river indicating that we should there find the casa and rancheria. They then continued their work with as much zeal and industry as if their lives were dependent upon the proceeds of their labour, and I suppose they were.

Crossing the river, we struck a trail which led us to the casa and rancheria, about two miles distant. The casa was a small adobe building, about twelve feet square, and was locked up. Finding that admission was not to be gained here, we hailed at the rancheria, and presently some dozen squalid and naked men, women, and children, made their appearance. We inquired for the mayor domo, or overseer. The chief speaker signified that he was absent, and that he did not expect hint to return until several suns rose and set. We then signified we were hungry, and very soon a loaf made of pulverized acorns, mingled with wild fruit of some kind, was brought to us with a basket of water. These Indians manufacture small baskets which are impervious to water, and they are used as basins to drink from, and for other purposes.

I knew that we had been travelling out of our course all day, and it was now three o'clock, P.M. Rain and mist had succeeded each other, and the sun was hidden from us by dark and threatening masses of clouds. We had no compass with us, and could not determine the course to Nappa Valley or Sonoma. Believing that the Indian would have some knowledge of the latter place, we made him comprehend that we wished to go there, and inquired the route. He pointed in a direction which he signified would take us to Sonoma. We pointed in another course, which it seemed to us was the right one. But he persisted in asserting that he was right. After some further talk, for the shirt on my back he promised to guide us, and, placing a ragged skin on one of our horses, he mounted the animal and led the way over the next range of hills. The rain soon poured down so hard upon the poor fellow's bare skin, that he begged permission to return, to which we would not consent; but, out of compassion to him, I took off my over-coat, with which he covered his swarthy hide, and seemed highly delighted with the shelter from the pitiless storm it afforded him, or with the supposition that I intended to present it to him.

Crossing several elevated and rocky hills, just before sunset, we had a view of a large timbered valley and a sheet of water, the extent of which we could not compass with the eye, on account of the thickness of the atmosphere. When we came in sight of the water, the Indian uttered various exclamations of pleasure; and, although I had felt but little faith in him as a pilot from the first, I began now to think that we were approaching the Bay of San Francisco. Descending into the valley, we travelled along a small stream two or three miles, and were continuing on in the twilight, when we heard the tinkling of a cow-bell on the opposite side of the stream. Certain, from this sound, that there must be an encampment near, I halted and hallooed at the top of my voice. The halloo called forth a similar response, with an interrogation in English, "Who the d——l are you—Spaniards or Americans?" "Americans." "Show yourselves, then, d——n you, and let us see the colour of your hide," was the answer.

"Tell us where we can cross the stream, and you shall soon see us," was our reply.

"Ride back and follow the sound of my voice, and be d——d to you, and you can cross the stream with a deer's jump."

Accordingly, following the sound of the voice of this rough colloquist, who shouted repeatedly, we rode back in the dark several hundred yards, and, plunging into the stream, the channel of which was deep, we gained the other side, where we found three men standing ready to receive us. We soon discovered them to be a party of professional hunters, or trappers, at the head of which was Mr. Greenwood, a famed mountaineer, commonly known as "Old Greenwood." They invited us to their camp, situated across a small opening in the timber about half a mile distant. Having unsaddled our tired animals and turned them loose to graze for the night, we placed our baggage under the cover of a small tent, and, taking our seats by the huge camp fire, made known as far as was expedient our business. We soon ascertained that we had ridden the entire day (about 40 miles) directly out of our course to Nappa Valley and Sonoma, and that the Indian's information was all wrong. We were now near the shore of a large lake, called the Laguna by Californians, some fifty or sixty miles in length, which lake is situated about sixty or seventy miles north of the Bay of San Francisco; consequently, to-morrow we shall be compelled to retrace our steps and find the trail that leads from Harriett's house to Nappa, which escaped us this morning. We received such directions, however, from Mr. Greenwood, that we could not fail to find it.

We found in the camp, much to our gratification after a long fast, an abundance of fat grisly bear-meat and the most delicious and tender deer-meat. The camp looked like a butcher's stall. The pot filled with bear-flesh was boiled again and again, and the choice pieces of the tender venison were roasting, and disappearing with singular rapidity for a long time. Bread there was none of course. Such a delicacy is unknown to the mountain trappers, nor is it much desired by them.

The hunting party consisted of Mr. Greenwood, Mr. Turner, Mr. Adams, and three sons of Mr. G., one grown, and the other two boys 10 or 12 years of age, half-bred Indians, the mother being a Crow. One of these boys is named "Governor Boggs," after ex-governor Boggs of Missouri, an old friend of the father. Mr. Greenwood, or "Old Greenwood," as he is familiarly called, according to his own statement, is 83 years of age, and has been a mountain trapper between 40 and 50 years. He lived among the Crow Indians, where he married his wife, between thirty and forty years. He is about six feet in height, raw-boned and spare in flesh, but muscular, and, notwithstanding his old age, walks with all the erect-ness and elasticity of youth. His dress was of tanned buckskin, and from its appearance one would suppose its antiquity to be nearly equal to the age of its wearer. It had probably never been off his body since he first put it on. "I am," said he, "an old man—eighty-three years—it is a long time to live;—eighty-three years last—. I have seen all the Injun varmints of the Rocky Mountains,—have fout them—lived with them. I have many children—I don't know how many, they are scattered; but my wife was a Crow. The Crows are a brave nation,—the bravest of all the Injuns; they fight like the white man; they don't kill you in the dark like the Black-foot varmint, and then take your scalp and run, the cowardly reptiles. Eighty-three years last——; and yet old Greenwood could handle the rifle as well as the best on 'em, but for this infernal humour in my eyes, caught three years ago in bringing the emigrators over the de-sart." (A circle of scarlet sur-rounded his weeping eyeballs.) "I can't see jist now as well as I did fifty years ago, but I can always bring the game or the slinking and skulking Injun. I have jist come over the mountains from Sweetwater with the emigrators as pilot, living upon bacon, bread, milk, and sich like mushy stuff. It don't agree with me; it never will agree with a man of my age, eighty-three last ——; that is a long time to live. I thought I would take a small hunt to get a little exercise for my old bones, and some good fresh meat. The grisly bear, fat deer, and poultry and fish— them are such things as a man should eat. I came up here, where I knew there was plenty. I was here twenty years ago, before any white man see this lake and the rich land about it. It's filled with big fish. That's beer-springs here, better than them in the Rocky Mountains; thar's a mountain of solid brimstone, and thar's mines of gold and silver, all of which I know'd many years ago, and I can show them to you if you will go with me in the morning. These black-skinned Spaniards have rebelled again. Wall, they can make a fuss, d—m 'em, and have revolutions every year, but they can't fight. It's no use to go after 'em, unless when you ketch 'em you kill 'em. They won't stand an' fight like men, an' when they can't fight longer give up; but the skared varmints run away and then make another fuss, d—m 'em." Such was the discourse of our host.

The camp consisted of two small tents, which had probably been obtained from the emigrants. They were pitched so as to face each other, and between them there was a large pile of blazing logs. On the trees surrounding the camp were stretched the skins of various animals which had been killed in the hunt; some preserved for their hides, others for the fur. Bear-meat and venison enough for a winter's supply were hanging from the limbs. The swearing of Turner, a man of immense frame and muscular power, during our evening's conversation, was almost terrific. I had heard mountain swearing before, but his went far beyond all former examples. He could do all the swearing for our army in Mexico, and then have a surplus.

The next morning (Nov. 3rd), after partaking of a hearty breakfast, and suspending from our saddles a sufficient supply of venison and bear-meat for two days' journey, we started back on our own trail. We left our miserable Indian pilot at his rancheria. I gave him the shirt from my back, out of compassion for his sufferings—he well deserved a dressing of another kind. It rained all day, and, when we reached Barnett's (the empty house) after four o'clock, P.M., the black masses of clouds which hung over the valley portended a storm so furious, that we thought it prudent to take shelter under a roof for the night. Securing our animals in one of the inclosures, we encamped in the deserted dwelling. The storm soon commenced, and raged and roared with a fierceness and strength rarely witnessed. The hogs and pigs came squealing about the door for admission; and the cattle and horses in the valley, terrified by the violence of elemental battle, ran backwards and forwards, bellowing and snorting. In comfortable quarters, we roasted and enjoyed our bear-meat and venison, and left the wind, rain, lightning, and thunder to play their pranks as best suited them, which they did all night.

On the morning of the fourth, we found the trail described to us by Mr. Greenwood, and, crossing a ridge of mountains, descended into the valley of Nappa creek, which empties into the Bay of San Francisco just below the Straits of Carquinez. This is a most beautiful and fertile valley, and is already occupied by several American settlers. Among the first who established themselves here is Mr. Yount, who soon after erected a flouring-mill and saw-mill. These have been in operation several years. Before reaching Mr. Yount's settlement we passed a saw-mill more recently erected, by Dr. Bale. There seems to be an abundance of pine and red-wood (a species of fir), in the canadas. No lumber can be superior for building purposes than that sawed from the red-wood. The trees are of immense size, straight, free from knots and twists, and the wood is soft, and eas-ily cut with plane and saw. Arriving at the residence of Dr. Bale, in Nappa Valley, we were hospitably entertained by him with a late breakfast of coffee, boiled eggs, steaks, and tortillas, served up in American style. Leaving Nappa, after travelling down it some ten or twelve miles, we crossed another range of hills or mountains, and reached Sonoma after dark, our clothing thoroughly drenched with the rain, which, with intermissions, had fallen the whole day. I put up at the same quarters as when here before. The house was covered with a dilapidated thatch, and the rain dripped through it, not leaving a dry spot on the floor of the room where we slept. But there was an advantage in this—the inundation of water had com-pletely discomfited the army of fleas that infested the building when we were here before.

It rained incessantly on the fifth. Col. Russell arrived at Sonoma early in the morning, having arrived from San Francisco last night. Procuring a boat belong-ing to Messrs. Howard and Mellus, lying at the embarcadero, I left for San Francisco, but, owing to the storm and contrary winds, did not arrive there until the morning of the seventh, being two nights and a day in the creek, and churn-ing on the bay. Purchasing a quantity of clothing, and other supplies for volun-teers, I sailed early on the morning of the eighth for New Helvetia, in a boat belonging to the sloop-of-war Portsmouth, manned by U.S. sailors, under the command of Midshipman Byres, a native of Maysville, Ky. We encamped that night at the head of "Soeson," having sailed about fifty miles in a severe storm of wind and rain. The waves frequently dashed entirely over our little craft. The rain continued during the ninth, and we encamped at night about the mouth of the Sacramento. On the night of the tenth we encamped at "Meritt's camp," the rain still falling, and the river rising rapidly, rendering navigation up-stream impossi-ble, except with the aid of the tide. On the night of the eleventh we encamped fif-teen miles below New Helvetia, still raining. On the morning of the twelfth the clouds cleared away, and the sun burst out warm and spring-like. After having been exposed to the rain for ten or twelve days, without having the clothing upon me once dry, the sight of the sun, and the influence of his beams, were cheering and most agreeable. We arrived at New Helvetia about twelve o'clock.

CHAPTER VIII.

On my arrival at New Helvetia, I found there Mr. Jacob. Mr. Reed had not yet returned from the mountains. Nothing had been heard from Mr. Lippincott, or Mr. Grayson, since I left the latter at Sonoma. An authorized agent of Col. Fremont had arrived at the fort the day that I left it, with power to take the caballada of public horses, and to enroll volunteers for the expedition to the south. He had left two or three days before my arrival, taking with him all the horses and trappings suitable for service, and all the men who had previously rendezvoused at the fort, numbering about sixty, as I understood. At my request messengers were sent by Mr. Kern, commandant of the fort, and by Captain Sutter, to the Indian chiefs on the San Joaquin River and its tributaries, to meet me at the most convenient points on the trail, with such warriors of their tribes as chose to volunteer as soldiers of the United States, and perform military service during the campaign. I believed that they would be useful as scouts and spies. On the 14th and 15th eight men (emigrants who had just arrived in the country, and had been enrolled at Johnson's settlement by Messrs. Reed and Jacob) arrived at the fort; and on the morning of the 16th, with these, we started to join Colonel Fremont, supposed to be at Monterey; and we encamped at night on the Coscumne River.

The weather is now pleasant. We are occasionally drenched with a shower of rain, after which the sun shines warm and bright; the fresh grass is springing up, and the birds sing and chatter in the groves and thickets as we pass through them. I rode forward, on the morning of the 17th, to the Mickelemes River (twenty-five miles from the Coscumne), where I met Antonio, an Indian chief, with twelve warriors, who had assembled hero for the purpose of joining us. The names of the warriors were as follows;—Santiago, Masua, Kiubu, Tocoso, Nonelo, Michael, Weala, Arkell, Nicolas, Heel, Kasheano, Estephen. Our party coming up in the afternoon, we encamped here for the day, in order to give the Indians time to make further preparations for the march. On the 18th we met, at the ford of the San Joaquin River, another party of eighteen Indians, including their chiefs. Their names were—Jose Jesus, Filipe, Ray-mundo, and Carlos, chiefs; Huligario, Bonefasio, Francisco, Nicolas, Pablo, Feliciano, San Antonio, Polinario, Manuel, Graviano, Salinordio, Romero, and Merikeeldo, warriors. The chiefs and some of the warriors of these parties were partially clothed, but most of them were naked, except a small garment around the loins. They were armed with bows and arrows. We encamped with our sable companions on the east bank of the San Joaquin.

The next morning (Nov. 19), the river being too high to ford, we constructed, by the aid of the Indians, tule-boats, upon which our baggage was ferried over the stream. The tule-boat consists of bundles of tule firmly hound together with willow withes. When completed, in shape it is not unlike a small keel-boat. The buoyancy of one of these craft is surprising. Six men, as many as could sit upon the deck, were passed over, in the largest of our three boats, at a time. The boats were towed backwards and forwards by Indian swimmers—one at the bow, and one at the stern as steersman, and two on each side as propellers. The poor fellows, when they came out of the cold water, trembled as if attacked with an ague. We encamped near the house of Mr. Livermore (previously described), where, after considerable difficulty, I obtained sufficient beef for supper, Mr. L. being absent. Most of the Indians did not get into camp until a late hour of the night, and some of them not until morning. They complained very much of sore feet, and wanted horses to ride, which I promised them as soon as they reached the Pueblo de San Jose.

About ten o'clock on the morning of the 20th, we slaughtered a beef in the hills between Mr. Livermore's and the mission of San Jose; and, leaving the hungry party to regale themselves upon it and then follow on, I proceeded immediately to the Pueblo de San Jose to make further arrangements, reaching that place just after sunset. On the 21st I procured clothing for the Indians, which, when they arrived with Mr. Jacob in the afternoon, was distributed among them.

On my arrival at the Pueblo, I found the American population there much excited by intelligence just received of the capture on the 15th, between Monterey and the mission of San Juan, of Thos. O. Larkin, Esq., late U.S. Consul in California, by a party of Californians, and of an engagement between the same Californians and a party of Americans escorting a caballada of 400 horses to Colonel Fremont's camp in Monterey. In this affair three Americans were killed, viz.: Capt. Burroughs, Capt. Foster, and Mr. Eames, late of St. Louis, Mo. The mission of San Juan lies on the road between the Pueblo de San Jose and Monterey, about fifty miles from the former place, and thirty from the latter. The skirmish took place ten miles south of San Juan, near the Monterey road. I extract the following account of this affair from a journal of his captivity published by Mr. Larkin:—

"On the 10th of November, from information received of the sickness of my family in San Francisco, where they had gone to escape the expected revolutionary troubles in Monterey, and from letters from Captain Montgomery requesting my presence respecting some stores for the Portsmouth, I, with one servant, left Monterey for San Francisco, knowing that for one month no Californian forces had been within 100 miles of us. That night I put up at the house of Don Joaquin Gomez, sending my servant to San Juan, six miles beyond, to request Mr. J. Thompson to wait for me, as he was on the road for San Francisco. About midnight I was aroused from my bed by the noise made by ten Californians (unshaved and unwashed for months, being in the mountains) rushing into my chamber with guns, swords, pistols, and torches in their hands. I needed but a moment to be fully awake and know my exact situation; the first cry was, 'Como estamos, Senor Consul.' 'Vamos, Senor Larkin.' At my bedside were several letters that I had re-read before going to bed. On dressing myself, while my captors were saddling my horse, I assorted these letters, and put them into different pockets. After taking my own time to dress and arrange my valise, we started, and rode to a camp of seventy or eighty men on the banks of the Monterey River; there each officer and principal person passed the time of night with me, and a remark or two. The commandante took me on one side, and informed me that his people demanded that I should write to San Juan, to the American captain of volunteers, saying that I had left Monterey to visit the distressed families of the river, and request or demand that twenty men should meet me before daylight, that I could station them, before my return to town, in a manner to protect these families. The natives, he said, were determined on the act being accomplished. I at first endeav-oured to reason with him on the infamy and the impossibility of the deed, but to no avail; he said my life depended on the letter; that he was willing, nay, anxious to preserve my life as an old acquaintance, but could not control his people in this affair. From argument I came to a refusal; he advised, urged, and demanded. At this period an officer called out * * * * (Come here, those who are named.) I then said, 'In this manner you may act and threaten night by night; my life on such condition is of no value or pleasure to me. I am by accident your prisoner—make the most of me—write, I will not; shoot as you see fit, and I am done talking on the subject.' I left him, and went to the camp fire. For a half-hour or more there was some commotion around me, when all disturbance subsided.

"At daylight we started, with a flag flying and a drum beating, and travelled eight or ten miles, when we camped in a low valley or hollow. There they caught with the lasso three or four head of cattle belonging to the nearest rancho, and break-fasted. The whole day their outriders rode in every direction, on the look-out, to see if the American company left the mission of San Juan, or Lieutenant-Colonel Fremont left Monterey; they also rode to all the neighbouring ranches, and forced the rancheros to join them. At one o'clock, they began their march with one hun-dred and thirty men (and two or three hundred extra horses); they marched in four single files, occupying four positions, myself under charge of an officer and five or six men in the centre. Their plan of operation for the night was, to rush into San Juan ten or fifteen men, who were to retreat, under the expectation that the Americans would follow them, in which case the whole party outside was to cut them off. I was to be retained in the centre of the party. Ten miles south of the mission, they encountered eight or ten Americans, a part of whom retreated into a low ground covered with oaks, the others returned to the house of Senor Gomez, to alarm their companions. For over one hour the hundred and thirty Californians surrounded the six or eight Americans, occasionally giving and receiving shots. During this period, I was several times requested, then com-manded, to go among the oaks and bring out my countrymen, and offer them their lives on giving up their rifles and persons. I at last offered to go and call them out, on condition that they should return to San Juan or go to Monterey, with their arms; this being refused, I told the commandante to go in and bring them out himself. While they were consulting how this could be done, fifty Americans came down on them, which caused an action of about twenty or thirty minutes. Thirty or forty of the natives leaving the field at the first fire, they remained drawn off by fives and tens until the Americans had the field to themselves. Both parties remained within a mile of each other until dark. Our countrymen lost Captain Burroughs of St. Louis, Missouri, Captain Foster, and two others, with two or three wounded. The Californians lost two of their countrymen, and Jose Garcia, of Val., Chili, with seven wounded."

The following additional particulars I extract from the "Californian" newspaper of November 21, 1846, published at Monterey: "Burroughs and Foster were killed at the first onset. The Americans fired, and then charged on the enemy with their empty rifles, and ran them off. However, they still kept rallying, and firing now and then a musket at the Americans until about eleven o'clock at night, when one of the Walla-Walla Indians offered his services to come into Monterey and give Colonel Fremont notice of what was passing. Soon after he started he was pursued by a party of the enemy. The foremost in pursuit drove a lance at the Indian, who, trying to parry it, received the lance through his hand; he immediately, with his other hand, seized his tomahawk, and struck his opponent, splitting his head from the crown to the mouth. By this time the others had come up, and, with the most extraordinary dexterity and bravery, the Indian vanquished two more, and the rest ran away. He rode on towards this town as far as his horse was able to carry him, and then left his horse and saddle, and came in on foot. He arrived here about eight o'clock on Tuesday morning, December 17th."

The Americans engaged in this affair were principally the volunteer emigrants just arrived in the country, and who had left New Helvetia a few days in advance of me.

Colonel Fremont marched from Monterey as soon as he heard of this skirmish, in pursuit of the Californians, but did not meet with them. He then encamped at the mission of San Juan, waiting there the arrival of the remaining volunteers from above.

Leaving the Pueblo on the afternoon of the 25th, in conjunction with a small force commanded by Captain Weber, we made an excursion into the hills, near a rancho owned by Captain W., where were herded some two or three hundred public horses. It had been rumoured that a party of Californians were hovering about here, intending to capture and drive off these horses. The next day (November 26th), without having met any hostile force, driving these horses before us, we encamped at Mr. Murphy's rancho. Mr. Murphy is the father of a large and respectable family, who emigrated to this country some three or four years since from, the United States, being originally from Canada. His daughter, Miss Helen, who did the honours of the rude cabin, in manners, conversation, and personal charms, would grace any drawing-room. On the 28th, we proceeded down the Pueblo valley, passing Gilroy's rancho, and reaching the mission of San Juan just before dark. The hills and valleys are becoming verdant with fresh grass and wild oats, the latter being, in places, two or three inches high. So tender is it, however, that it affords but little nourishment to our horses.

The mission of San Juan Bautista has been one of the most extensive of these establishments. The principal buildings are more durably constructed than those of other missions I have visited, and they are in better condition. Square bricks are used in paving the corridors and the ground floors. During the twilight, I strayed accidentally through a half-opened gate into a cemetery, inclosed by a high wall in the rear of the church. The spectacle was ghastly enough. The exhumed skeletons of those who had been deposited here lay thickly strewn around, showing but little respect for the sanctity of the grave, or the rights of the dead from the living. The cool damp night-breeze sighed and moaned through the shrubbery and ruinous arches and corridors, planted and reared by those whose neglected bones were now exposed to the rude insults of man and beast. I could not but imagine that the voices of complaining spirits mingled with these dismal and mournful tones; and plucking a cluster of roses, the fragrance of which was delicious, I left the spot, to drive away the sadness and melancholy produced by the scene.

The valley contiguous to the mission is extensive, well watered by a large arroyo, and highly fertile. The gardens and other lands for tillage are inclosed by willow hedges. Elevated hills, or mountains, bound this valley on the east and west. Large herds of cattle were scattered over the valley, greedily cropping the fresh green herbage, which now carpets mountain and plain.

Colonel Fremont marched from San Juan this morning, and encamped, as we learned on our arrival, ten miles south. Proceeding up the arroyo on the 29th, we reached the camp of Colonel F. about noon. I immediately reported, and delivered over to him the men and horses under my charge. The men were afterwards organized into a separate corps, of which Mr. R.T. Jacob, my travelling companion, was appointed the captain by Colonel Fremont.

CHAPTER IX.

November 30.—The battalion of mounted riflemen, under the command of Lieutenant-Colonel Fremont, numbers, rank and file, including Indians, and servants, 428. With the exception of the exploring party, which left the United States with Colonel F., they are composed of volunteers from the American settlers, and the emigrants who have arrived in the country within a few weeks. The latter have generally furnished their own ammunition and other equipments for the expedition. Most of these are practised riflemen, men of undoubted courage, and capable of bearing any fatigue and privations endurable by veteran troops. The Indians are composed of a party of Walla-Wallas from Oregon, and a party of native Californians. Attached to the battalion are two pieces of artillery, under the command of Lieutenant McLane, of the navy. In the appearance of our small army there is presented but little of "the pomp and circumstance of glorious war." There are no plumes nodding over brazen helmets, nor coats of broadcloth spangled with lace and buttons. A broad-brimmed low-crowned hat, a shirt of blue flannel, or buckskin, with pantaloons and mocassins of the same, all generally much the worse for wear, and smeared with mud and dust, make up the costume of the party, officers as well as men. A leathern girdle surrounds the waist, from which are suspended a bowie and a hunter's knife, and sometimes a brace of pistols. These, with the rifle and holster-pistols, are the arms carried by officers and privates. A single bugle (and a sorry one it is) composes the band. Many an embryo Napoleon, in his own conceit, whose martial spirit has been excited to flaming intensity of heat by the peacock-plumage and gaudy trappings of our militia companies, when marching through the streets to the sound of drum, fife, and brass band, if he could have looked upon us, and then consulted the state of the military thermometer within him, would probably have discovered that the mercury of his heroism had fallen several degrees below zero. He might even have desired that we should not come

"Between the wind and his nobility."

War, stripped of its pageantry, possesses but few of the attractions with which poetry and painting have embellished it. The following is a list of the officers composing the California Battalion:—Lieut.-colonel J.G. Fremont, commanding; A.H. Gillespie, major; P.B. Reading, paymaster; H. King, commissary; J.R. Snyder, quartermaster, since appointed a land-surveyor by Colonel Mason; Wm. H. Russell, ordnance officer; T. Talbot, lieutenant and adjutant; J.J. Myers, sergeant-major, appointed lieutenant in January, 1847.

Company A.—Richard Owens, captain; Wm. N. Loker, 1st lieutenant, appointed adjutant, Feb. 10th, 1847; B.M. Hudspeth, 2d lieutenant, appointed captain, Feb. 1847, Wm. Findlay, 2d lieutenant, appointed captain, Feb. 1847.

Company B.—Henry Ford, captain; Andrew Copeland, 1st lieutenant.

Company C.—Granville P. Swift, captain; Wm. Baldridge, 1st lieutenant; Wm. Hartgrove, 2d do.

Company D.—John Sears, captain; Wm. Bradshaw, 1st lieutenant.

Company E.—John Grigsby, captain; Archibald Jesse, 1st lieutenant.

Company F.—L.W. Hastings, captain (author of a work on California); Wornbough, 1st lieutenant; J.M. Hudspeth, 2d do.

Company G.—Thompson, captain; Davis 1st lieutenant; Rock, 2d do.

Company H.—R.T. Jacobs, captain; Edwin Bryant, 1st lieutenant (afterwards alcalde at San Francisco); Geo. M. Lippincott, 2d do., of New York.

Artillery Company.—Louis McLane, captain (afterwards major); John. K. Wilson, 1st lieutenant, appointed captain in January, 1847; Wm. Blackburn, 2d do. (now alcalde of Santa Cruz).

Officers on detached Service and doing Duty at the South.—S. Hensley, captain; S. Gibson, do. (lanced through the body at San Pascual); Miguel Pedrorena, do., Spaniard (appointed by Stockton); Stgo. Arguello, do., Californian (appointed by do.); Bell, do. (appointed by do.), old resident of California (Los Angeles); H. Rhenshaw, 1st lieutenant, (appointed by do.); A. Godey, do. (appointed by do.); Jas. Barton, do. (appointed by do.); L. Arguello, do., Californian (appointed by do.).

After a march of six or eight hours, up the valley of the arroyo, through a heavy rain, and mud so deep that several of our horses gave out from exhaustion, we encamped in a circular bottom, near a deserted adobe house. A caballada, of some 500 or 600 loose horses and mules is driven along with us, but many of them are miserable sore-backed skeletons, having been exhausted with hard usage and bad fare during the summer campaign. Besides these, we have a large number of pack-mules, upon which all our baggage and provisions are transported. Distance 10 miles.

We did not move on the 1st and 2d of December. There being no cattle in the vicinity of our camp, a party was sent back to the mission, on the morning of the 1st, who in the afternoon returned, driving before them about 100 head, most of them in good condition. After a sufficient number were slaughtered to supply the camp with meat for the day, the remainder were confined in a corral prepared for the purpose, to be driven along with us, and slaughtered from day to day. The rain has continued, with short intermissions, since we commenced our march on the 30th of November. The ground has become saturated with water, and the small branches are swollen into large streams. Notwithstanding these discomforts, the men are in good spirits, and enjoy themselves in singing, telling stories, and playing monte.

December 3.—The rain ceased falling about 8 o'clock this morning; and, the clouds breaking away, the sun cheered us once more with his pleasant beams. The battalion was formed into a hollow square, and, the order of the day being read, we resumed our march. Our progress, through the deep mud, was very slow. The horses were constantly giving out, and many were left behind. The young and tender grass upon which they feed affords but little nourishment, and hard labour soon exhausts them. We encamped on a low bluff, near the arroyo, timbered with evergreen oak. Distance 8 miles.

December 4.—I was ordered with a small party in advance this morning. Proceeding up the valley a few miles, we left it, crossing several steep hills sparsely timbered with oak, from which we descended into another small valley, down which we continued to the point of its termination, near some narrow and difficult mountain gorges. In exploring the gorges, we discovered the trail of a party of Californians, which had passed south several days before us, and found a horse which they had left in their march. This, doubtless, was a portion of the party which captured Mr. Larkin, and had the engagement between Monterey and St. Juan, on the 17th ult. The main body coming up, we encamped at three o'clock. The old grass around our camp is abundant; but having been so much washed by the rains, and consequently exhausted of its nutritious qualities, the animals refused to eat it. The country over which we have travelled to-day, and as far as I can see, is mountainous and broken, little of it being adapted to other agricultural purposes than grazing.

Thirteen beeves are slaughtered every afternoon for the consumption of the battalion. These beeves are generally of good size, and in fair condition. Other provisions being entirely exhausted, beef constitutes the only subsistence for the men, and most of the officers. Under these circumstances, the consumption of beef is astonishing. I do not know that I shall be believed when I state a fact, derived from observation and calculation, that the average consumption per man of fresh beef is at least ten pounds per day. Many of them, I believe, consume much more, and some of them less. Nor does this quantity appear to be injurious to health, or fully to satisfy the appetite. I have seen some of the men roast their meat and devour it by the fire from the hour of encamping until late bed-time. They would then sleep until one or two o'clock in the morning, when, the cravings of hunger being greater than the desire for repose, the same occupation would be resumed, and continued until the order was given to march. The Californian beef is generally fat, juicy, and tender, and surpasses in flavour any which I ever tasted elsewhere. Distance 10 miles.

December 5.—I rose before daylight. The moon shone brightly. The temperature was cold. The vapour in the atmosphere had congealed and fallen upon the ground in feathery flakes, covering it with a white semi-transparent veil, or crystal sheen, sparkling in the moonbeams. The smoke from the numerous camp-fires soon began to curl languidly up in graceful wreaths, settling upon the mountain summits. The scene was one for the pencil and brush of the artist; but, when the envious sun rose, he soon stripped Madam Earth of her gauzy holiday morning-gown, and exposed her every-day petticoat of mud.

Our march to-day has been one of great difficulty, through a deep brushy mountain gorge, through which it was almost impossible to force the field-pieces. In one place they were lowered with ropes down a steep and nearly perpendicular precipice of great height and depth. We encamped about three o'clock, P.M., in a small valley. Many of the horses gave out on the march, and were left behind by the men, who came straggling into camp until a late hour of the evening, bringing their saddles and baggage upon their shoulders. I noticed, while crossing an elevated ridge of hills, flakes of snow flying in the air, but melting before they reached the ground. The small spring-branch on which we encamped empties into the Salinas River. The country surrounding us is elevated and broken, and the soil sandy, with but little timber or grass upon it. Distance 12 miles.

December 6.—Morning clear and cool. Crossed an undulating country, destitute of timber and water, and encamped in a circular valley surrounded by elevated hills, through which flows a small tributary of the Salinas. The summits of the mountains in sight are covered with snow, but the temperature in the valleys is pleasant. Distance 15 miles.

December 7.—Ice, the first I have seen since entering California, formed in the branch, of the thickness of window-glass. We reached the valley of the Salinas about eleven o'clock A.M., and encamped for the day. The river Salinas (laid down in some maps as Rio San Buenaventura) rises in the mountains to the south, and has a course of some sixty or eighty miles, emptying into the Pacific about twelve miles north of Monterey. The valley, as it approaches the ocean, is broad and fertile, and there are many fine ranchos upon it. But, higher up, the stream becomes dry in the summer, and the soil of the valley is arid and sandy. The width of the stream at this point is about thirty yards. Its banks are skirted by narrow belts of small timber. A range of elevated mountains rises between this valley and the coast. A court-martial was held to-day, for the trial of sundry offenders. Distance 8 miles.

December 8.—Morning cool, clear, and pleasant. Two Californians were arrested by the rear-guard near a deserted rancho, and brought into camp. One of them turned out to be a person known to be friendly to the Americans. There has been but little variation in the soil or scenery. But few attempts appear to have been made to settle this portion of California. The thefts and hostilities of the Tular Indians are said to be one of the causes preventing its settlement. Distance 15 miles.

December 9.—The mornings are cool, but the middle of the day is too warm to ride comfortably with our coats on. Our march has been fatiguing and difficult, through several brushy ravines and over steep and elevated hills. Many horses gave out as usual, and were left, from inability to travel. Our caballada is diminishing rapidly. Distance 10 miles.

December 10.—Our march has been on the main beaten trail, dry and hard, and over a comparatively level country. We passed the mission of San Miguel about three o'clock, and encamped in a grove of large oak timber, three or four miles south of it. This mission is situated on the upper waters of the Salinas, in an extensive plain. Under the administration of the padres it was a wealthy establishment, and manufactures of various kinds were carried on. They raised immense numbers of sheep, the fleeces of which were manufactured by the Indians into blankets and coarse cloths. Their granaries were filled with an abundance of maize and frijoles, and their store-rooms with other necessaries of life, from the ranchos belonging to the mission lands in the vicinity. Now all the buildings, except the church and the principal range of houses contiguous, have fallen into ruins, and an Englishman, his wife, and one small child, with two or three Indian servants, are the sole inhabitants. The church is the largest I have seen in the country, and its interior is in good repair, although it has not probably been used for the purpose of public worship for many years. The Englishman professes to have purchased the mission and all the lands belonging to it for 300 dollars.

Our stock of cattle being exhausted, we feasted on Californian mutton, sheep being more abundant than cattle at this mission. The wool, I noticed, was coarse, but the mutton was of an excellent quality. The country over which we have travelled to-day shows the marks of long drought previous to the recent rains. The soil is sandy and gravelly, and the dead vegetation upon it is thin and stunted. About eighty of our horses are reported to have given out and been left behind. Distance 20 miles.

December 12.—To relieve our horses, which are constantly giving out from exhaustion, the grass being insufficient for their sustenance while performing labour, the entire battalion, officers and men, were ordered to march on foot, turning their horses, with the saddles and bridles upon them, into the general caballada, to be driven along by the horse-guard. The day has been drizzly, cold, and disagreeable. The country has a barren and naked appearance; but this, I believe, is attributable to the extreme drought that has prevailed in this region for one or two years past. We encamped near the rancho of a friendly Californian— the man who was taken prisoner the other day and set at large. An Indian, said to be the servant of Tortoria Pico, was captured here by the advance party. A letter was found upon him, but the contents of which I never learned. This being the first foot-march, there were, of course, many galled and blistered feet in the battalion. My servant obtained, with some difficulty, from the Indians at the rancho, a pint-cup of pinole, or parched corn-meal, and a quart or two of wheat, which, being boiled, furnished some variety in our viands at supper, fresh beef having been our only subsistence since the commencement of the march from San Juan. Distance 12 miles.

December 13.—A rainy disagreeable morning. Mr. Stanley, one of the volunteers, and one of the gentlemen who so kindly supplied us with provisions on Mary's River, died last night. He has been suffering from an attack of typhoid fever since the commencement of our march, and unable most of the time to sit upon his horse. He was buried this morning in a small circular opening in the timber near our camp. The battalion was formed in a hollow square surrounding the grave which had been excavated for the final resting-place of our deceased friend and comrade. There was neither bier, nor coffin, nor pall—

"Not a drum was heard, nor a funeral note."

The cold earth was heaped upon his mortal remains in silent solemnity, and the ashes of a braver or a better man will never repose in the lonely hills of California.

After the funeral the battalion was marched a short distance to witness another scene, not more mournful, but more harrowing than the last. The Indian captured at the rancho yesterday was condemned to die. He was brought from his place of confinement and tied to a tree. Here he stood some fifteen or twenty minutes, until the Indians from a neighbouring rancheria could be brought to witness the execution. A file of soldiers were then ordered to fire upon him. He fell upon his knees, and remained in that position several minutes without uttering a groan, and then sank upon the earth. No human being could have met his fate with more composure, or with stronger manifestations of courage. It was a scene such as I desire never to witness again.

A cold rain fell upon us during the entire day's march. We encamped at four o'clock, P.M.; but the rain poured down in such torrents that it was impossible to light our camp-fires and keep them burning. This continued nearly the whole night, and I have rarely passed a night more uncomfortably. A scouting party brought in two additional prisoners this evening. Another returned, and reported the capture of a number of horses, and the destruction of a rancho by fire. Distance 12 miles.

December 14.—The battalion commenced its march on foot and in a heavy rain. The mud is very deep, and we have been compelled to wade several streams of considerable depth, being swollen by the recent rains. At one o'clock a halt was ordered, and beef slaughtered and cooked for dinner. The march was resumed late in the afternoon, and the plain surrounding the mission of San Luis Obispo was reached in the pitch darkness of the night, a family in the canada having been taken prisoners by the advance party to prevent them from giving the alarm. The battalion was so disposed as to surround the mission and take prisoners all contained within it. The place was entered in great confusion, on account of the darkness, about nine o'clock. There was no military force at the mission, and the few inhabitants were greatly alarmed, as may well be supposed, by this sudden invasion. They made no resistance, and were all taken prisoners except one or two, who managed to escape and fled in great terror, no one knew where or how. It being ascertained that Tortoria Pico, a man who has figured conspicuously in most of the Californian revolutions, was in the neighbourhood, a party was despatched immediately to the place, and he was brought in a prisoner. The night was rainy and boisterous, and the soldiers were quartered to the best advantage in the miserable mud houses, and no acts of violence or outrage of any kind were committed.

The men composing the Californian battalion, as I have before stated, have been drawn from many sources, and are roughly clad, and weather-beaten in their exterior appearance; but I feel it but justice here to state my belief, that no military party ever passed through an enemy's country and observed the same strict regard for the rights of its population. I never heard of an outrage, or even a trespass being committed by one of the American volunteers during our entire march. Every American appeared to understand perfectly the duty which he owed to himself and others in this respect, and the deportment of the battalion might be cited as a model for imitation. Distance 18 miles.

CHAPTER X.

Tremendous rain
Mission of San Luis Obispo
Gardens
Various fruits
Farm
Cactus tuna
Caliche
Pumpkins
Trial of Tortoria Pico
Procession of women
Pico's pardon
Leave San Luis
Surf of the Pacific
Captain Dana
Tempestuous night
Mission of St. Ynes
Effects of drought
Horses exhausted
St. Ynes Mountain
View of the plain of Santa Barbara and the Pacific
A wretched Christmas-day
Descent of St. Ynes Mountain
Terrible storm
Frightful destruction of horses
Dark night

What we are fighting for
Arrive at Santa Barbara
Town deserted.

December 15.—The rain fell in cataracts the entire day. The small streams which flow from the mountains through, and water the valley of, San Luis Obispo, are swollen by the deluge of water from the clouds into foaming unfordable torrents. In order not to trespass upon the population at the mission, in their miserable abodes of mud, the church was opened, and a large number of the soldiers were quartered in it. A guard, however, was set day and night, over the chancel and all other property contained in the building, to prevent its being injured or disturbed. The decorations of the church are much the same as I have before described. The edifice is large, and the interior in good repair. The floor is paved with square bricks. I noticed a common hand-organ in the church, which played the airs we usually hear from organ-grinders in the street.

Besides the main large buildings connected with the church, there are standing, and partially occupied, several small squares of adobe houses, belonging to this mission. The heaps of mud, and crumbling walls outside of these, are evidence that the place was once of much greater extent, and probably one of the most opulent and prosperous establishments of the kind in the country. The lands surrounding the mission are finely situated for cultivation and irrigation if necessary. There are several large gardens, inclosed by high and substantial walls, which now contain a great variety of fruit-trees and shrubbery. I noticed the orange, fig, palm, olive, and grape. There are also large inclosures hedged in by the prickly-pear (cactus), which grows to an enormous size, and makes an impervious barrier against man or beast. The stalks of some of these plants are of the thickness of a man's body, and grow to the height of fifteen feet. A juicy fruit is produced by the prickly-pear, named tuna, from which a beverage is sometimes made, called calinche. It has a pleasant flavour, as has also the fruit, which, when ripe, is blood-red. A small quantity of pounded wheat was found here, which, being purchased, was served out to the troops, about a pound to the man. Frijoles and pumpkins were also obtained, delicacies of no common order.

December 16.—A court-martial was convened this morning for the trial of Pico, the principal prisoner, on the charge, I understood, of the forfeiture of his parole which had been taken on a former occasion. The sentence of the court was, that he should be shot or hung, I do not know which. A rumour is current among the population here, that there has been an engagement between a party of Americans and Californians, near Los Angeles, in which the former were defeated with the loss of thirty men killed.

December 17.—Cool, with a hazy sky. While standing in one of the corridors this morning, a procession of females passed by me, headed by a lady of fine appearance and dressed with remarkable taste and neatness, compared with those who followed her. Their rebosos concealed the faces of most of them, except the leader, whose beautiful features, dare say, she thought (and justly) required no concealment. They proceeded to the quarters of Colonel Fremont, and their object, I understood, was to petition for the reprieve or pardon of Pico, who had been condemned to death by the court-martial yesterday, and whose execution was expected to take place this morning. Their intercession was successful, as no execution took place, and in a short time all the prisoners were discharged, and the order to saddle up and march given. We resumed our march at ten o'clock, and encamped just before sunset in a small but picturesque and fertile valley timbered with oak, so near the coast that the roar of the surf breaking against the shore could be heard distinctly. Distance seven miles.

December 18.—Clear, with a delightful temperature. Before the sun rose the grass was covered with a white frost. The day throughout has been calm and beautiful. A march of four miles brought us to the shore of a small indentation in the coast of the Pacific, where vessels can anchor, and boats can land when the wind is not too fresh. The surf is now rolling and foaming with prodigious energy—breaking upon the beach in long lines one behind the other, and striking the shore like cataracts. The hills and plains are verdant with a carpet of fresh grass, and the scattered live-oaks on all sides, appearing like orchards of fruit-trees, give to the country an old and cultivated aspect. The mountains bench away on our left, the low hills rising in gentle conical forms, beyond which are the more elevated and precipitous peaks covered with snow. We encamped about three o'clock near the rancho of Captain Dana, in a large and handsome valley well watered by an arroyo.

Captain Dana is a native of Massachusetts, and has resided in this country about thirty years. He is known and esteemed throughout California for his intelligence and private virtues, and his unbounded generosity and hospitality. I purchased here a few loaves of wheat bread, and distributed them among the men belonging to our company as far as they would go, a luxury which they have not indulged in since the commencement of the march. Distance 15 miles.

December 19.—The night was cold and tempestuous, with a slight fall of rain. The clouds broke away after sunrise, and the day became warm and pleasant. We continued our march up the valley, and encamped near its head. The table-land and hills are generally gravelly, but appear to be productive of fine grass. The soil of the bottom is of the richest and most productive composition. We crossed in the course of the day a wide flat plain, upon which were grazing large herds of brood-mares (manadas) and cattle. In the distance they resembled large armies approaching us. The peaks of the elevated mountains in sight are covered with snow. A large number of horses gave out, strayed, and were left behind to-day, estimated at one hundred. The men came into camp bringing their saddles on their backs, and some of them arriving late in the evening. Distance 18 miles.

December 20.—Parties were sent back this morning to gather up horses and baggage left on the march yesterday, and it was one o'clock before the rear-guard, waiting for the return of those, left camp. The main body made a short march and encamped early, in a small hollow near the rancho of Mr. Faxon, through which flows an arroyo, the surrounding hills being timbered with evergreen oaks. The men amused themselves during the afternoon in target-shooting. Many of the battalion are fine marksmen with the rifle, and the average of shots could not easily be surpassed. The camp spread over an undulating surface of half a mile in diameter, and at night, when the fires were lighted, illuminating the grove, with its drapery of drooping Spanish moss, it presented a most picturesque appearance. Distance 3 miles.

December 21.—Clear and pleasant. A foot march was ordered, with the exception of the horse and baggage guard. We marched several miles through a winding hollow, passing a deserted rancho, and ascending with much labour a steep ridge of hills, descending which we entered a handsome valley, and encamped upon a small stream about four miles from the mission of St. Ynes. The banks of the arroyo are strewn with dead and prostrate timber, the trees, large and small, having been overthrown by tornados. The plain has suffered, like much of the country we have passed through, by a long-continued drought, but the composition of the soil is such as indicates fertility, and from the effects of the late rains the grass is springing up with great luxuriance, from places which before were entirely denuded of vegetation. A party was sent from camp to inspect the mission, but returned without making any important discoveries. Our horses are so weak that many of them are unable to carry their saddles, and were left on the road as usual. A man had his leg broken on the march to-day, by the kick of a mule. He was sent back to the rancho of Mr. Faxon. Distance 15 miles.

December 22.—Clear and pleasant. Being of the party which performed rear-guard duty to-day, with orders to bring in all stragglers, we did not leave camp until several hours after the main body had left. The horses of the caballada and the pack-animals were continually giving out and refusing to proceed. Parties of men, exhausted, lay down upon the ground, and it was with much urging, and sometimes with peremptory commands only, that they could be prevailed upon to proceed. The country bears the same marks of drought heretofore described, but fresh vegetation is now springing up and appears vigorous. A large horse-trail loading into one of the canadas of the mountains on our left was discovered by the scouts, and a party was dispatched to trace it. We passed one deserted rancho, and reached camp between nine and ten o'clock at night, having forced in all the men and most of the horses and pack-mules. Distance 15 miles.

December 23.—Rain fell steadily and heavily the entire day. A small party of men was in advance. Discovering in a brushy valley two Indians armed with bows and arrows, they were taken prisoners. Learning from them that there was a caballada of horses secreted in one of the canadas, they continued on about ten miles, and found about twenty-five fresh fat horses, belonging to a Californian now among the insurgents below. They were taken and delivered at the camp near the eastern base of the St. Ynes Mountain. Passed this morning a rancho inhabited by a foreigner, an Englishman.

December 24.—Cloudy and cool, with an occasional sprinkling rain. Our route to-day lay directly over the St. Ynes Mountain, by an elevated and most difficult pass. The height of this mountain is several thousand feet. We reached the summit about twelve o'clock, and, our company composing the advance-guard, we encamped about a mile and a half in advance of the main body of the battalion, at a point which overlooks the beautiful plain of Santa Barbara, of which, and the ocean beyond, we had a most extended and interesting view. With the spy-glass, we could see, in the plain far below us, herds of cattle quietly grazing upon the green herbage that carpets its gentle undulations. The plain is dotted with groves, surrounding the springs and belting the small water-courses, of which there are many flowing from this range of mountains. Ranchos are scattered far up and down the plain, but not one human being could be seen stirring. About ten or twelve miles to the south, the white towers of the mission of Santa Barbara raise themselves. Beyond is the illimitable waste of waters. A more lovely and picturesque landscape I never beheld. On the summit of the mountain, and surrounding us, there is a growth of hawthorn, manzinita (in bloom), and other small shrubbery. The rock is soft sandstone and conglomerate, immense masses of which, piled one upon another, form a wall along the western brow of the mountain, through which there is a single pass or gateway about eight or ten feet in width. The descent on the western side is precipitous, and appears almost impassable. Distance 4 miles.

December 25.—Christmas-day, and a memorable one to me. Owing to the difficulty in hauling the cannon up the steep acclivities of the mountain, the main body of the battalion did not come up with us until twelve o'clock, and before we commenced the descent of the mountain a furious storm commenced, raging with a violence rarely surpassed. The rain fell in torrents, and the wind blew almost with the force of a tornado. This fierce strife of the elements continued without abatement the entire afternoon, and until two o'clock at night. Driving our horses before us, we were compelled to slide down the steep and slippery rocks, or wade through deep gullies and ravines filled with mud and foaming torrents of water, that rushed downwards with such force as to carry along the loose rocks and tear up the trees and shrubbery by the roots. Many of the horses falling into the ravines refused to make an effort to extricate themselves, and were swept downwards and drowned. Others, bewildered by the fierceness and terrors of the storm, rushed or fell headlong over the steep precipices and were killed. Others obstinately refused to proceed, but stood quaking with fear or shivering with cold, and many of these perished in the night from the severity of the storm. The advance party did not reach the foot of the mountain and find a place to encamp until night—and a night of more impenetrable and terrific darkness I never witnessed. The ground upon which our camp was made, although sloping from the hills to a small stream, was so saturated with water that men as well as horses sunk deep at every step. The rain fell in such quantities, that fires with great difficulty could be lighted, and most of them were immediately extinguished.

The officers and men belonging to the company having the cannon in charge laboured until nine or ten o'clock to bring them down the mountain, but they were finally compelled to leave them. Much of the baggage also remained on the side of the mountain, with the pack-mules and horses conveying them, all efforts to force the animals down being fruitless. The men continued to straggle into the camp until a late hour of the night;—some crept under the shelving rocks and did not come in until the next morning. We were so fortunate as to find our tent, and after much difficulty pitched it under an oak-tree. All efforts to light a fire and keep it blazing proving abortive, we spread our blankets upon the ground and endeavoured to sleep, although we could feel the cold streams of water running through the tent and between and around our bodies.

In this condition we remained until about two o'clock in the morning, when the storm having abated I rose, and shaking from my garments the dripping water, after many unsuccessful efforts succeeded in kindling a fire. Near our tent I found three soldiers who had reached camp at a late hour. They were fast asleep on the ground, the water around them being two or three inches deep; but they had taken care to keep their heads above water, by using a log of wood for a pillow. The fire beginning to blaze freely, I dug a ditch with my hands and a sharp stick of wood, which drained off the pool surrounding the tent. One of the men, when he felt the sensation consequent upon being "high and dry," roused himself, and, sitting upright, looked around for some time with an expression of bewildered amazement. At length he seemed to realize the true state of the case, and exclaimed, in a tone of energetic soliloquy,—

"Well, who wouldn't be a soldier and fight for California?"

"You are mistaken," I replied.

Rubbing his eyes, he gazed at me with astonishment, as if having been entirely unconscious of my presence; but, reassuring himself, he said:

"How mistaken?"

"Why," I answered, "you are not fighting for California."

"What the d——l, then, am I fighting for?" he inquired.

"For TEXAS."

"Texas be d——d; but hurrah for General Jackson!" and with this exclamation he threw himself back again upon his wooden pillow, and was soon snoring in a profound slumber.

Making a platform composed of sticks of wood upon the soft mud, I stripped myself to the skin, wringing the water from each garment as I proceeded. I then commenced drying them by the fire in the order that they were replaced upon my body, an employment that occupied me until daylight, which sign, above the high mountain to the east, down which we had rolled rather than marched yesterday, I was truly rejoiced to see. Distance 3 miles.

December 26.—Parties were detailed early this morning, and despatched up the mountain to bring down the cannon, and collect the living horses and baggage. The destruction of horse-flesh, by those who witnessed the scene by daylight, is described as frightful. In some places large numbers of dead horses were piled together. In others, horses half buried in the mud of the ravines, or among the rocks, were gasping in the agonies of death. The number of dead animals is variously estimated at from seventy-five to one hundred and fifty, by different persons. The cannon, most of the missing baggage, and the living horses, were all brought in by noon. The day was busily employed in cleansing our rifles and pistols, and drying our drenched baggage.

December 27.—Preparations were commenced early for the resumption of our march; but such was the condition of everything around us, that it was two o'clock, P.M., before the battalion was in readiness; and then so great had been the loss of horses in various ways, that the number remaining was insufficient to mount the men. One or two companies, and portions of others, were compelled to march on foot. We were visited during the forenoon by Mr. Sparks, an American, Dr. Den, an Irishman, and Mr. Burton, another American, residents of Santa Barbara. They had been suffered by the Californians to remain in the place. Their information communicated to us was, that the town was deserted of nearly all its population. A few houses only were occupied. Passing down a beautiful and fertile undulating plain, we encamped just before sunset in a live-oak grove, about half a mile from the town of Santa Barbara. Strict orders were issued by Col. Fremont, that the property and the persons of Californians, not found in arms, should be sacredly respected. To prevent all collisions, no soldier was allowed to pass the lines of the camp without special permission, or orders from his officers.

I visited the town before dark, but found the houses, with few exceptions, closed, and the streets deserted. After hunting about some time, we discovered a miserable dwelling, occupied by a shoemaker and his family, open. Entering it, we were very kindly received by its occupants, who, with a princely supply of civility, possessed but a beggarly array of comforts. At our request they provided for us a supper of tortillas, frijoles, and stewed carne seasoned with chile colorado, for which, paying them dos pesos for four, we bade them good evening, all parties being well satisfied. The family consisted, exclusive of the shoemaker, of a dozen women and children, of all ages. The women, from the accounts they had received of the intentions of the Americans, were evidently unprepared for civil treatment from them. They expected to be dealt with in a very barbarous manner, in all respects; but they were disappointed, and invited us to visit them again. Distance 8 miles.

CHAPTER XI.

The battalion remained encamped at Santa Barbara, from the 27th of December to the 3rd of January, 1847. The U.S. flag was raised in the public square of the town the day after our arrival.

The town of Santa Barbara is beautifully situated for the picturesque, about one mile from the shore of a roadstead, which affords anchorage for vessels of any size, and a landing for boats in calm weather. During stormy weather, or the prevalence of strong winds from the south-east, vessels, for safety, are compelled to stand out to sea. A fertile plain extends some twenty or thirty miles up and down the coast, varying in breadth from two to ten miles, and bounded on the east by a range of high mountains. The population of the town I should judge, from the number of houses, to be about 1200 souls. Most of the houses are constructed of adobes, in the usual architectural style of Mexican buildings. Some of them, however, are more Americanized, and have some pretensions to tasteful architecture, and comfortable and convenient interior arrangement. Its commerce, I presume, is limited to the export of hides and tallow produced upon the surrounding plain; and the commodities received in exchange for these from the traders on the coast. Doubtless, new and yet undeveloped sources of wealth will be discovered hereafter that will render this town of much greater importance than it is at present.

On the coast, a few miles above Santa Barbara, there are, I have been told, immense quantities of pure bitumen or mineral tar, which, rising in the ocean, has been thrown upon the shore by the waves, where in a concrete state, like resin, it has accumulated in inexhaustible masses. There are, doubtless, many valuable minerals in the neighbouring mountains, which, when developed by enterprise, will add greatly to the wealth and importance of the town. For intelligence, refinement, and civilization, the population, it is said, will compare advantageously with any in California. Some old and influential Spanish families are residents of this place; but their casas, with the exception of that of Senor Don Jose Noriega, the largest house in the place, are now closed and deserted. Senor N. is one of the oldest and most respectable citizens of California, having filled the highest offices in the government of the country. One of his daughters is a resident of New York, having married Alfred Robinson, Esq., of that city, author of "Life in California."

The climate, judging from the indications while we remained here, must be delightful, even in winter. With the exception of one day, which was tempestuous, the temperature at night did not fall below 50 deg., and during the day the average was between 60 deg. and 70 deg. The atmosphere was perfectly clear and serene, the weather resembling that of the pleasant days of April in the same latitude on the Atlantic side of the continent. It is a peculiarity of the Mexicans that they allow no shade or ornamental trees to grow near their houses. In none of the streets of the towns or missions through which I have passed has there been a solitary tree standing. I noticed very few horticultural attempts in Santa Barbara. At the mission, about two miles distant, which is an extensive establishment and in good preservation, I was told that there were fine gardens, producing most of the varieties of fruits of the tropical and temperate climates.

Several Californians came into camp and offered to deliver themselves up. They were permitted to go at large. They represented that the Californian force at the south was daily growing weaker from dissensions and desertions. The United States prize-schooner Julia arrived on the 30th, from which was landed a cannon for the use of the battalion. It has, however, to be mounted on wheels, and the gear necessary for hauling it has to be made in the camp. Reports were current in camp on the 31st, that the Californians intended to meet and fight us at San Buenaventura, about thirty miles distant. On the 1st of January, the Indians of the mission and town celebrated new-year's day, by a procession, music, etc., etc. They marched from the mission to the town, and through most of the empty and otherwise silent streets. Among the airs they played was "Yankee Doodle."

January 3.—A beautiful spring-like day. We resumed our march at 11 o'clock, and encamped in a live-oak grove about ten miles south of Santa-Barbara. Our route has been generally near the shore of the ocean. Timber is abundant, and the grass and other vegetation luxuriant. Distance 10 miles.

January 4.—At the "Rincon," or passage between two points of land jutting into the ocean, so narrow that at high tides the surf dashes against the neatly perpendicular bases of the mountains which bound the shore, it has been supposed the hostile Californians would make a stand, the position being so advantageous to them. The road, if road it can be called, where all marks of hoofs or wheels are erased by each succeeding tide, runs along a hard sand-beach, with occasional projections of small points of level ground, ten or fifteen miles, and the surf, even when the tide has fallen considerably, frequently reaches to the bellies of the horses. Some demonstration has been confidently expected here, but we encamped in this pass the first day without meeting an enemy or seeing a sign of one. Our camp is close to the ocean, and the roar of the surf, as it dashes against the shore, is like that of an immense cataract. Hundreds of the grampus whale are sporting a mile or two distant from the land, spouting up water and spray to a great height, in columns resembling steam from the escape-pipes of steam-boats. Distance 6 miles.

January 5.—The prize-schooner Julia was lying off in sight this morning, for the purpose of co-operating with us, should there be any attempt on the part of the enemy to interrupt the march of the battalion. We reached the mission of San Buenaventura, and encamped a short distance from it at two o'clock. Soon after, a small party of Californians exhibited themselves on an elevation just beyond the mission. The battalion was immediately called to arms, and marched out to meet them. But, after the discharge of the two field-pieces, they scampered away like a flock of antelopes, and the battalion returned to camp, with none killed or wounded on either side. Under the belief that there was a larger force of Californians encamped at a distance of some five or six miles, and that during the night they might attempt a surprise, or plant cannon on the summit of a hill about a mile from camp, so as to annoy us, a party, of which I was one, was detached, after dark, to occupy the hill secretly. We marched around the mission as privately as possible, and took our position on the hill, where we remained all night without the least disturbance, except by the tempestuous wind, which blew a blast so cold and piercing as almost to congeal the blood. When the sun rose in the morning, I could see, far out in the ocean, three vessels scudding before the gale like phantom ships. One of these was the little schooner that had been waiting upon us while marching along the "Rincon." Distance 14 miles.

January 6.—The wind has blown a gale in our faces all day, and the clouds of dust have been almost blinding. The mission of San Buenaventura does not differ, in its general features, from those of other establishments of the same kind heretofore described. There is a large garden, inclosed by a high wall, attached to the mission, in which I noticed a great variety of fruit-trees and ornamental shrubbery. There are also numerous inclosures, for cultivation, by willow hedges. The soil, when properly tilled, appears to be highly productive. This mission is situated about two miles from the shore of a small bay or indentation of the coast, on the edge of a plain or valley watered by the Rio Santa Clara, which empties into the Pacific at this point. A chain of small islands, from ten to twenty miles from the shore, commences at Santa Barbara, and extends south along the coast, to the bay of San Pedro. These islands present to the eye a barren appearance. At present the only inhabitants of the mission are a few Indians, the white population having abandoned it on our approach, with the exception of one man, who met us yesterday and surrendered himself a prisoner.

Proceeding up the valley about seven miles from the mission, we discovered at a distance a party of sixty or seventy mounted Californians, drawn up in order on the bank of the river. This, it was conjectured, might be only a portion of a much larger force stationed here, and concealed in a deep ravine which runs across the valley, or in the canadas of the hills on our left. Scouting-parties mounted the hills, for the purpose of ascertaining if such was the case. In the mean time, the party of Californians on our right scattered themselves over the plain, prancing their horses, waving their swords, banners, and lances, and performing a great variety of equestrian feats. They were mounted on fine horses, and there are no better horsemen, if as good, in the world, than Californians. They took especial care, however, to keep beyond the reach of cannon-shot. The battalion wheeled to the left for the purpose of crossing a point of hills jutting into the plain, and taking the supposed concealed party of the enemy on their flank. It was, however, found impracticable to cross the hills with the cannon; and, returning to the plain, the march was continued, the Californians still prancing and performing their antics in our faces. Our horses were so poor and feeble that it was impossible to chase them with any hope of success. As we proceeded, they retreated. Some of the Indian scouts, among whom were a Delaware named Tom, who distinguished himself in the engagement near San Juan, and a Californian Indian named Gregorio, rode towards them; and two or three guns were discharged on both sides, but without any damage, the parties not being within dangerous gunshot distance of each other. The Californians then formed themselves in a body, and soon disappeared behind some hills on our right. We encamped about four o'clock in the valley, the wind blowing almost a hurricane, and the dust flying so as nearly to blind us. Distance 9 miles.

January 7.—Continuing our march up the valley, we encamped near the rancho of Carrillo, where we found an abundance of corn, wheat, and frijoles. The house was shut up, having been deserted by its proprietor, who is said to be connected with the rebellion. Californian scouts were seen occasionally to-day on the summits of the hills south of us. Distance 7 miles.

January 8.—Another tempestuous day. I do not remember ever to have experienced such disagreeable effects from the wind and the clouds of dust in which we were constantly enveloped, driving into our faces without intermission. We encamped this afternoon in a grove of willows near a rancho, where, as yesterday, we found corn and beans in abundance. Our horses, consequently, fare well, and we fare better than we have done. One-fourth of the battalion, exclusive of the regular guard, is kept under arms during the night, to be prepared against surprises and night-attacks. Distance 12 miles.

January 9.—Early this morning Captain Hamley, accompanied by a Californian as a guide, came into camp, with despatches from Commodore Stockton. The exact purport of these despatches I never learned, but it was understood that the commodore, in conjunction with General Kearny, was marching upon Los Angeles, and that, if they had not already reached and taken that town (the present capital of California), they were by this time in its neighbourhood. Captain Hamley passed, last night, the encampment of a party of Californians in our rear.

He landed from a vessel at Santa Barbara, and from thence followed us to this place by land. We encamped this afternoon at a rancho, situated on the edge of a fertile and finely watered plain of considerable extent, where we found corn, wheat, and frijoles in great abundance. The rancho was owned and occupied by an aged Californian, of commanding and respectable appearance; I could not but feel compassion for the venerable old man, whose sons were now all absent and engaged in the war, while he, at home and unsupported, was suffering the unavoidable inconveniences and calamities resulting from an army being quartered upon him.

As we march south there appears to be a larger supply of wheat, maize, beans, and barley in the granaries of the ranchos. More attention is evidently given to the cultivation of the soil here than farther north, although neither the soil nor climate is so well adapted to the raising of crops. The Californian spies have shown themselves at various times to-day, on the summits of the hills on our right. Distance 12 miles.

January 10.—Crossing the plain, we encamped, about two o'clock P.M., in the mouth of a canada, through which we ascend over a difficult pass in a range of elevated hills between us and the plain of San Fernando, or Couenga. Some forty or fifty mounted Californians exhibited themselves on the summit of the pass during the afternoon. They were doubtless a portion of the same party that we met several days ago, just below San Buenaventura. A large number of cattle were collected in the plain and corralled, to be driven along to-morrow for subsistence. Distance 10 miles.

January 11.—The battalion this morning was divided into two parties; the main body, on foot, marching over a ridge of hills to the right of the road or trail; and the artillery, horses and baggage, with an advance-guard and escort, marching by the direct route. We found the pass narrow, and easily to be defended by brave and determined men against a greatly superior force; but when we had mounted the summit of the ridge there was no enemy, nor the sign of one, in sight. Descending into a canada on the other side, we halted until the main body came up to us, and then the whole force was again reunited, and the march continued.

Emerging from the hills, the advance party to which I was attached met two Californians, bareheaded, riding in great haste. They stated that they were from the mission of San Fernando; that the Californian forces had met the American forces under the command of General Kearny and Commodore Stockton, and had been defeated after two days' fighting; and that the Americans had yesterday marched into Los Angeles. They requested to be conducted immediately to

Colonel Fremont, which request was complied with. A little farther on we met a Frenchman, who stated that he was the bearer of a letter from General Kearny, at Los Angeles, to Colonel Fremont. He confirmed the statement we had just heard, and was permitted to pass. Continuing our march, we entered the mission of San Fernando at one o'clock, and in about two hours the main body arrived, and the whole battalion encamped in the mission buildings.

The buildings and gardens belonging to this mission are in better condition than those of any of these establishments I have seen. There are two extensive gardens, surrounded by high walls; and a stroll through them afforded a most delightful contrast from the usually uncultivated landscape we have been travelling through for so long a time. Here were brought together most of the fruits and many of the plants of the temperate and tropical climates. Although not the season of flowers, still the roses were in bloom. Oranges, lemons, figs, and olives hung upon the trees, and the blood-red tuna, or prickly-pear, looked very tempting. Among the plants I noticed the American aloe (argave Americana), which is otherwise called maguey. From this plant, when it attains maturity, a saccharine liquor is extracted, which is manufactured into a beverage called pulque, and is much prized by Mexicans. The season of grapes has passed, but there are extensive vineyards at this mission. I drank, soon after my arrival, a glass of red wine manufactured here, of a good quality.

The mission of San Fernando is situated at the head of an extensive and very fertile plain, judging from the luxuriance of the grass and other vegetation now springing up. I noticed in the granary from which our horses were supplied with food many thousand bushels of corn. The ear is smaller than that of the corn of the Southern States. It resembles the maize cultivated in the Northern States, the kernel being hard and polished. Large herds of cattle and sheep were grazing upon the plain in sight of the mission.

January 12.—This morning two Californian officers, accompanied by Tortaria Pico, who marched with us from San Luis Obispo, came to the mission to treat for peace. A consultation was held and terms were suggested, and, as I understand, partly agreed upon, but not concluded. The officers left in the afternoon.

January 13.—We continued our march, and encamped near a deserted rancho at the foot of Couenga plain. Soon after we halted, the Californian peace-commissioners appeared, and the terms of peace and capitulation were finally agreed upon and signed by the respective parties. They were as follows:—

ARTICLES OF CAPITULATION,

Made and entered into at the Ranch of Couenga, this thirteenth day of January, eighteen hundred and forty-seven, between P.B. Reading, major; Louis McLane, junr., commanding 3rd Artillery; William H. Russell, ordnance officer—commissioners appointed by J.C. Fremont, Colonel United States Army, and Military Commandant of California; and Jose Antonio Carillo, commandant esquadron; Augustin Olivera, deputado—commissioners appointed by Don Andres Pico, Commander-in-chief of the Californian forces under the Mexican flag.

Article 1st. The Commissioners on the part of the Californians agree that their entire force shall, on presentation of themselves to Lieutenant-Colonel Fremont, deliver up their artillery and public arms, and that they shall return peaceably to their homes, conforming to the laws and regulations of the United States, and not again take up arms during the war between the United States and Mexico, but will assist and aid in placing the country in a state of peace and tranquillity.

Art. 2nd. The Commissioners on the part of Lieutenant-Colonel Fremont agree and bind themselves, on the fulfilment of the 1st Article by the Californians, that they shall be guaranteed protection of life and property, whether on parole or otherwise.

Article 3rd. That until a Treaty of Peace be made and signed between the United States of North America and the Republic of Mexico, no Californian or other Mexican citizen shall be bound to take the oath of allegiance.

Article 4th. That any Californian or citizen of Mexico, desiring, is permitted by this capitulation to leave the country without let or hinderance.

Article 5th. That, in virtue of the aforesaid articles, equal rights and privileges are vouchsafed to every citizen of California, as are enjoyed by the citizens of the United States of North America.

Article 6th. All officers, citizens, foreigners or others, shall receive the protection guaranteed by the 2nd Article.

Article 7th. This capitulation is intended to be no bar in effecting such arrangements as may in future be in justice required by both parties.

ADDITIONAL ARTICLE.

Ciudad de Los Angeles, Jan. 16th, 1847.

That the paroles of all officers, citizens and others, of the United States, and naturalized citizens of Mexico, are by this foregoing capitulation cancelled, and every condition of said paroles, from and after this date, are of no further force and effect, and all prisoners of both parties are hereby released.

P.B. READING, Maj. Cal'a. Battalion. LOUIS McLANE, Com'd. Artillery. WM. H. RUSSELL, Ordnance Officer. JOSE ANTONIO CARILLO, Comd't. of Squadron. AUGUSTIN OLIVERA, Deputado.

Approved,

J.C. FREMONT, Lieut.-Col.U.S. Army, and Military Commandant of California.

ANDRES PICO, Commandant of Squadron and Chief of the National Forces of California.

The next morning a brass howitzer was brought into camp, and delivered. What other arms were given up I cannot say, for I saw none. Nor can I speak as to the number of Californians who were in the field under the command of Andres Pico when the articles of capitulation were signed, for they were never in sight of us after we reached San Fernando. Distance 12 miles.

January 14.—It commenced raining heavily this morning. Crossing a ridge of hills, we entered the magnificent undulating plain surrounding the city of Angels, now verdant with a carpet of fresh vegetation. Among other plants I noticed the mustard, and an immense quantity of the common pepper-grass of our gardens. We passed several warm springs which throw up large quantities of bitumen or mineral tar. Urging our jaded animals through the mud and water, which in places was very deep, we reached the town about 3 o'clock.

A more miserably clad, wretchedly provided, and unprepossessing military host, probably never entered a civilized city. In all, except our order, deportment, and arms, we might have been mistaken for a procession of tatterdemalions, or a tribe of Nomades from Tartary. There were not many of us so fortunate as to have in our possession an entire outside garment; and several were without hats or shoes, or a complete covering to their bodies. But that we had at last reached the terminus of a long and laborious march, attended with hardships, exposure, and privation rarely suffered, was a matter of such heartfelt congratulation, that these comparatively trifling inconveniences were not thought of. Men never, probably, in

the entire history of military transactions, bore these privations with more forti-
tude or uttered fewer complaints.

We had now arrived at the abode of the celestials, if the interpretation of the name
of the place could be considered as indicative of the character of its population,
and drenched with rain and plastered with mud, we entered the "City of the
Angels," and marched through its principal street to our temporary quarters. We
found the town, as we expected, in the possession of the United States naval and
military forces under the command of Commodore Stockton and General
Kearny, who, after two engagements with six hundred mounted Californians on
the 8th and 9th, had marched into the city on the 10th. The town was almost
entirely deserted by its inhabitants, and most of the houses, except those belonging to foreigners, or occupied as quarters for the troops, were closed. I met here
many of the naval officers whose agreeable acquaintance I had made at San
Francisco. Among others were Lieutenants Thompson, Hunter, Gray and
Rhenshaw, and Captain Zeilin of the marines, all of whom had marched from San
Diego. Distance 12 miles.

CHAPTER XII.

La Ciudad de los Angeles is the largest town in California, containing between fifteen hundred and two thousand inhabitants. Its streets are laid out without any regard to regularity. The buildings are generally constructed of adobes one and two stories high, with flat roofs. The public buildings are a church, quartel, and government house. Some of the dwelling-houses are frames, and large. Few of them, interiorly or exteriorly, have any pretensions to architectural taste, finish, or convenience of plan and arrangement. The town is situated about 20 miles from the ocean, in a extensive undulating plain, bounded on the north by a ridge of elevated hills, on the east by high mountains whose summits are now covered with snow, on the west by the ocean, and stretching to the south and the southeast as far as the eye can reach. The Rio St. Gabriel flows near the town. This stream is skirted with numerous vineyards and gardens, inclosed by willow-hedges. The gardens produce a great variety of tropical fruits and plants. The yield of the vineyards is very abundant; and a large quantity of wines of a good quality and flavour, and aguardiente, are manufactured here. Some of the vineyards, I understand, contain as many as twenty thousand vines. The produce of the vine in California will, undoubtedly, in a short time form an important item, in its exports and commerce. The soil and climate, especially of the southern portion of the country, appear to be peculiarly adapted to the culture of the grape.

We found in Los Angeles an abundance of maize, wheat, and frijoles, showing that the surrounding country is highly productive of these important articles of subsistence. There are no mills, however, in this vicinity, the universal practice of Californian families being to grind their corn by hand; and consequently flour and bread are very scarce, and not to be obtained in any considerable quantities. The only garden vegetables which I saw while here were onions, potatoes, and chile colorado, or red pepper, which enters very largely into the cuisine of the country. I do not doubt, however, that every description of garden vegetables can be produced here, in perfection and abundance.

While I remained at Los Angeles, I boarded with two or three other officers at the house of a Mexican Californian, the late alcalde of the town, whose political functions had ceased. He was a thin, delicate, amiable, and very polite gentleman, treating us with much courtesy, for which we paid him, when his bill was presented, a very liberal compensation. In the morning we were served, on a common deal table, with a cup of coffee and a plate of tortillas. At eleven o'clock, a more substantial meal was provided, consisting of stewed beef, seasoned with chile colorado, a rib of roasted beef, and a plate of frijoles with tortillas, and a bottle of native wine. Our supper was a second edition of the eleven o'clock entertainment.

The town being abandoned by most of its population, and especially by the better class of the female portion of it, those who remained, which I saw, could not, without injustice, be considered as fair specimens of the angels, which are reputed here to inhabit. I did not happen to see one beautiful or even comely-looking woman in the place; but, as the fair descendants of Eve at Los Angeles have an exalted reputation for personal charms, doubtless the reason of the invisibility of the examples of feminine attractions, so far-famed and so much looked for by the sojourner, is to be ascribed to their "unavoidable absence," on account of the dangers and casualties of war. At this time, of course, everything in regard to society, as it usually exists here, is in a state of confusion and disorganization, and no correct conclusions in reference to it can be drawn from observation under such circumstances.

The bay of San Pedro, about twenty-five miles south of Los Angeles, is the port of the town. The bay affords a good anchorage for vessels of any size; but it is not a safe harbour at all times, as I have been informed by experienced nautical men on this coast. San Gabriel River empties into the bay. The mission of San Gabriel is about twelve miles east of Los Angeles. It is represented as an extensive establishment of this kind, the lands surrounding and belonging to it being highly fertile. The mission of San Luis Rey is situated to the south, about midway between Los Angeles and San Diego. This mission, according to the descriptions which I have received of it, is more substantial and tasteful in its construction than any other in the country; and the gardens and grounds belonging to it are now in a high state of cultivation.

San Diego is the most southern town in Upper California. It is situated on the Bay of San Diego, in latitude 33 deg. north. The country back of it is described by those who have travelled through it as sandy and arid, and incapable of supporting any considerable population. There are, however, it is reported on authority regarded as reliable, rich mines of quicksilver, copper, gold, and coal, in the neighbourhood, which, if such be the fact, will before long render the place one of considerable importance. The harbour, next to that of San Francisco, is the best on the Pacific coast of North America, between the Straits of Fuca and Acapulco.

For the following interesting account of Lower California I am indebted to Rodman M. Price, Esq., purser of the U.S. sloop-of-war Cyane, who has been connected with most of the important events which have recently taken place in Upper and Lower California, and whose observations and opinions are valuable and reliable. It will be seen that the observations of Mr. Price differ materially from the generally received opinions in reference to Lower California.

"Burlington, N.J., June 7, 1848.

"Dear Sir,—It affords me pleasure to give you all the information I have about Lower California, derived from personal observation at several of its ports that I have visited, in the U.S. ship Cyane, in 1846-47.

"Cape St. Lucas, the southern extremity of the peninsula of Lower California, is in lat. 22 deg. 45' N., has a bay that affords a good harbour and anchorage, perfectly safe nine months in the year; but it is open to the eastward, and the hurricanes which sometimes occur during July, August, and September, blow the strongest from the southeast, so that vessels will not venture in the bay during the hurricane season. I have landed twice at the Cape in a small boat, and I think a breakwater can be built, at small cost, so as to make a safe harbour at all seasons. Stone can be obtained with great ease from three cones of rocks rising from the sea, and forming the extreme southerly point of the Cape, called the Frayles. Looking to the future trade and commerce of the Pacific Ocean, this great headland must become a most important point as a depot for coal and merchandise, and a most convenient location for vessels trading on that coast to get their supplies. Mr. Ritchie, now residing there, supplies a large number of whale-ships that cruise off the Cape, annually, with fresh provisions, fruits, and water. The supplies are drawn from the valley of San Jose twenty miles north of the Cape, as the land in its immediate vicinity is mountainous and sterile; but the valley of San Jose is extensive and well cultivated, producing the greatest variety of vegetables and fruits. The sweet and Irish potato, tomato, cabbage, lettuce, beans, peas, beets, and carrots are the vegetables; oranges, lemons, bananas, plantains, figs, dates, grapes, pomegranates, and olives are its fruits. Good beef and mutton are cheap. A large amount of sugar-cane is grown, from which is made panoche, a favourite sugar with the natives; it is the syrup from the cane boiled down, and run into cakes of a pound weight, and in appearance is like our maple-sugar.

"Panoche, cheese, olives, raisins, dried figs, and dates, put up in ceroons of hide, with the great staples of the Californians—hides and tallow—make the export of San Jose, which is carried to San Blas and Mazatlan, on the opposite coast. This commerce the presence of the Cyane interrupted, finding and capturing in the Bay of La Paz, just after the receipt of the news of war on that coast in September, 1846, sixteen small craft, laid up during the stormy season, engaged in this trade.

"I cannot dismiss the valley of San Jose, from which the crew of the Cyane have drawn so many luxuries, without alluding to the never-failing stream of excellent water that runs through it (to which it owes its productiveness) and empties into the Gulf here, and is easily obtained for shipping when the surf is low. It is now frequented by some of our whale ships, and European vessels bound to Mazatlan with cargoes usually stop here to get instructions from their consignees before appearing off the port; but vessels do not anchor during the three hurricane months. The view from seaward, up this valley, is beautiful indeed, being surrounded by high barren mountains, which is the general appearance of the whole peninsula, and gives the impression that the whole country is without soil, and unproductive. When your eye gets a view of this beautiful, fertile, cultivated, rich, green valley, producing all the fruits and vegetables of the earth, Lower California stock rises. To one that has been at sea for months, on salt grub, the sight of this bright spot of cultivated acres, with the turkeys, ducks, chickens, eggs, vegetables, and fruit, makes him believe the country an Eldorado. Following up the coast on the Gulf side, after passing Cape Polmo, good anchorage is found between the peninsula and the island of Cerralbo. Immediately to the north of this island is the entrance to the great and beautiful bay of La Paz. It has two entrances, one to the north and one to the south of the island of Espiritu Santo. The northern one is the boldest and safest for all craft drawing over twelve feet. The town of La Paz is at the bottom or south side of the bay, about twenty miles from the mouth. The bay is a large and beautiful sheet of water. The harbour of Pichelinque, of perfect mill-pond stillness, is formed inside of this bay. The Cyane lay at this quiet anchorage several days.

"Pearl-fishing is the chief employment of the inhabitants about the bay, and the pearls are said to be of superior quality. I was shown a necklace, valued at two thousand dollars, taken in this water. They are all found by diving. The Yake Indians are the best divers, going down in eight-fathom water. The pearl shells are sent to China, and are worth, at La Paz, one dollar and a half the arroba, or twenty-five pounds. Why it is a submarine diving apparatus has not been employed in this fishery, with all its advantages over Indian diving, I cannot say. Yankee enterprise has not yet reached this new world. I cannot say this either, as a countryman of ours, Mr. Davis, living at Loretta, has been a most successful pearl-fisher, employing more Indians than any one else engaged in the business. I am sorry to add that he has suffered greatly by the war. The country about La Paz is a good grazing country, but very dry. The mountains in the vicinity are said to be very rich in minerals. Some silver mines near San Antonio, about forty miles south, are worked, and produce well. La Paz may export one hundred thousand dollars a-year of platapina. Gold-dust and virgin gold are brought to La Paz. The copper and lead mines are numerous and rich. To the north of La Paz are numerous safe and good harbours. Escondida, Loretta, and Muleje are all good harbours, formed by the islands in front of the main land.

"The island of Carmen, lying in front of Loretta, has a large salt lake, which has a solid salt surface of several feet thickness. The salt is of good quality, is cut out like ice, and it could supply the world. It has heretofore been a monopoly to the governor of Lower California, who employed convicts to get out the salt and put it on the beach ready for shipping. It is carried about a quarter of a mile, and is sent to Mazatlan and San Blas. A large quantity of salt is used in producing silver. To the north of Muleje, which is nearly opposite Guymas, the gulf is so much narrower that it is a harbour itself. No accurate survey has ever been made of it—indeed, all the peninsula, as well as the coast of Upper California, is laid down wrong on the charts, being about twelve miles too far easterly. The English Government now have two naval ships engaged in surveying the Gulf of California.

"On the Pacific coast of the peninsula there is the great Bay of Magdalena, which has fine harbours, but no water, provisions, or inhabitants. Its shores are high barren mountains, said to possess great mineral wealth. A fleet of whale-ships have been there during the winter months of the last two years, for a new species of whale that are found there, represented as rather a small whale, producing forty or fifty barrels of oil; and, what is most singular, I was assured, by most respectable whaling captains, that the oil is a good paint-oil (an entire new quality for fish-oil). Geographically and commercially, Lower California must become very valuable. It will be a constant source of regret to this country, that it is not included in the treaty of peace just made with Mexico. We have held and governed it during the war, and the boundary of Upper California cuts the head of the Gulf of California, so that Lower California is left entirely disconnected with the Mexican territory.

"Cape St. Lucas is the great headland of the Pacific Ocean, and is destined to be the Gibraltar and entrepot of that coast, or perhaps La Paz may be preferred, on account of its superior harbour. As a possession to any foreign power, I think Lower California more valuable than the group of the Sandwich Islands. It has as many arable acres as that group of islands, with rich mines, pearl-fishing, fine bays and harbours, with equal health, and all their productions. As a country, it is dry, mountainous, and sterile, yet possessing many fine valleys like San Jose, as the old mission establishments indicate. I have heard Todas Santos, Commondee, Santa Guadalupe, and others, spoken of as being more extensive, and as productive as San Jose.

"I am, most faithfully and truly, yours,

"RODMAN M. PRICE."

In the vicinity of Los Angeles there are a number of warm springs which throw out and deposit large quantities of bitumen or mineral tar. This substance, when it cools, becomes hard and brittle like resin. Around some of these springs many acres of ground are covered with this deposit to the depth of several feet. It is a principal material in the roofing of houses. When thrown upon the fire, it ignites immediately, emitting a smoke like that from turpentine, and an odour like that from bituminous coal. This mineral, so abundant in California, may one day become a valuable article of commerce.

There are no reliable statistics in California. The traveller is obliged to form his estimate of matters and things chiefly from his own observation. You can place but little reliance upon information derived from the population, even when they choose to answer your questions; and most generally the response to your inquiries is—"Quien sabe?" (who knows?) No Californian troubles his brains about these matters. The quantity of wines and aguardiente produced by the vine-yards and distilleries, at and near Los Angeles, must be considerable—basing my estimate upon the statement of Mr. Wolfskill, an American gentleman residing here, and whose house and vineyard I visited. Mr. W.'s vineyard is young, and covers about forty acres of ground, the number of vines being 4,000 or 5,000. From the produce of these, he told me, that last year he made 180 casks of wine, and the same quantity of aguardiente. A cask here is sixteen gallons. When the vines mature, their produce will be greatly increased. Mr. W.'s vineyard is doubtless a model of its kind. It was a delightful recreation to stroll through it, and among the tropical fruit-trees bordering its walks. His house, too, exhibited an air of cleanliness and comfort, and a convenience of arrangement not often met with in this country. He set out for our refreshment three or four specimens of his wines, some of which would compare favourably with the best French and Madeira wines. The aguardiente and peach-brandy, which I tasted, of his manufacture, being mellowed by age, were of an excellent flavour. The quantity of wine and aguardiente produced in California, I would suppose, amounted to 100,000 casks of sixteen gallons, or 1,600,000 gallons. This quantity by culture can be increased indefinitely.

It was not possible to obtain at Los Angeles a piece of woollen cloth sufficiently large for a pair of pantaloons, or a pair of shoes, which would last a week. I succeeded, after searching through all the shops of the town, in procuring some black cotton velvet, for four yards of which I paid the sum of 12 dollars. In the United States the same article would probably have cost 1.50 dollar. For four dollars more I succeeded in getting the pantaloons made up by an American tailor, who came into the country with General Kearny's forces. A Rocky Mountain trapper and trader (Mr. Goodyear), who has established himself near the Salt Lake since I passed there last year, fortunately arrived at Los Angeles, bringing with him a quantity of dressed deer and elk skins, which were purchased for clothing for the nearly naked soldiers.

Among the houses I visited while here, was that of Mr. Pryor, an American, and a native of Louisville, Ky. He has been a resident of the country between twenty and thirty years, but his Kentucky manners, frankness, and hospitality still adhere to him.

I remained at Los Angeles from the 14th to the 29th of January. During this time, with the exception of three days, the weather and temperature were pleasant. It rained one day, and during two days the winds blew strong and cold from the north-west. The nights are cool, but fires are not requisite to comfort. The snow-clad mountains, about twenty-five or thirty miles to the east of us, contrast singularly with the brilliant fresh verdure of the plain.

On the 18th of January General Kearny, with the dragoons, left for San Diego. There was understood to be a difference between General Kearny and Commodore Stockton, and General Kearny and Colonel Fremont, in regard to their respective powers and duties; which, as the whole subject has subsequently undergone a thorough investigation, and the result made public, it is unnecessary for me to allude to more particularly. I did not converse with General Kearny while he was at Los Angeles, and consequently possessed no other knowledge of his views and intentions, or of the powers with which he had been invested by the President, than what I derived from report.

On the 19th, Commodore Stockton and suite, with a small escort, left for San Diego. Soon after his departure the battalion was paraded, and the appointment of Colonel Fremont as governor of California, and Colonel W.H. Russell, as secretary of state, by Commodore Stockton, was read to them by Colonel Russell. It was announced, also, that, although Colonel Fremont had accepted the office of chief civil magistrate of California, he would still retain his military office, and command the battalion as heretofore.

Commodore Shubrick, however, arrived at Monterey on the 23rd of January, in the U.S. ship Independence, and, ranking above Commodore Stockton, assumed the chief command, as appears by the date of a general order published at Monterey, and written on board the United States ship Independence, on February 1st, thanking the volunteers for their services, and announcing the restoration of order. For I should state that an insurrection, headed by Don Francisco Sanchez, had broken out in the upper portion of California some time towards the last of December, which had been put down by a detachment of marines and volunteers. The insurgents had committed some outrages, and among other acts had taken prisoner Lieutenant W.A. Bartlett, acting Alcalde of San Francisco, with some other Americans. An account of the suppression of this affair I find in the "Californian" newspaper of February 6th, 1847, from which it appears, "that a party of one hundred and one men, commanded by Captain

Ward Marston, of the United States marines, marched from San Francisco on the 29th December in search of the enemy, whom they discovered on the 2nd of January, about one hundred in number, on the plains of Santa Clara, under the command of Francisco Sanchez. An attack was immediately ordered. The enemy was forced to retire, which they were able to do in safety, after some resistance, in consequence of their superior horses. The affair lasted about an hour, during which time we had one marine slightly wounded in the head, one volunteer of Captain Weber's command in the leg; and the enemy had one horse killed, and some of their forces supposed to be killed or wounded. In the evening the enemy sent in a flag of truce, with a communication, requesting an interview with the commanding officer of the expedition the next day, which was granted, when an armistice was entered into, preparatory to a settlement of the difficulties. On the 3rd, the expedition was reinforced by the mounted Monterey volunteers, fifty-five men, under the command of Captain W.A.T. Maddox, and on the 7th, by the arrival of Lieutenant Grayson with fifteen men, attached to Captain Maddox's company. On the 8th a treaty was concluded, by which the enemy surrendered Lieutenant Bartlett, and the other prisoners, as well as all their arms, including one small field-piece, their ammunition and accoutrements, and were permitted to return peaceably to their homes, and the expedition to their respective posts."

A list of the expedition which marched from San Francisco is given as follows:— Captain Ward Marston, commandant; Assistant-surgeon J. Duval, aide-de-camp. A detachment of United States marines, under command of Lieutenant Tansil, thirty-four men; artillery, consisting of one field-piece, under the charge of Master William F. De Iongh, assisted by Mid. John M. Kell, ten men; Interpreter John Pray; mounted company of San Jose volunteers, under command of Captain C.M. Weber, Lieutenant John Murphy, and acting Lieutenant John Reed, thirty-three men; mounted company of Yerba Buena volunteers, under command of Captain William M. Smith, Lieutenant John Rose, with a small detachment under Captain J. Martin, twelve men.

Thus ended the insurrections, if resistance against invasion can properly be so called, in Upper California.

On the 20th January, the force of sailors and marines which had marched with Commodore Stockton and General Kearny left Los Angeles, to embark at San Pedro for San Diego. On the 21st a national salute was fired by the artillery company belonging to the battalion, in honour of Governor Fremont. On the 22nd, letters were received from San Diego, stating that Colonel Cooke, who followed General Kearny from Santa Fe with a force of four hundred Mormon volunteers, had reached the neighbourhood of that place. Having applied for my discharge from the battalion as soon as we reached Los Angeles, I received it on the 29th, on which day, in company with Captain Hastings, I set out on my return to San Francisco, designing to leave that place on the first favourable opportunity for the United States.

CHAPTER XIII.

We left Los Angeles late in the afternoon of the 29th of January, with two Indian vaqueros, on miserable broken-down horses (the best we could obtain), and encamped at the deserted rancho at the foot of Couenga plain, where the treaty of peace had been concluded. After we had been here some time, two Indians came to the house, who had been sent by the proprietor of the rancho to herd the cattle. Having nothing to eat with us, a tempting offer prevailed upon the Indians to milk one of the cows; and we made our supper and our breakfast next morning on milk. Both of our Indian vaqueros deserted in the night, carrying with them sundry articles of clothing placed in their charge. A few days have made a great change in the appearance of the country. The fresh grass is now several inches in height, and many flowers are in bloom. The sky is bright, and the temperature is delightful.

On the 30th of January, leaving the mission of San Fernando on our right, at a distance of eight or ten miles, we followed the usually travelled trail next to the hills, on the western side of the plain. As we were passing near a rancho, a well-dressed Californian rode out to us, and, after examining the horses of our miserable caballada, politely claimed one of them as his property. He was told that the horse was drawn from the public caballada, at Los Angeles, and could not be given up. This seemed to satisfy him. After some further conversation, he informed us, that he was Don Andres Pico, the late leader and general of the Californians. The expression of his countenance is intelligent and prepossessing, and his address and manners courteous and pleasing. Shaking hands, and bidding us a very earnest adios, he put spurs to his horse and galloped away.

We were soon after overtaken by a young Californian, who appeared at first rather doubtful whether or not he should make our acquaintance. The ice being broken, however, he became very loquacious and communicative. He stated that he was returning to his home near Santa Barbara, from the wars, in which he had been engaged against his will. The language that he used was, that he, with many others of his acquaintances, were forced to take up arms by the leading men of the country. He was in the two battles of the 8th and 9th of January, below Los Angeles; and he desired never to be in any more battles. He was heartily rejoiced that there was peace, and hoped that there would never be any more wars. He travelled along with us until afternoon, when he fell behind, and we did not see him again until the next day.

After passing two or three deserted houses, we reached an inhabited rancho, situated at the extremity of a valley, and near a narrow gorge in the hills, about four o'clock, and, our jaded animals performing duty with reluctance, we determined to halt for the night, if the prospect of obtaining anything to eat (of which we stood in much need) was flattering. Riding up to the house, a small adobe, with one room, and a shed for a kitchen, the ranchero and the ranchera came out and greeted us with a hearty "Buenas tardes, Senores, paisanos amigos," shaking hands, and inviting us at the same time to alight and remain for the night, which invitation we accepted. The kind-hearted ranchera immediately set about preparing supper for us. An Indian muchacha was seated at the metate (hand-mill), which is one of the most important articles of the Californian culinary apparatus. While the muchacha ground, or rather crushed, the wheat between the stones, the ranchera, with a platter-shaped basket, cleansed it of dust, chaff, and all impure particles, by tossing the grain in the basket. The flour being manufactured and sifted through a cedazo, or coarse sieve, the labour of kneading the dough was performed by the muchacha. An iron plate was then placed over a rudely-constructed furnace, and the dough, being beaten by hand into tortillas (thin cakes), was baked upon this. What would American housewives say to such a system as this? The viands being prepared, they were set out upon a small table, at which we were invited to seat ourselves. The meal consisted of tortillas, stewed jerk beef, with chile seasoning, milk, and quesadillas, or cheesecakes, green and tough as leather. However, our appetites were excellent, and we enjoyed the repast with a high relish.

Our host and hostess were very inquisitive in regard to the news from below, and as to what would be the effects of the conquest of the country by the Americans. The man stated that he and all his family had refused to join in the late insurrection. We told them that all was peaceable now; that there would be no more wars in California; that we were all Americans, all Californians—hermanos, hermanas, amigos. They expressed their delight at this information by numerous exclamations.

We asked the woman how much the dress which she wore, a miserable calico, cost her? She answered, "Seis pesos" (six dollars). When we told her that in a short time, under the American government, she could purchase as good a one "por un peso," she threw up her hands in astonishment, expressing by her features at the same time the most unbounded delight. Her entire wardrobe was soon brought forth, and the price paid for every article named. She then inquired what would be the cost of similar clothing under the American government, which we told her. As we replied, exclamation followed upon exclamation, expressive of her surprise and pleasure, and the whole was concluded with "Viva los Americanos— viva los Americanos!" I wore a large coarse woollen pea-jacket, which the man was very desirous to obtain, offering for it a fine horse. I declined the trade.

In the evening several of the brothers, sisters, and brothers and sisters-in-law of the family collected, and the guitar and violin, which were suspended from a beam in the house, were taken down, and we were entertained by a concert of instrumental and vocal music. Most of the tunes were such as are performed at fandangos. Some plaintive airs were played and sung with much pathos and expression, the whole party joining in the choruses. Although invited to occupy the only room in the house, we declined it, and spread our blankets on the outside.

The next morning (January 31st), when we woke, the sun was shining bright and warm, and the birds were singing gayly in the grove of evergreen oaks near the house. Having made ready to resume our journey, as delicately as possible we offered our kind hostess compensation for the trouble we had given her, which she declined, saying, that although they were not rich, they nevertheless had enough and to spare. We however insisted, and she finally accepted, with the condition that we would also accept of some of her quesadillas and tortillas to carry along with us. The ranchero mounted his horse and rode with us about three or four miles, to place us on the right trail, when, after inviting us very earnestly to call and see him again, and bidding us an affectionate adios, he galloped away.

Travelling over a hilly country, and passing the ruins of several deserted ranchos, the grounds surrounding which were strewn with the bones of slaughtered cattle, we reached, about five o'clock P.M., a cluster of houses in the valley of Santa Clara River, ten miles east of the mission of San Buenaventura. Here we stopped at the house of a man named Sanchez. Our arrival was thought to be worthy of notice, and it was accordingly celebrated in the evening by a fandango given at one of the houses, to which we were invited. The company, to the number of some thirty or forty persons, young and old, were assembled in the largest room of the house, the floor being hard clay. The only furniture contained in the room was a bed and some benches, upon which the company seated themselves when not engaged in dancing.

Among the senoritas assembled were two daughters of an American named Chapman, who has been a resident of the country for many years. They were fair-skinned, and might be called handsome. An elder and married sister was also present. They called themselves Americans, although they did not speak our language, and seemed to be more proud of their American than their Spanish blood.

A singular custom prevails at these fandangos. It is this: during the intervals between the waltzes, quadrilles, and other dances, when the company is seated, a young lady takes the floor solus, and, after showing off her graces for general observation a few minutes, she approaches any gentleman she may select, and performs a variety of pirouettes and other Terpsichorean movements before him for his especial amusement and admiration, until he places on her head his hat or cap, as the case may be, when she dances away with it. The hat or cap has afterwards to be redeemed by some present, and this usually is in money. Not dancing ourselves, we were favoured with numerous special exhibitions of this kind, the cost of each of which was un peso. With a long journey before us, and with purses in a nearly collapsed condition, the drafts upon us became so frequent, that at an early hour, under a plea of fatigue and want of rest, we thought it prudent to beat a retreat, leaving our fair and partial fandangueras to bestow their favours upon others better able to bear them. The motions of the Californian females of all classes in the dance are highly graceful. The waltz is their favourite measure, and in this they appear to excel as much as the men do in horsemanship. During the progress of the dance, the males and females improvise doggerel rhymes complimentary of the personal beauties and graces of those whom they admire, or expressive of their love and devotion, which are chanted with the music of the instruments, and the whole company join in the general chorus at the end of each verse. The din of voices is sometimes almost deafening.

Our host accompanied us to our lodgings on the opposite side of the way. Beds were spread down under the small porch outside, and we laid our bodies upon them, but not to sleep, for the noise of the fandango dancers kept us awake until broad daylight, at which time it broke up.

Hiring fresh horses here, and a vaquero to drive our tired animals after us, we started about 9 o'clock in the morning, and, passing through San Buenaventura, reached Santa Barbara, 45 miles, a little after two in the afternoon. We stopped at the house of Mr. Sparks, who received us with genuine hospitality. Santa Barbara presented a more lively appearance than when we passed here on our way down, most of its population having returned to their homes. Procuring fresh but miserably poor horses, we resumed our journey on the afternoon of the 2nd of February, and encamped at the rancho of Dr. Deu, situated on the plain of Santa Barbara, near the sea shore. The soil of this plain is of the most fertile composition. The fresh grass is now six or eight inches high, and the varieties are numerous. Many of the early flowers are in bloom. I noticed a large wheat field near the house, and its appearance was such as to promise a rich harvest.

The rain fell heavily on the morning of the 3rd, but continuing our journey we crossed the St. Ynes Mountain, and, passing the mission by that name, reached the rancho of Mr. Faxon after dark, where we halted for the night. Around the mission of St. Ynes I noticed, as we passed, immense quantities of cattle bones thickly strewn in all directions. Acres of ground were white with these remains of the immense herds belonging to this mission in the days of its prosperity, slaughtered for their hides and tallow. We met two or three elegantly dressed Californians to-day, who accosted us with much civility and apparent friendliness.

Mr. Faxon is an Englishman by birth, and has resided in California about thirty years. He is married to a Californian lady, and has a family of interesting and beautiful children. A large portion of the land belonging to his rancho is admirably adapted to agriculture, and he raises crops of corn and vegetables as well as wheat without irrigation. He informed me that the yield of wheat on his rancho was fully seventy bushels to the acre. Mr. F. showed me specimens of lead ore from which he moulds his bullets, taken from an inexhaustible mine in the Tular Valley, some fifty miles distant from this. It is certainly the richest ore that

I have ever seen, appearing almost like the pure metal. He also showed me a caustic alkali, produced by burning a plant or shrub which grows in great abundance in the Tular Valley. This substance is used by him in the manufacture of soap.

About noon on the 4th, we halted at the rancho of Captain Dana, where we procured fresh horses, leaving our wretchedly lean and tired animals, and, proceeding on, stopped for the night at the rancho of Mr. Branch, an intelligent American, originally from the state of New York, who has been settled in the country a number of years. His rancho is situated on what is called the arroyo grande, a small stream which empties into the Pacific some two or three miles from the house. The house is new, and constructed after American models of farm-houses, with neat and comfortable apartments, chimneys and fireplaces. The arable lands here are finely adapted to the culture of maize, wheat, and potatoes.

Our horses straying, it was twelve o'clock on the 5th before we found them. The rain had fallen steadily and heavily all night, and during the forenoon, and was pouring down when we started. We passed through the mission of San Luis Obispo just before sunset, intending to halt at a rancho about three miles distant in a canada. But, the storm increasing in strength, it became suddenly so dark in the mountain-gorge, that we could not distinguish the trail, and, after wandering about some time, vainly attempting to find the house, we were compelled to bivouac, wet to our skins, without fire or shelter, and the rain pouring down in torrents.

The next morning (Feb. 6.), in hunting up our loose horses, we discovered the house about half a mile distant from our camp. Continuing our journey, we halted about nine o'clock at a rancho near the ruins of Santa Margarita. A solitary Indian was the only occupant of the house, and only inhabitant of the place; and he could furnish us with no food. Passing two or three other deserted ranches, we reached the house of a Mexican about one o'clock, where we obtained a meal of fried eggs and tortillas, after having been without food thirty hours. Late in the afternoon we arrived at the mission of San Miguel, now occupied by an Englishman named Reed, his mestiza wife, and one child, with two or three Indian vaqueros. Crossing the Salinas in the morning (Feb. 7), we continued down its eastern side, and encamped in a wide bottom under a large live oak. A quesadilla was all we had to eat. This was divided, one-half being reserved for breakfast. The fresh vegetation has so much changed the face of the country on this river since we passed along here in December, that I scarcely recognise it. The grass is six or eight inches high in the bottom, the blades standing so thick as to present a matted appearance, and the hills are brilliant with flowers—pink, purple, blue, and yellow.

On the 8th we continued down the eastern bank of the Salinas, passing through several large and fertile bottoms, and reaching the rancho of San Lorenzo about twelve o'clock. This rancho, as we learned from the proprietors, is owned by two bachelor brothers, one of whom told me that he had not been off his lands but once or twice for several years. Large herds of fat cattle and horses were grazing upon the luxuriant grasses of the plain, and there were several extensive inclosures sowed in wheat, which presented all the indications of an abundant harvest. But, with all these natural resources surrounding him the elder brother told us that he had nothing to eat in his house but fresh beef. A quantity of the choice pieces of a fat beef was roasted by an Indian boy, which we enjoyed with all the relish of hungry men. Our host, a gentleman of intelligence and politeness, made apology after apology for his rude style of living, a principal excuse being that he had no wife. He inquired, with apparent earnestness, if we could not send him two pretty accomplished and capable American women, whom they could marry; and then they would build a fine house, have bread, butter, cheese, and all the delicacies, luxuries, and elegancies of life in abundance. He appeared to be well pleased with the conquest of the country by the Americans, and desirous that they should not give it up. When we resumed our journey in the afternoon, he rode with us four or five miles to show us the way, and, on taking his leave, invited us to return again, when he said he hoped his accommodations would be much improved. Riding 15 miles, we halted at a tule-cabin, where we remained until two o'clock in the morning, when, the moon shining brightly, we mounted our horses, and continued our journey.

We reached the Monterey road just at daylight. My intention had been to visit Monterey; but the Salinas being unfordable, and there being no ferry, it was not possible to do it without swimming the river, which I did not feel inclined to do. Monterey is situated on the bay by that name, about 90 miles by water south of San Francisco. The bay affords a good anchorage and landing in calm weather, being exposed only to the northers, which blow violently. The town contains about 1500 inhabitants, and is rapidly increasing in wealth and population. Arriving at the rancho of Don Joaquin Gomez, we found no one but a mestiza servant at home, and could obtain nothing to eat but a quesadilla. All the streams, large and small, are much swollen by late heavy rains, and the travelling is consequently very laborious and difficult. Resting our horses a short time, we crossed the mountains, and reached the mission of San Juan Bautista about noon.

At San Juan we met with Messrs. Grayson, Boggs, and a party of volunteers returning from Monterey to San Francisco, having been discharged since the suppression of the rebellion in this part of California, headed by Francisco Sanchez.

Here we learned, for the first time, the arrival at Monterey of Commodore Shubrick in the ship Independence, and of the Lexington with Captain Tomkins's company of artillery, and freighted otherwise with munitions, stores, and tools necessary to the erection and defence of durable fortifications at Monterey and San Francisco.

Seven or eight miles beyond San Juan, we found that the waters of the arroyo had risen so as to inundate a wide valley which we were compelled to cross. After making several ineffectual attempts to reach the opposite side, wading through the water, and sometimes falling into deep holes from which it was difficult for either men or horses to extricate themselves, we encamped for the night on a small elevation in the valley, entirely surrounded by water. Our condition was miserable enough. Tired, wet, and hungry, we laid down for the night on the damp ground. The next day (Feb. 10), about eleven o'clock, we succeeded in finding a ford across the valley and stream, and procured dinner at a soap-factory on the opposite side, belonging to T.O. Larkin, Esq. Continuing on, we encamped at a rancho occupied by an Englishman as mayor domo. He was very glad to see us, and treated us with unbounded hospitality, furnishing a superabundance of beef and frijoles for our consumption. On the 11th, about three P.M., we arrived at the Pueblo de San Jose, and, finding there a launch employed by Messrs. Howard and Mellus in collecting hides, bound for San Francisco, we embarked in her, and on the morning of the 13th arrived at that place. We found lying here the U.S. sloop Warren, and Lieutenant Radford politely furnished us with a boat to land. In the afternoon the Cyane, Commander Dupont, with Gen. Kearny on board, and the store-ship Erie, with Col. Mason on board, arrived in the harbour. Col. Mason is from the United States direct, via Panama, and brings late and interesting intelligence.

The Cyane and Warren have just returned from a cruise on the southern Pacific coast of Mexico. The town of Guymas had been taken by bombardment. The Cyane had captured, during her cruize, fourteen prizes, besides several guns at San Blas. The boats of the Warren, under the command of Lieut. Radford, performed the gallant feat of cutting out of the harbour of Mazatlan the Mexican schooner Malek Abdel.

Landing in San Francisco, I found my wardrobe, which I had deposited in the care of Capt. Leidesdorff, and the first time for nearly five months dressed myself in a civilized costume. Having been during that time almost constantly in motion, and exposed to many hardships and privations, it was, as may be supposed, no small satisfaction to find once more a place where I could repose for a short time at least.

CHAPTER XIV.

Wherever the Anglo-Saxon race plant themselves, progress is certain to be displayed in some form or other. Such is their "go-ahead" energy, that things cannot stand still where they are, whatever may be the circumstances surrounding them. Notwithstanding the wars and insurrections, I found the town of San Francisco, on my arrival here, visibly improved. An American population had flowed into it; lots, which heretofore have been considered almost valueless, were selling at high prices; new houses had been built, and were in progress; new commercial houses had been established; hotels had been opened for the accommodation of the travelling and business public; and the publication of a newspaper had been commenced. The little village of two hundred souls, when I arrived here in September last, is fast becoming a town of importance. Ships freighted with full cargoes are entering the port, and landing their merchandise to be disposed of at wholesale and retail on shore, instead of the former mode of vending them afloat in the harbour. There is a prevailing air of activity, enterprise, and energy; and men, in view of the advantageous position of the town for commerce, are making large calculations upon the future; calculations which I believe will be fully realized.

On the 15th I dined on board the sloop-of-war Cyane, with Commander Dupont, to whom I had the good fortune to be the bearer from home of a letter of introduction. I say "good fortune," because I conceive it to be one of the greatest of social blessings, as well as pleasures, to be made acquainted with a truly upright and honourable man—one whose integrity never bends to wrongful or pusillanimous expediency;—one who, armed intellectually with the panoply of justice, has courage to sustain it under any and all circumstances;—one whose ambition is, in a public capacity, to serve his country, and not to serve himself;—one who waits for his country to judge of his acts, and, if worthy, to place the laurel wreath upon his head, disdaining a self-wrought and self-assumed coronal. Capt. Dupont is a native of Delaware; and that gallant and patriotic state should feel proud of such a son. He is one of whom all men, on sea or on land, with whom his duties as an officer or citizen of our republic brings him in contact, speak well; and whose private virtues, as well as professional merits, are deserving of the warmest admiration and the highest honours.

Although I have long known Gen. S.W. Kearny from reputation, and saw him at Los Angeles, I was here introduced to him for the first time. Gen. K. is a man rising fifty years of age. His height is about five feet ten or eleven inches. His figure is all that is required by symmetry. His features are regular, almost Grecian; his eye is blue, and has an eagle-like expression, when excited by stern or angry emotion; but, in ordinary social intercourse, the whole expression of his countenance is mild and pleasing, and his manners and conversation are unaffected, urbane, and conciliatory, without the slightest exhibition of vanity or egotism. He appears the cool, brave, and energetic soldier; the strict disciplinarian, without tyranny; the man, in short, determined to perform his duty, in whatever situation he may be placed, leaving consequences to follow in their natural course. These, my first impressions, were fully confirmed by subsequent intercourse, in situations and under circumstances which, by experience, I have found an unfailing alembic for the trial of character—a crucible wherein, if the metal be impure, the drossy substances are sure to display themselves. It is not my province to extol or pronounce judgment upon his acts; they are a part of the military and civil history of our country, and as such will be applauded or condemned, according to the estimate that may be placed upon them. But I may be allowed to express the opinion, that no man, placed under the same circumstances, ever aimed to perform his duty with more uprightness and more fidelity to the interests and honour of his country, or who, to shed lustre upon his country, ever braved greater dangers, or endured more hardships and privations, and all without vaunting his performances and sacrifices.

On the 16th, in company of Gen. Kearny, Capt. Turner, and Lieuts. Warner and Hallock, of the U.S. Engineer Corps, I rode to the Presidio of San Francisco, and the old fortification at the mouth of the bay. The presidio is about three miles from the town, and consists of several blocks of adobe buildings, covered with files. The walls of most of the buildings are crumbling for the want of care in protecting them from the annual rains; and without this care they will soon become heaps of mud. The fort is erected upon a commanding position, about a mile and a half from the entrance to the bay. Its walls are substantially constructed of burnt brick, and are of sufficient thickness and strength to resist heavy battering. There are nine or ten embrasures. Like everything else in the country belonging to the public, the fort is fast falling into ruins. There has been no garrison here for several years; the guns are dismounted, and half decomposed by long exposure to the weather, and from want of care. Some of them have sunk into the ground.

On the 20th I was waited upon by Gen. Kearny, and requested to accept the office of alcalde, or chief magistrate, of the district of San Francisco. There being no opportunity of returning to the United States immediately, I accepted of the proposed appointment, and on the 22d was sworn into office, my predecessor, Lieut. W.A. Bartlett, of the navy, being ordered to his ship by the commanding officer of the squadron.

The annual salute in celebration of the birthday of the immortal and illustrious founder of our republic, required by law from all the ships of the navy in commission, in whatever part of the world they may be at the time, strikes us more forcibly when in a far-off country, as being a beautiful and appropriate tribute to the unapproachable virtues and heroism of that great benefactor of the human race, than when we are nearer home, or upon our own soil. The U.S. ships in the harbour, at twelve o'clock on the 22d, each fired a national salute; and the day being calm and beautiful, the reports bounded from hill to hill, and were echoed and re-echoed until the sound died away, apparently in the distant gorges of the Sierra Nevada. This was a voice from the soul of WASHINGTON, speaking in majestic and thunder-tones to the green and flowery valley, the gentle hills and lofty mountains of California, and consecrating them as the future abode of millions upon millions of the sons of liberty. The merchant and whale ships lying at anchor, catching the enthusiasm, joined in the salute; and for a time the harbour and bay in front of the town were enveloped in clouds of gunpowder smoke.

General Kearny left San Francisco, in the frigate Savannah, Captain Mervine, on the 23d, for Monterey, and soon after his arrival at that place issued the following proclamation:—

PROCLAMATION TO THE PEOPLE OF CALIFORNIA.

The President of the United States having instructed the undersigned to take charge of the civil government of California, he enters upon his duties with an ardent desire to promote, as far as he is able, the interests of the country and the welfare of its inhabitants.

The undersigned has instructions from the President to respect and protect the religious institutions of California, and to see that the religious rights of the people are in the amplest manner preserved to them, the constitution of the United States allowing every man to worship his Creator in such a manner as his own conscience may dictate to him.

The undersigned is also instructed to protect the persons and property of the quiet and peaceable inhabitants of the country against all or any of their enemies, whether from abroad or at home; and when he now assures the Californians that it will be his duty and his pleasure to comply with those instructions, he calls upon them all to exert themselves in preserving order and tranquillity, in promoting harmony and concord, and in maintaining the authority and efficiency of the laws.

It is the wish and design of the United States to provide for California, with the least possible delay, a free government, similar to those in her other territories; and the people will soon be called upon to exercise their rights as freemen, in electing their own representatives, to make such laws as may be deemed best for their interest and welfare. But until this can be done, the laws now in existence, and not in conflict with the constitution of the United States, will be continued until changed by competent authority; and those persons who hold office will continue in the same for the present, provided they swear to support that constitution, and to faithfully perform their duty.

The undersigned hereby absolves all the inhabitants of California from any further allegiance to the republic of Mexico, and will consider them as citizens of the United States; those who remain quiet and peaceable will be respected in their rights and protected in them. Should any take up arms against or oppose the government of this territory, or instigate others to do so, they will be considered as enemies, and treated accordingly.

When Mexico forced a war upon the United States, time did not permit the latter to invite the Californians as friends to join her standard, but compelled her to take possession of the country to prevent any European power from seizing upon it, and, in doing so, some excesses and unauthorized acts were no doubt committed by persons employed in the service of the United States, by which a few of the inhabitants have met with a loss of property; such losses will be duly investigated, and those entitled to remuneration will receive it.

California has for many years suffered greatly from domestic troubles; civil wars have been the poisoned fountains which have sent forth trouble and pestilence over her beautiful land. Now those fountains are dried up; the star-spangled banner floats over California, and as long as the sun continues to shine upon her, so long will it float there, over the natives of the land, as well as others who have found a home in her bosom; and under it agriculture must improve, and the arts and sciences flourish, as seed in a rich and fertile soil.

The Americans and Californians are now but one people; let us cherish one wish, one hope, and let that be for the peace and quiet of our country. Let us, as a band of brothers, unite and emulate each other in our exertions to benefit and improve this our beautiful, and which soon must be our happy and prosperous, home.

Done at Monterey, capital of California, this first day of March, A.D. 1847, and in the seventy-first year of independence of the United Suites.

S.W. KEARNY Brig.-Gen., U.S.A., and Governor of California.

The proclamation of General Kearny gave great satisfaction to the native as well as the emigrant population of the country. Several of the alcaldes of the district of my jurisdiction, as well as private individuals (natives of the country), expressed, by letter and orally, their approbation of the sentiments of the proclamation in the warmest terms. They said that they were heartily willing to become Americans upon these terms, and hoped that there would be the least possible delay in admitting them to the rights of American citizenship. There was a general expectation among natives as well as foreigners, that a representative form of territorial government would be immediately established by General Kearny. Why this was not done, is explained by the recent publication of General Scott's letter to General Kearny, dated November 3rd, 1846, of which Colonel Mason was the bearer, he having left the United States on the 7th November. In this letter General Scott says:—

"As a guide to the civil governor of Upper California, in our hands, see the letter of June 3rd (last), addressed to you by the Secretary of War. You will not, however, formally declare the province to be annexed. Permanent incorporation of the territory must depend on the government of the United States.

"After occupying with our forces all necessary points in Upper California, and establishing a temporary civil government therein, as well as assuring yourself of its internal tranquillity, and the absence of any danger of reconquest on the part of Mexico, you may charge Colonel Mason, United States first dragoons, the bearer of this open letter, or land officer next in rank to your own, with your several duties, and return yourself, with a sufficient escort of troops, to St. Louis, Missouri; but the body of the United States dragoons that accompanied you to California will remain there until further orders."

The transport ships Thomas H. Perkins, Loo Choo, Susan Drew, and Brutus, with Colonel Stevenson's regiment, arrived at San Francisco during the months of March and April. These vessels were freighted with a vast quantity of munitions, stores, tools, saw-mills, grist-mills, etc., etc., to be employed in the fortification of the principal harbours on the coast—San Francisco, Monterey, and San Diego. The regiment of Col. Stevenson was separated into different commands, portions of it being stationed at San Francisco, Sonoma, Monterey, Santa Barbara, and Los Angeles; and some companies employed against the horse-thief Indians of the Sierra Nevada and the Tulares.

As good an account of these horse-thief Indians, and their depredations, as I have seen, I find in the "California Star," of March 28th, 1847, written by a gentleman who has been a resident of California for a number of years, and who has been a sufferer. It is subjoined:—

"During the Spanish regime, such a thing as a horse-thief was unknown in the country; but as soon as the Mexicans took possession, their characteristic anarchy began to prevail, and the Indians to desert from the missions. The first Indian horse-thief known in this part of the country was a neophyte of the mission of Santa Clara, George, who flourished about twenty years ago. He absconded from his mission to the river of Stanislaus, of which he was a native. From thence he returned to the settlements, and began to steal horses, which at that time were very numerous. After pursuing his depredations for some time, he was at last pursued and killed on his return from one of his forages. The mission of Santa Clara has been, from that time to the present day, the greatest nursery for horse thieves, as the Stanislaus river has been and is their principal rendezvous. I have taken some pains to inquire among some of the most intelligent and respectable of the native inhabitants, as to the probable number of horses that have been stolen between Monterey and San Francisco within the last twenty years, and the result has been that more than one hundred thousand can be distinctly enumerated, and that the total amount would probably be double that number. Nearly all these horses have been eaten! From the river of Stanislaus, as a central point, the evil has spread to the north and south, and at present extends from the vicinity of the Mickelemes River on the north, to the sources of the St. Joaquin on the south. These Indians inhabit all the western declivity of the great snowy mountains, within these limits, and have become so habituated to living on horseflesh, that it is now with them the principal means of subsistence.

"In past time they have been repeatedly pursued, and many of them killed, and whole villages destroyed, but, so far from being deterred, they are continually becoming more bold and daring in their robberies, as horses become scarcer and more carefully guarded. About twenty persons have been killed by them within the knowledge of the writer. Among others, Mr. Lindsay and Mr. Wilson were killed by them not long ago. Only about one month since, they shot and dangerously wounded four persons employed on the farm of Mr. Weber, near the Pueblo of St. Joseph, and at the same time stole the horses of the farm, and those also from the farms of Captain Fisher and Mr. Burnal, in the same vicinity; in all, about two hundred head. Within the last ten days numerous parties of them have been committing depredations on many of the farms in the jurisdiction of the Contra Costa, and scarcely a night passes but we hear of their having stolen horses from some one. Three days ago, a party of them were met by some young men who had been out catching wild horses on the plains of the St. Joaquin, but as they were mounted on tired animals, they were only able to recapture the stolen horses, but could not overtake the thieves."

It has not been within the scope of my design, in writing out those notes, to enter into the minute details of the conquest and occupation of California by the forces of the United States. To do so would require more space than I have allowed myself, and the matter would be more voluminous than interesting or important. My intention has been to give such a sketch of the military operations in California, during my residence and travels in the country, as to afford to the reader a general and correct idea of the events transpiring at the time. No important circumstance, I think, has escaped my attention.

Among the officers of the army stationed at San Francisco, with whom I became acquainted, were Major Hardie, in command of the troops, Captain Folsom, acting quartermaster-general in California, and Lieutenant Warner, of the engineer corps. Lieutenant Warner marched with General Kearny from the United States, and was at the battle of San Pasqual. I have seen the coat which he wore on that occasion, pierced in seven different places by the lances of the enemy. He did not make this exhibition himself; and I never heard him refer to the subject but once, and then it was with the modesty of a veteran campaigner.

The corps of topographical engineers accompanying General Kearny, under the command of Captain Emory, will, doubtless, furnish in their report much interesting and valuable information. Mr. Stanley, the artist Of the expedition, completed his sketches in oil, at San Francisco; and a more truthful, interesting, and valuable series of paintings, delineating mountain scenery, the floral exhibitions on the route, the savage tribes between Santa Fe and California—combined with camp-life and marches through the desert and wilderness—has never been, and probably never will be, exhibited. Mr. Stanley informed me that he was preparing a work on the savage tribes of North America and of the islands of the Pacific, which, when completed on his plan, will be the most comprehensive and descriptive of the subject of any that has been published.

Legal proceedings are much less complex in California than in the United States. There is no written statute law in the country. The only law books I could find were a digested code entitled, "Laws of Spain and the Indies," published in Spain about a hundred years ago, and a small pamphlet defining the powers of various judicial officers, emanating from the Mexican government since the revolution. A late Mexican governor of California, on being required by a magistrate to instruct him as to the manner in which he should administer the law within his jurisdiction, replied, "Administer it in accordance with the principles of natural right and justice," and this is the foundation of Californian jurisprudence. The local bandos, or laws, are enacted, adjudicated, and executed by the local magistrates, or alcaldes. The alcalde has jurisdiction in all municipal matters, and in cases for minor offences, and for debt in sums not over one hundred dollars. In cases of heinous or capital offences, the alcalde has simply an examining power, the testimony being taken down in writing, and transmit-to the juez de primera instancia, or first judge of the district, before whom the case is tried. Civil actions, for sums over one hundred dollars, must also be tried before the juez de primera instancia, and from him there is an appeal to the prefect, or the governor of the province. The trial by hombres buenos, or good men, is one of the established legal tribunals when either of the parties demand it, and is similar to our trial by jury; the difference being in the number, the hombres buenos usually consisting of three or five, as they may be ordered by the magistrate, or requested by the litigants, and our jury of twelve. With honest and intelligent magistrates, the system operates advantageously, as justice is speedy and certain; but the reverse of this, with corrupt and ignorant magistrates, too frequently in power, the consequences of the system are as bad as can well be imagined.

The policy of the Mexican government has been to encourage in certain localities the erection of pueblos, or towns, and for this purpose they have made grants of land to the local authorities, or municipalities, within certain defined limits, to be regranted upon application, in lots of fifty or one hundred varass, as the case may be, to persons declaring their intention to settle and to do business in the town. For these grants to individuals a certain sum of money is paid, which goes into the treasury of the municipality. The magistrates, however, without special permission, have no power to grant lots of land within a certain number of feet of or below high-water mark. The power is reserved to be exercised by the governor of the province. It being necessary for the convenient landing of ships, and for the discharging and receiving of their cargoes, that the beach in front of the town of San Francisco should be improved with wharfs, etc., etc., and that titles should be granted to individuals who otherwise would make no durable improvements. As magistrate of the town, in compliance with the request of numerous citizens, I solicited from General Kearny, the acting governor, a relinquishment, on the part of the general government, of the beach lands in front of the town in favour of the municipality, under certain conditions. This was granted by the Governor, who issued a decree dated 10th March, permitting the sales by auction of all such grounds adjacent to the water-side as might be found adapted to commercial purposes, with the exception of such lots as might be selected for the use of the United States government, by its proper officers. The sales accordingly took place, the lots were eagerly purchased, and the port has already become a place of considerable commercial activity.

CHAPTER XV.

GENERAL OBSERVATIONS UPON THE COUNTRY.

First settlement of the missionaries
Population
Characteristics of white population
Employments
Pleasures and amusements
Position of women
Soil
Grasses
Vegetable productions
Agriculture
Fruits
Cattle
Horses
Wild animals
Minerals
Climate
Flora
Water-power
Timber
Religion.

It was during the month of November, 1602, the sun just retiring behind the distant high land which forms the background of a spacious harbour at the southernmost point of Alta California, that a small fleet of vessels might have been seen directing their course as if in search of a place of anchorage; their light sails drawn up, while the larger ones, swelling now and then to the action of the breeze, bore them majestically along, forcing their way through the immense and almost impenetrable barrier of sea-weed, to a haven which, at the remote period stated, was considered the unexplored region of the North. The fleet referred to hauled their wind to the shore, and, passing a bluff point of land on their left, soon came to anchor; but not until the shades of night had cast a gloom over the scene so recently lighted up with the gorgeous rays of a setting sun.

This was the commencement, or rather preliminary mark, of civilization in this country, by the Spaniards, (if so it can be called,) and on the following morning a detachment was landed, accompanied by a friar, to make careful investigation of the long ridge of high land which serves as a protection to the harbour from the heavy north-west gales. They found, as reported, an abundance of small oak and other trees, together with a great variety of useful and aromatic herbs; and from its summit they beheld the extent and beauty of the port, reaching, as they said, full three leagues from where the vessel lay at anchor. A large tent was erected on the sandy beach, to answer the purposes of a church, where the friar might perform mass, and by directions of the commanding officers, the boats were drawn up for repairing, wells were dug, parties were sent off to cut wood, while guards were placed at convenient distances to give notice of the approach of any hostile force. The latter precaution was hardly carried into effect, ere a large body of naked Indians were seen moving along the shore, armed with bows and arrows. A friar, protected by six soldiers, was dispatched to meet them, who, making signs of peace by exhibiting a white flag and throwing handfuls of sand high into the air, influenced them to lay aside their arms, when, affectionately embracing them, the good old friar distributed presents of beads and necklaces, with which they eagerly adorned their persons. This manifestation of good feeling induced them to draw near to where the commander had landed with his men, but perceiving so large a number, they retreated to a neighbouring knoll, and from thence sent forward to the Spaniards ten aged females, who, possessing apparently so much affability, were presented immediately with gifts, and instructed to go and inform their people of the friendly disposition cherished for them by the white strangers. This was sufficient to implant a free intercourse with the Indians, who daily visited the Spaniards, and bartered off their skins and furs in exchange for bread and trinkets. But at length the time arrived for the fleet to depart, and they proceeded northward, visiting in their course Monterey and Mendocino, where the same favourable result attended the enterprise as at other places, and they returned in safety to New Spain.

So successful had been the character of this expedition throughout the entire peri-od of its execution, that an enthusiasm prevailed in the minds of the Spaniards, which could only be assuaged by an attempt to conquer and christianize the inhabitants of that distant portion of the American continent. Many were the fruitless results of the Spanish adventurer—numerous were the statements of his toil and labour, till at length a formidable attempt, under the patronage and direc-tion of Don Gaspar de Portala and Father Junipero Serra, successfully achieved the desired object for which it was planned and executed.

At San Diego, where, a century and a half before, the primitive navigators under Cortez communed with the rude and unsophisticated native—there, where the zealous devotee erected his altar on the burning sand, and with offerings of incense and prayer hallowed it to God, as the birthplace of Christianity in that region—upon that sainted spot commenced the spiritual conquest, the cross was erected, and the holy missionaries who accompanied the expedition entered heart and soul upon their religious duties. Successful in all they undertook, their first establishment in a short time was completed, and drawing around it the convert-ed Indians in large numbers, the rude and uncultivated fields gave place to agri-cultural improvement—the arts and sciences gradually obtained foundation where before all was darkness, and day after day hundreds were added to the folds of the holy and apostolic church. Thus triumphantly proceeded the labours of the Spanish conquerors! In course of time other institutions were founded at Santa Barbara, Monterey, and San Francisco, where at each place a military fortress was erected, which served for their protection, and to keep in check such of the natives who were disinclined to observe the regulations of the community.

The natives formed an ardent and almost adorable attachment for their spiritual fathers, and were happy, quite happy, under their jurisdiction. Ever ready to obey them, the labour in the field and workshop met with ready compliance, and so prosperous were the institutions that many of them became wealthy, in the increase of their cattle and great abundance of their granaries. It was no unusual sight to behold the plains for leagues literally spotted with bullocks, and large fields of corn and wheat covering acres of ground. This state of things continued until the period when Mexico underwent a change in its political form of gov-ernment, which so disheartened the feelings of the loyal missionaries, that they became regardless of their establishments, and suffered them to decline for want of attention to their interests. At length, civil discord and anarchy among the Californians prepared a more effective measure for their destruction, and they were left to the superintendence of individuals who plundered them of all that was desirable or capable of removal. Thus, the government commenced the rob-bery, and its hirelings carried it out to the letter, destroying and laying waste wherever they were placed. In order to give the inhabitants a share of the spoils, some of them were permitted to slaughter the cattle by contract, which was an equal division of the proceeds, and the contractors were careful, when they delivered one hide to a mission, to reserve two for themselves, in this way following up the example of their superiors.

This important revolution in the systematic order of the monastic institutions took place in 1836, at which period the most important of them possessed property, exclusive of their lands and tenements, to the value of two hundred and fifty thousand dollars. At the present day they have but a little more than dilapidated walls and restricted boundaries of territory. Notwithstanding this wanton devastation of property, contrary to the opinion of many who were strongly in favour of supporting these religious institutions, the result proved beneficial to the country at large. Individual enterprise succeeded as the lands became distributed, so that the Californian beheld himself no longer dependent on the bounty of his spiritual directors, but, on the contrary, he was enabled to give support to them, from the increase and abundance of his own possessions.

Subsequent to the expulsion of the Mexicans, numbers of new farms were created, and hundreds of Americans were scattered over the country. Previous to 1830, the actual possessions of horned cattle by the rancheros did not exceed one hundred thousand; but in 1842, according to a fair estimate, made by one on the spot, the number had increased to four hundred thousand; so that the aggregate is equal to that held by the missions when in their most flourishing condition. The present number is not much, if any, short of one million.

Presuming a statistical knowledge of this country, before and after the missionary institutions were secularized, may be interesting, I will insert the following returns of 1831 and 1842, to contrast the same with its present condition:—

1st. In 1832 the white population throughout Alta-California did not exceed 4,500, while the Indians of the twenty-one missions amounted to 19,000; in 1842, the former had increased to 7,000, and the latter decreased to about 5,000.

2nd. In the former year, the number of horned cattle, including individual possessions, amounted to 500,000; in the latter, to 40,000.

3rd. At the same period, the number of sheep, goats, and pigs, was 321,000; at the latter, 32,000.

4th. In 1831 the number of horses, asses, mules, etc., was 64,000; in 1842 it was 30,000.

5th. The produce in corn, etc., had decreased in a much greater proportion—that of seventy to four.

The amount of duties raised at the customhouse in Monterey, from 1839 to 1842, was as follows, viz.:—

1839	85,613 dollars.
1840	72,308 dollars
1841	101,150 dollars
1842	73,729 dollars.

The net amount of revenue seldom exceeding in any year eighty thousand dollars; so that, when a deficiency took place, to supply the expenditures of government, it had been usual to call upon the missions for aid.

The value of the hides and tallow derived from the annual matanzas may be estimated at 372,000 dollars. These two commodities, with the exception of some beaver, sea-otter, and other furs, comprise the most important part of the exportations, which in addition, would augment the value of exports to 400,000 dollars.

The permanent population of that portion of Upper California situated between the Sierra Nevada and the Pacific, I estimate at 25,000. Of this number, 8,000 are Hispano-Americans, 5,000 foreigners, chiefly from the United States, and 12,000 christianized Indians. There are considerable numbers of wild or Gentile Indians, inhabiting the valley of the San Joaquin and the gorges of the Sierra, not included in this estimate. They are probably as numerous as the Christian Indians. The Indian population inhabiting the region of the Great Salt Lake, Mary's River, the oases of the Great Desert Basin, and the country bordering the Rio Colorado and its tributaries, being spread over a vast extent of territory, are scarcely seen, although the aggregate number is considerable.

The Californians do not differ materially from the Mexicans, from whom they are descended, in other provinces of that country. Physically and intellectually, the men, probably, are superior to the same race farther south, and inhabiting the countries contiguous to the city of Mexico. The intermixture of blood with the Indian and negro races has been less, although it is very perceptible.

The men, as a general fact, are well made, with pleasing sprightly countenances, and possessing much grace and ease of manners, and vivacity of conversation. But hitherto they have had little knowledge of the world and of events, beyond what they have heard through Mexico, and derived from the supercargoes of merchant-ships and whalemen touching upon the coast. There are no public schools in the country—at least I never heard of one. There are but few books. General Vallejo has a library with many valuable books, and this is the only one I saw, although there are others; but they are rare, and confined to a few families.

The men are almost constantly on horseback, and as horsemen excel any I have seen in other parts of the world. From the nature of their pursuits and amuse-ments, they have brought horsemanship to a perfection challenging admiration and exciting astonishment. They are trained to the horse and the use of the lasso (riata, as it is here called) from their infancy. The first act of a child, when he is able to stand alone, is to throw his toy lasso around the neck of a kitten; his next feat is performed on the dog; his next upon a goat or calf; and so on, until he mounts the horse, and demonstrates his skill upon horses and cattle. The crown-ing feat of dexterity with the riata, and of horsemanship, combined with daring courage, is the lassoing of the grisly bear. This feat is performed frequently upon this large and ferocious animal, but it is sometimes fatal to the performer and his horse. Well drilled, with experienced military leaders, such as would inspire them with confidence in their skill and prowess, the Californians ought to be the finest cavalry in the world. The Californian saddle is, I venture to assert, the best that has been invented, for the horse and the rider. Seated in one of these, it is scarce-ly possible to be unseated by any ordinary casualty. The bridle bit is clumsily made, but so constructed that the horse is compelled to obey the rider upon the slightest intimation. The spurs are of immense size, but they answer to an experi-enced horseman the double purpose of exciting the horse, and of maintaining the rider in his seat under difficult circumstances.

For the pleasures of the table they care but little. With his horse and trappings, his sarape and blanket, a piece of beef and a tortilla, the Californian is content, so far as his personal comforts are concerned. But he is ardent in his pursuit of amusement and pleasure, and these consist chiefly in the fandango, the game of monte, horse-racing, and bull and bear-baiting. They gamble freely and desper-ately, but pay their losses with the most strict punctuality, at any and every sacri-fice, and manifest but little concern about them. They are obedient to their mag-istrates, and in all disputed cases decided by them, acquiesce without uttering a word of complaint. They have been accused of treachery and insincerity. Whatever may have been the grounds for these accusations in particular instances, I know not; but, judging from my own observation and experience, they are as free from these qualities as our own people.

While the men are employed in attending to the herds of cattle and horses, and engaged in their other amusements, the women (I speak of the middle classes on the ranchos) superintend and perform most of the drudgery appertaining to housekeeping, and the cultivation of the gardens, from whence are drawn such vegetables as are consumed at the table. These are few, consisting of frijoles, potatoes, onions, and chiles. The assistants in these labours are the Indian men and women, legally reduced to servitude.

The soil of that portion of California between the Sierra Nevada and the Pacific will compare, in point of fertility, with any that I have seen elsewhere. As I have already described such portions of it as have come under my observation, it is unnecessary for me here to descend to particulars. Wheat, barley, and other small grains, with hemp, flax, and tobacco, can be produced in all the valleys, without irrigation. To produce maize, potatoes, and other garden vegetables, irrigation is necessary. Oats and mustard grow spontaneously, with such rankness as to be considered nuisances upon the soil. I have forced my way through thousands of acres of these, higher than my head when mounted on a horse. The oats grow to the summits of the hills, but they are not here so tall and rank as in the valleys.

The varieties of grasses are greater than on the Atlantic side of the continent, and far more nutritious. I have seen seven different kinds of clover, several of them in a dry state, depositing a seed upon the ground so abundant as to cover it, which is lapped up by the cattle and horses and other animals, as corn or oats, when threshed, would be with us. All the grasses, and they cover the entire country, are heavily seeded, and, when ripe, are as fattening to stock as the grains which we feed to our beef, horses, and hogs. Hence it is unnecessary to the sustenance or fattening of stock to raise corn for their consumption.

Agriculture is in its rudest state. The farming implements which have been used by the Californians, with few exceptions, are the same as were used three hundred years ago, when Mexico was conquered by Cortez. A description of them would be tedious. The plough, however, which merely scratches the ground, is the fork of a small tree. It is the same pattern as the Roman plough, two thousand years ago. Other agricultural implements are of the same description. The Americans, and other foreigners, are, however, introducing the American plough, and other American farming tools, the consequence of which has already been, to some extent, to produce a revolution in agriculture. The crops of wheat and barley, which I saw about the 1st of June, while passing through the country on my journey to the United States, exceeded in promise any which I have seen in the United States. It was reported to me that Captain Sutter's crop of wheat, for 1847, would amount to 75,000 bushels.

The natural vegetable productions of California have been sufficiently noticed in the course of this work, for the reader to form a correct estimate of the capabilities of the soil and climate. It is supposed by some, that cotton, sugar, and rice, could be produced here. I do not doubt but there are portions of the country where these crops would thrive; but I question whether, generally, they could be cultivated to advantage. Nearly all the fruits of the temperate and tropical climates are produced in perfection in California, as has before been stated.

The principal product of the country has been its cattle and horses. The cattle are, I think, the largest and finest I ever saw, and the beef is more delicious. There are immense herds of these, to which I have previously referred; and their hides and tallow, when slaughtered, have hitherto composed the principal exports from the country. If I were to hazard an estimate of the number of hides annually exported, it would be conjectural, and not worth much. I would suppose, however, at this time (1847), that the number would not fall much short of 150,000, and a corresponding number of arrobas (25 pounds) of tallow. The average value of cattle is about five dollars per head.

The horses and mules are correspondingly numerous with the cattle; and although the most of them are used in the country, considerable numbers are driven to Sonora, New Mexico, and other southern provinces, and some of them to the United States, for a market. They are smaller than American horses, and I do not think them equal for continuous hard service; but on short trips, for riding, their speed and endurance are not often, if ever, equalled by our breed of horses. The value of good horses is from ten to twenty-five dollars; of mares, five dollars. The prices have, however, since the Americans came into the country, become fluctuating, and the value of both horses and cattle is increasing rapidly.

The wild animals of California are the wild-horse, the elk, the black-tailed deer, antelope, grizly bear, all in large numbers. Added to these are the beaver, otter, coyote, hare, squirrel, and the usual variety of other small animals. There is not so great a variety of small birds as I have seen elsewhere. I do not consider that the country presents strong attractions for the ornithologist. But what is wanting in variety is made up in numbers. The bays and indentations on the coast, as well as the rivers and lakes interior, swarm with myriads of wild geese, ducks, swans, and other water birds. The geese and ducks are a mongrel race, their plumage being variegated, the same as our barn-yard fowls. Some of the islands in the harbour, near San Francisco, are white with the guano deposited by these birds; and boat-loads of eggs are taken from them. The pheasant and partridge are abundant in the mountains.

In regard to the minerals of California, not much is yet known. It has been the policy of the owners of land upon which there existed minerals to conceal them as much as possible. A reason for this has been, that the law of Mexico is such, that if one man discovers a mine of any kind upon another man's land, and the proprietor does not work it, the former may denounce the mine, and take possession of it, and hold it so long as he continues to work it. Hence the proprietors of land upon which there are valuable mineral ores conceal their existence as much as possible. While in California I saw quicksilver, silver, lead, and iron ores, and the specimens were taken from mines said to be inexhaustible. From good authority I learned the existence of gold and copper mines, the metals being combined; and I saw specimens of coal taken from two or three different points, but I do not know what the indications were as to quality. Brimstone, saltpetre, muriate and carbonate of soda, and bitumen, are abundant. There is little doubt that California is as rich in minerals of all kinds as any portion of Mexico.

I have taken much pains to describe to the reader, from day to day, and at different points during my travels in California, the temperature and weather. It is rarely so cold in the settled portions of California as to congeal water. But twice only while here I saw ice, and then not thicker than window-glass. I saw no snow resting upon the ground. The annual rains commence in November, and continue, with intervals of pleasant springlike weather, until May. From May to November, usually, no rain falls. There are, however, exceptions. Rain sometimes falls in August. The thermometer, at any season of the year, rarely sinks below 50 deg. or rises above 80 deg.. In certain positions on the coast, and especially at San Francisco, the winds rise diurnally, and blowing fresh upon the shore render the temperature cool in midsummer. In the winter the wind blows from the land, and the temperature at these points is warmer. These local peculiarities of climate are not descriptive of the general climate of the interior.

For salubrity I do not think there is any climate in the world superior to that of the coast of California. I was in the country nearly a year, exposed much of the time to great hardships and privations, sleeping, for the most part, in the open air, and I never felt while there the first pang of disease, or the slightest indication of bad health. On some portions of the Sacramento and San Joaquin Rivers, where vegetation is rank, and decays in the autumn, the malaria produces chills and fever, but generally the attacks are slight, and yield easily to medicine. The atmosphere is so pure and preservative along the coast, that I never saw putrified flesh, although I have seen, in midsummer, dead carcasses lying exposed to the sun and weather for months. They emitted no offensive smell. There is but little disease in the country arising from the climate.

The botany and flora of California are rich, and will hereafter form a fruitful field of discovery to the naturalist. There are numerous plants reported to possess extraordinary medical virtues. The "soap-plant" (amole) is one which appears to be among the most serviceable. The root, which is the saponaceous portion of the plant, resembles the onion, but possesses the quality of cleansing linen equal to any "oleic soap" manufactured by my friends Cornwall and Brother, of Louisville, Ky.

There is another plant in high estimation with the Californians, called canchalagua, which is held by them as an antidote for all the diseases to which they are subject, but in particular for cases of fever and ague. For purifying the blood, and regulating the system, I think it surpasses all the medicinal herbs that have been brought into notice, and it must become, in time, one of the most important articles in the practice of medicine. In the season for flowers, which is generally during the months of May and June, its pretty pink-coloured blossoms form a conspicuous display in the great variety which adorn the fields of California.

The water-power in California is ample for any required mill purposes. Timber for lumber is not so convenient as is desirable. There is, however, a sufficiency of it, which, when improvements are made, will be more accessible. The timber on the Sierra Nevada, the most magnificent in the world, cannot be, at present, available. The evergreen oak, that grows generally in the valleys, is not valuable, except for fuel. But in the canadas of the hills, and at several places on the coast, particularly at Santa Cruz and Bodega, there is an amount of pine and fir, adapted for lumber, that will not be consumed for a long time.

The religion of the Californians is the Roman Catholic, and, like the people of all Roman Catholic countries, they appear to be devotedly attached to the forms of their religion. That there are some, I will not say how many, paganish grafts upon the laws, formalities, and ceremonies, as prescribed by the "Holy Church Universal" for its government and observance, is undeniable, but these probably do not materially affect the system. The females, I noticed, were nearly all devoutly attached to their religious institutions. I have seen, on festival or saint days, the entire floor of a church occupied by pious women, with their children, kneeling in devout worship, and chanting with much fervency some dismal hymn appertaining to the service. There are but few of the Jesuit fathers who established the missions now remaining in the country. The services are performed at several of the churches that I visited, by native Indians, educated by the padres previous to their expulsion by the Mexican government.

CHAPTER XVI.

OFFICIAL REPORT ON THE GOLD MINES.

The following is an official account of a visit paid to the gold region in July by Colonel Mason, who had been appointed to the military command in California, and made his report to the authorities at Washington. It is dated from head-quarters at Monterey, August 17, 1848.

"Sir,—I have the honour to inform you that, accompanied by Lieut. W.T. Sherman, 3rd Artillery, A.A.A. General, I started on the 12th of June last to make a tour through the northern part of California. We reached San Francisco on the 20th, and found that all, or nearly all, its male inhabitants had gone to the mines. The town, which a few months before was so busy and thriving, was then almost deserted. Along the whole route mills were lying idle, fields of wheat were open to cattle and horses, houses vacant, and farms going to waste.

"On the 5th we arrived in the neighbourhood of the mines, and proceeded twenty-five miles up the American Fork, to a point on it now known as the Lower Mines, or Mormon Diggings. The hill sides were thickly strewn with canvas tents and bush-harbours; a store was erected, and several boarding shanties in operation. The day was intensely hot, yet about 200 men were at work in the full glare of the sun, washing for gold—some with tin pans, some with close woven Indian baskets, but the greater part had a rude machine known as the cradle. This is on rockers, six or eight feet long, open at the foot, and its head had a coarse grate, or sieve; the bottom is rounded, with small cleets nailed across. Four men are required to work this machine; one digs the ground in the bank close by the stream; another carries it to the cradle, and empties it on the grate; a third gives a violent rocking motion to the machine, whilst a fourth dashes on water from the stream itself. The sieve keeps the coarse stones from entering the cradle, the current of water washes off the earthy matter, and the gravel is gradually carried out at the foot of the machine, leaving the gold mixed with a heavy fine black sand above the first cleets. The sand and gold mixed together are then drawn off through auger holes into a pan below, are dried in the sun, and afterwards separated by blowing off the sand. A party of four men, thus employed at the Lower Mines, average 100 dollars a-day. The Indians, and those who have nothing but pans or willow baskets, gradually wash out the earth, and separate the gravel by hand, leaving nothing but the gold mixed with sand, which is separated in the manner before described. The gold in the Lower Mines is in fine bright scales, of which I send several specimens.

"As we ascended the south branch of the American fork, the country became more broken and mountainous, and twenty-five miles below the lower washings the hills rise to about 1000 feet above the level of the Sacramento Plain. Here a species of pine occurs, which led to the discovery of the gold. Captain Sutter, feeling the great want of lumber, contracted in September last with a Mr. Marshall to build a saw-mill at that place. It was erected in the course of the past winter and spring—a dam and race constructed; but when the water was let on the wheel, the tail race was found to be too narrow to permit the water to escape with sufficient rapidity. Mr. Marshall, to save labour, let the water directly into the race with a strong current, so as to wash it wider and deeper. He effected his purpose, and a large bed of mud and gravel was carried to the foot of the race. One day Mr. Marshall, as he was walking down the race to this deposit of mud, observed some glittering particles at its upper edge; he gathered a few, examined them, and became satisfied of their value. He then went to the fort, told Captain Sutter of his discovery, and they agreed to keep it secret until a certain grist-mill of Sutter's was finished. It, however, got out and spread like magic. Remarkable success attended the labours of the first explorers, and, in a few weeks, hundreds of men were drawn thither. At the time of my visit, but little more than three months after its first discovery, it was estimated that upwards of four thousand people were employed. At the mill there is a fine deposit or bank of gravel, which the people respect as the property of Captain Sutter, though he pretends to no right to it, and would be perfectly satisfied with the simple promise of a pre-emption on account of the mill which he has built there at a considerable cost. Mr. Marshall was living near the mill, and informed me that many persons were employed above and below him; that they used the same machines as at the lower washings, and that their success was about the same—ranging from one to three ounces of gold per man daily. This gold, too, is in scales a little coarser than those of the lower mines. From the mill Mr. Marshall guided me up the mountain on the opposite or north bank of the south fork, where in the bed of small streams or ravines, now dry, a great deal of coarse gold has been found. I there saw several parties at work, all of whom were doing very well; a great many specimens were shown me, some as heavy as four or five ounces in weight; and I send three pieces, labelled No. 5, presented by a Mr. Spence. You will perceive that some of the specimens accompanying this hold mechanically pieces of quartz—that the surface is rough, and evidently moulded in the crevice of a rock. This gold cannot have been carried far by water, but must have remained near where it was first deposited from the rock that once bound it. I inquired of many if they had encountered the metal in its matrix, but in every instance they said they had not; but that the gold was invariably mixed with wash-gravel, or lodged in the crevices of other rocks. All bore testimony that they had found gold in greater or less quantities in the numerous small gullies or ravines that occur in that mountainous region. On the 7th of July I left the mill, and crossed to a small stream emptying into the American fork, three or four miles below the saw-mill. I struck the stream (now known as Weber's Creek) at the washings of Sunol and Company. They had about thirty Indians employed, whom they pay in merchandise. They were getting gold of a character similar to that found in the main fork, and doubtless in sufficient quantities to satisfy them. I send you a small specimen, presented by this Company, of their gold. From this point we proceeded up the stream about eight miles, where we found a great many people and Indians, some engaged in the bed of the stream, and others in the small side valleys that put into it. These latter are exceedingly rich, two ounces being considered an ordinary yield for a day's work. A small gutter, not more than 100 yards long by four feet wide, and two or three deep, was pointed out to me as the one where two men (W. Daly and Percy McCoon) had a short time before obtained. 17,000 dollars' worth of gold. Captain Weber informed me, that he knew that these two men had employed four white men and about 100 Indians, and that, at the end of one week's work, they paid off their party, and had left 10,000 dollars' worth of this gold. Another small ravine was shown me, from which had been taken upwards of 12,000 dollars' worth of gold. Hundreds of similar ravines, to all appearances, are as yet untouched. I could not have credited these reports had I not seen, in the abundance of the precious metal, evidence of their truth. Mr. Neligh, an agent of Commodore Stockton, had been at work about three weeks in the neighbourhood, and showed me, in bags and bottles, 2000 dollars' worth of gold; and Mr. Lyman, a gentleman of education, and worthy of every credit, said he had been engaged with four others, with a machine, on the American fork, just below Sutter's Mill, that they worked eight days, and that his share was at the rate of fifty dollars a-day, but hearing that others were doing better at Weber's Place, they had removed there, and were then on the point of resuming operations.

"The country on either side of Weber's Creek is much broken up by hills, and is intersected in every direction by small streams or ravines which contain more or less gold. Those that have been worked are barely scratched, and, although thousands of ounces have been carried away, I do not consider that a serious impression has been made upon the whole. Every day was developing new and richer deposits; and the only impression seemed to be, that the metal would be found in such abundance as seriously to depreciate in value.

"On the 8th July I returned to the lower mines, and eventually to Monterey, where I arrived on the 17th of July. Before leaving Sutter's, I satisfied myself that gold existed in the bed of the Feather River, in the Yubah and Bear, and in many of the small streams that lie between the latter and the American fork; also, that it had been found in the Consummes, to the south of the American fork. In each of these streams the gold is found in small scales, whereas in the intervening mountains it occurs in coarser lumps.

"Mr. Sinclair, whose rancho is three miles above Sutter's on the north side of the American, employs about fifty Indians on the north fork, not far from its junction with the main stream. He had been engaged about five weeks when I saw him, and up to that time his Indians had used simply closely-woven willow baskets. His net proceeds (which I saw) were about 16,000 dollars' worth of gold. He showed me the proceeds of his last week's work—14 lbs. avoirdupois of clean washed gold.

"The principal store at Sutter's fort, that of Brannan and Co., had received in payment for goods 36,000 dollars' worth of this gold from the 1st of May to the 10th of July. Other merchants had also made extensive sales. Large quantities of goods were daily sent forward to the mines, as the Indians, heretofore so poor and degraded, have suddenly become consumers of the luxuries of life. I before mentioned that the greater part of the farmers and rancheros had abandoned their fields to go to the mines. This is not the case with Captain Sutter, who was carefully gathering his wheat, estimated at 40,000 bushels. Flour is already worth, at Sutter's, 36 dollars a-barrel, and will soon be 50. Unless large quantities of breadstuffs reach the country much suffering will occur; but as each man is now able to pay a large price, it is believed the merchants will bring from Chili and the Oregon a plentiful supply for the coming winter.

"The most moderate estimate I could obtain from men acquainted with the subject was, that upwards of 4,000 men were working in the gold district, of whom more than one-half were Indians, and that from 30,000 to 50,000 dollars' worth of gold, if not more, were daily obtained. The entire gold district, with very few exceptions of grants made some years ago by the Mexican authorities, is on land belonging to the United States. It was a matter of serious reflection to me, how I could secure to the Government certain rents or fees for the privilege of securing this gold; but upon considering the large extent of country, the character of the people engaged, and the small scattered force at my command, I resolved not to interfere, but permit all to work freely, unless broils and crimes should call for interference.

"The discovery of these vast deposits of gold has entirely changed the character of Upper California. Its people, before engaged in cultivating their small patches of ground, and guarding their herds of cattle and horses, have all gone to the mines, or are on their way thither. Labourers of every trade have left their work-benches, and tradesmen their shops; sailors desert their ships as fast as they arrive on the coast; and several vessels have gone to sea with hardly enough hands to spread a sail. Two or three are now at anchor in San Francisco, with no crew on board. Many desertions, too, have taken place from the garrisons within the influence of these mines; twenty-six soldiers have deserted from the post of Sonoma, twenty-four from that of San Francisco, and twenty-four from Monterey. I have no hesitation now in saying, that there is more gold in the country drained by the Sacramento and San Joaquin Rivers than will pay the cost of the present war with Mexico a hundred times over. No capital is required to obtain this gold, as the labouring man wants nothing but his pick and shovel and tin pan, with which to dig and wash the gravel, and many frequently pick gold out of the crevices of rocks with their knives, in pieces of from one to six ounces.

"Gold is also believed to exist on the eastern slope of the Sierra Nevada; and, when at the mines, I was informed by an intelligent Mormon that it had been found near the Great Salt Lake by some of his fraternity. Nearly all the Mormons are leaving California to go to the Salt Lake; and this they surely would not do unless they were sure of finding gold there, in the same abundance as they now do on the Sacramento.

"I have the honour to be,

"Your most obedient Servant,

"R.B. MASON, Colonel 1st Dragoons, commanding.

"Brigadier-General R. Jones, Adjutant-General, U.S.A., Washington, D.C."

CHAPTER XVII.

Rate of Wages
Mode of procuring the Gold
Extent of Gold Region
Price of Provisions.

It will be seen, from the later accounts that each new report continues to realize the wildest expectation. The following letter dated Monterey, November 16th, is highly interesting—

"We can now call ourselves citizens of the United States. We have now only to go by law, as we formerly went by custom; that is, when Congress gives us a government and code. The old foreign residents of California, having done very well ten or twenty years without law, care but very little whether Congress pays early or late attention to the subject. Those who have emigrated from the Atlantic States within the last three or four years deem the subject an important one; I only call it difficult. The carrying out a code of laws, under existing circumstances, is far from being an easy task. The general Government may appoint governors, secretaries, and other public functionaries; and judges, marshals, collectors, etc., may accept offices with salaries of 3000 or 4000 dollars per annum; but how they are to obtain their petty officers, at half these sums, remains to be seen. The pay of a member of Congress will be accepted here by those alone who do not know enough to better themselves. Mechanics can now get 10 to 16 dollars per day; labourers on the wharfs or elsewhere, 5 to 10 dollars; clerks and storekeepers, 1000 to 3000 dollars per annum—some engage to keep store during their pleasure at 8 dollars per day, or 1 lb. or 1-1/2 lb. of gold per month; cooks and stewards, 60 to 100 dollars per month. In fact, labour of every description commands exorbitant prices.

"The Sandwich Islands, Oregon, and Lower California are fast parting with their inhabitants, all bound for this coast, and thence to the great 'placer' of the Sacramento Valley, where the digging and washing of one man that does not produce 100 troy ounces of gold, 23 carats, from the size of a half spangle to one pound in a month, sets the digger to 'prospecting,' that is, looking for better grounds. Your 'Paisano' can point out many a man who has, for fifteen to twenty days in succession, bagged up five to ten ounces of gold a-day. Our placer, or gold region, now extends over 300 or 400 miles of country, embracing all the creeks and branches on the east side of the river Sacramento and one side of the San Joaquin. In my travels I have, when resting under a tree and grazing my horse, seen pieces of pure gold taken from crevices of the rocks or slate where we were stopping. On one occasion, nooning or refreshing on the side of a stream entirely unknown to diggers or 'prospectors,' or rather, if known not attended to, one of my companions, while rolling in the sand, said, 'Give me a tin pan; why should we not be cooking in gold sand?' He took a pan, filled it with sand, washed it out, and produced in five minutes two or three dollars' worth of gold, merely saying, as he threw both pan and gold on the sand, 'I thought so.' Perhaps it is fair that your readers should learn, that, however plenty the Sacramento Valley may afford gold, the obtaining of it has its disadvantages. From the 1st of July to the 1st of October, more or less, one half of the people will have fever and ague, or intermittent fever. In the winter, it is too cold to work in the water. Some work in the sand by washing from the surface in a wooden bowl, or tin pan; some gouge it out from the rocks or slate; the more lazy ones roll about and pick up the large pieces, leaving the small gold for the next emigration. The extent of the gold region on the San Joaquin and Sacramento rivers extends a distance of 800 miles in length by 100 in width. It embraces not only gold, but quantities of quicksilver in almost general abundance. It is estimated that a small population actively engaged in mining operations in that region could export 100,000,000 dollars in gold in every year, and that an increased population might increase that amount to 300,000,000 dollars annually. You may believe me when I say that for some time to come California will export, yearly, nearly or quite 500,000 ounces of gold, 22 to 24 carats fine; some pieces of that will weigh 16 lbs., very many 1 lb. Many men who began last June to dig gold with a capital of 50 dollars can now show 5000 to 15,000 dollars. I saw a man to-day making purchases of dry goods, etc., for his family, lay on the counter a bag of raw hide, well sewed up, containing 109 ounces. I observed, 'That is a good way to pack gold dust.' He very innocently replied, 'All the bags I brought down are that way; I like the size!' Five such bags in New York would bring nearly 10,000 dollars. This man left his family last

August. Three months' digging and washing, producing four or five bags, of 100 ounces each, is better than being mate of a vessel at 40 dollars per month, as the man formerly was. His companion, a Mexican, who camped and worked with him, only had two or three cow-hide bags of gold. In this tough, but true, golden tale, you must not imagine that all men are equally successful. There are some who have done better, even to 4000 dollars in a month; many 1000 dollars during the summer; and others, who refused to join a company of gold-washers who had a cheap-made machine, and receive one ounce per day, that returned to the settlement with not a vest pocket-full of gold. Some left with only sufficient to pay for a horse and saddle, and pay the physician six ounces of gold for one ounce of quinine, calomel, and jalap in proportion. An ounce of gold for advice given, six ounces a visit, brings the fever and ague to be rather an expensive companion. A 'well' man has his proportionate heavy expenses also, to reduce his piles or bags of gold. Dry beef in the settlements, at 4 cents per lb., at the Placer, 1 to 2 dollars per lb.; salt beef and pork, 50 to 100 dollars per barrel; flour, 30 to 75 dollars per barrel; coffee, sugar, and rice, 50 cents to 1 dollar per lb. As washing is 50 cents to 1 dollar a garment, many prefer throwing away their used-up clothes to paying the washerwoman; that is, if they intend returning to the settlements soon, where they can purchase more. As to shaving, I have never seen a man at the Placer who had time to perform that operation. They do not work on Sundays, only brush up the tent, blow out the emery or fine black sand from the week's work. Horses that can travel only one day, and from that to a week, are from 100 to 300 dollars. Freight charge by launch owners for three days' run, 5 dollars per barrel. Wagoners charge 50 to 100 dollars per load, 20 to 50 miles, on good road. Corn, barley, peas, and beans, 10 dollars a-bushel. Common pistols, any price; powder and lead very dear. I know a physician who, in San Francisco, purchased a common made gold-washer at 20 or 30 dollars, made of 70 or 80 feet of boards. At a great expense he boated it up to the first landing on the Sacramento, and there met a wagoner bound to one of the diggings with an empty wagon, distant about 50 miles. The wagoner would not take up the machine under 100 dollars. The doctor had to consent, and bided his time. June passed over, rich in gold; all on that creek did wonders, when the wagoner fell sick, called on his friend the doctor, whose tent was in sight; the doctor came, but would not administer the first dose under the old sum of 100 dollars, which was agreed to, under a proviso that the following doses should be furnished more moderate. When a man's time is worth 100 dollars a-day, to use a spade and tin pan, neither doctors nor wagoners can think much of a pound of gold, and you may suppose merchants, traders, and pedlars are not slow to make their fortunes in these golden times. In San Francisco there is more merchandize sold now, monthly, than before in a year. Vessels after vessels arrive, land their cargoes, dispose of them, and bag up the dust and lay up the vessel, as the crew are soon among the missing. The cleanest clear out is where the captain follows the crew. There are many vessels in San Francisco that cannot weigh anchor, even with the assistance of three or four neighbouring vessels. Supercargoes must land cargo on arriving, or have no crew to do it for them. Some vessels continue to go to sea, with small crews, at 50 dollars per month for green hands. Old hands are too wise for them, and prefer digging an ounce or two a-day, and drinking hock and champagne at half an ounce a-bottle, and eating bad sea bread at 1 dollar per pound. I have seen a captain of a vessel, who, by his old contract in the port whence he sailed, was getting 60 dollars per month, paying his cook 75 dollars, and offering 100 dollars per month for a steward; his former crew, even to his mates, having gone a 'prospecting.' Uncle Sam's ships suffer a little the same way, although they offer from 200 to 500 dollars for the apprehension of a deserter. The Ohio, however, laid in the port of Monterey about a month, and lost only 20 or 30 men. Colonel Stevenson's regiment is disbanded, 99 out of 100 of whom have also gone 'prospecting,' including the colonel, who arrived in Monterey last month, from his last post, and was met by his men at the edge of the town, to escort and cheer him into the town. The captains, etc., have bought up country carts and oxen, turned drivers, and gone to the Placer. Our worthy governor, Colonel of the 1st Dragoons, etc., having plenty of carts, wagons, horses, and mules, with a few regulars left, has also gone, but under better advantages, for the second or third time, to see the Placer and the country, and have justice done to his countrymen or himself. Commodore Jones, lately arrived in Monterey, supposed it to be the capital, head-quarters, etc., but found not even the Governor left. Where head-quarters are may be uncertain, whether in Monterey, Sutter's Fort, or in a four-mule wagon travelling over the gold region. Now, whether headquarters are freighted with munitions of war, etc., or whether the cargo consists of blankets, shirts, etc., to clothe the suffering Indians, for the paltry consideration of gold, no one cares or knows; but the principle should be, that, if privates can or will be off making their thousands, those who are better able should not go goldless."

The Washington Union contains a letter from Lieutenant Larkin, dated Monterey, November 16, received at the State Department, containing further confirmation of the previous despatches, public and private, and far outstripping all other news in its exciting character. The gold was increasing in size and quality daily. Lumps were found weighing from one to two pounds. Several had been heard of weighing as high as 16 pounds, and one 25 pounds. Many men, who were poor in June, were worth 30,000 dollars, by digging and trading with the Indians. 100 dollars a-day is the average amount realized daily, from July to October. Half the diggers were sick with fevers, though not many deaths had occurred among them. The Indians would readily give an ounce of gold for a common calico shirt; others were selling for ten dollars each in specie. The gold region extends over a track of 300 miles, and it was not known that it did not extend 1000. A letter from Commodore Jones states that many of the petty officers and men had deserted and gone in search of the gold. He adds, the Indians were selling gold at 50 cents the ounce. Many vessels were deserted by captain, cook, and seamen. The ship Isaac Walton offered discharged soldiers 50 dollars per month to go to Callao, which was refused. She was supplied by government sailors. All the naval vessels on the coast were short of hands. Nearly the whole of the 3rd Artillery had deserted. Provisions were scarce and high; board, 4 dollars a-day; washing, 6 dollars a-dozen. Merchants' clerks get from 2000 to 3000 dollars a-year.

CHAPTER XVIII.

Route by land
Outfit, etc., and advice to intending Emigrants.

The route via Independence or St. Joseph, Mo., to Fort Laramie, South Pass, Fort Hall, the Sink of Mary's River, etc., etc., the old route. Let no emigrant, carrying his family with him, deviate from it, or imagine that he can find a better road. This road is the best that has yet been discovered, and to the Bay of San Francisco and the Gold Region it is much the shortest. The Indians, moreover, on this route, have, up to the present time, been so friendly as to commit no acts of hostility on the emigrants. The trail is plain and good where there are no physical obstructions, and the emigrant, by taking this route, will certainly reach his destination in good season and without disaster. From our information we would most earnestly advise all emigrants to take this trail, without deviation, if they would avoid the fatal calamities which almost invariably have attended those who have undertaken to explore new routes.

The lightest wagon that can be constructed, of sufficient strength to carry 2500 pounds' weight, is the vehicle most desirable. No wagon should be loaded over this weight, or if it is, it will be certain to stall in the muddy sloughs and crossings on the prairie in the first part of the journey. This wagon can be hauled by three or four yokes of oxen or six mules. Oxen are usually employed by the emigrants for hauling their wagons. They travel about 15 miles per day, and, all things considered, are perhaps equal to mules for this service, although they cannot travel so fast. They are, however, less expensive, and there is not so much danger of their straying and of being stolen by the Indians.

Pack-mules can only be employed by parties of men. It would be very difficult to transport a party of women and children on pack-mules, with the provisions, clothing, and other baggage necessary to their comfort. A party of men, however, with pack-mules, can make the journey in less time by one month than it can be done in wagons—carrying with them, however, nothing more than their provisions, clothing, and ammunition.

For parties of men going out, it would be well to haul their wagons, provisions, etc., as far as Fort Laramie, or Fort Hall, by mules, carrying with them pack-saddles and alforjases, or large saddle-bags, adapted to the pack-saddle, with ropes for packing, etc., when, if they saw proper, they could dispose of their wagons for Indian ponies, and pack into California, gaining perhaps two or three weeks' time.

The provisions actually necessary per man are as follows:—

   150 lbs. of flour.
   150 do. bacon.
   25 do. coffee.
   30 do. sugar.

Added to these, the main items, there should be a small quantity of rice, 50 or 75 lbs. of crackers, dried peaches, etc., and a keg of lard, with salt, pepper, etc., and such other luxuries of light weight as the person outfitting chooses to purchase. He will think of them before he starts.

Every man should be provided with a good rifle, and, if convenient, with a pair of pistols, five pounds of powder, and ten pounds of lead. A revolving belt-pistol may be found useful.

With the wagon, there should be carried such carpenter's tools as a hand-saw, auger, gimlet, chisel, shaving-knife, etc., an axe, hammer, and hatchet. This last weapon every man should have in his belt, with a hunter's or a bowie-knife.

From Independence to the first settlement in California, which is near the gold region, it is about 2050 miles—to San Francisco, 2290 miles.

The accounts that have been received and published in regard to the wealth and productiveness of the gold mines, and other mines in California, are undoubtedly true. They are derived from the most authentic and reliable sources, and from individuals whose veracity may be undoubtingly believed.

When a young man arrives there, he must turn his attention to whatever seems to promise the largest recompense for his labour. It is impossible in the new state of things produced by the late discoveries, and the influx of population, to foresee what this might be. The country is rich in agricultural resources, as well as in the precious metals, and, with proper enterprise and industry, he could scarcely fail to do well.

Families, as well as parties going out, should carry with them good tents, to be used after their arrival as houses. The influx of population will probably be so great that it will be difficult, if not impossible, to obtain other shelter for some time after their arrival. The climate of the country, however, even in winter, is so mild that, with good tents, comfort is attainable. They should be careful, also, to carry as much subsistence into the country as they can; as what they purchase there, after their arrival, they will be compelled to pay a high price for.

The shortest route to California is unquestionably by the West India Mail Packets, which leave Southampton on the 17th of every month. The point to which they take passengers is Chagres. This voyage is usually accomplished in about 22 to 26 days. From thence passengers proceed across the Isthmus, a distance of about 52 miles (say three or four days' journey) to Panama, and thence 3500 miles by sea in the Pacific to St. Francisco. From the vast number of eager emigrants that it is expected will assemble at Panama, it is very probable that great delay will be occasioned from there not being sufficient number of vessels to convey them to their destination. Unless such adventurers are abundantly supplied with money, they will not be able to live in the hot desolation of the tropics, where life is but little valued, and where death is even less regarded. The entire route by sea (round Cape Horn) cannot be less than 18,500 miles, and generally occupies from five to six months, yet this route is much cheaper, safer, and in the end (from the delay that will occur at Panama) quite as short. This route, particularly to parties from England, is universally allowed to be the best many, dangers and difficulties that attend the route across the Isthmus of Panama (not noticing the probable delay) will be avoided, and many a one will bitterly regret that he was ever induced to attempt (as he perceives ship after ship sailing gallantly on to these favoured regions) what he considered a shorter route, from the want of the means of transit, while he is himself compelled idly to waste his time, a prey to pestilence and to the "hope deferred that maketh the heart sick."

APPENDIX.

The following are letters addressed to the Government at Washington, and other communications, all of which, it will be seen, are fully confirmatory of the accounts given in the preceding pages; with other details of interest relative to the state of the gold districts:

Extract from a Letter from Mr. Larkin, United States Consul at Monterey, to Mr. Buchanan, Secretary of State at Washington.

"San Francisco (Upper California), June 1, 1848.

"Sir: * * * I have to report to the State Department one of the most astonishing excitements and state of affairs now existing in this country, that, perhaps, has ever been brought to the notice of the Government. On the American fork of the Sacramento and Feather River, another branch of the same, and the adjoining lands, there has been within the present year discovered a placer, a vast tract of land containing gold, in small particles. This gold, thus far, has been taken on the bank of the river, from the surface to eighteen inches in depth, and is supposed deeper, and to extend over the country.

"On account of the inconvenience of washing, the people have, up to this time, only gathered the metal on the banks, which is done simply with a shovel, filling a shallow dish, bowl, basket, or tin pan, with a quantity of black sand, similar to the class used on paper, and washing out the sand by movement of the vessel. It is now two or three weeks since the men employed in those washings have appeared in this town with gold, to exchange for merchandise and provisions. I presume nearly 20,000 dollars of this gold has as yet been so exchanged. Some 200 or 300 men have remained up the river, or are gone to their homes, for the purpose of returning to the Placer, and washing immediately with shovels, picks, and baskets; many of them, for the first few weeks, depending on borrowing from others. I have seen the written statement of the work of one man for sixteen days, which averaged 25 dollars per day; others have, with a shovel and pan, or wooden bowl, washed out 10 dollars to even 50 dollars in a day. There are now some men yet washing who have 500 dollars to 1,000 dollars. As they have to stand two feet deep in the river, they work but a few hours in the day, and not every day in the week.

"A few men have been down in boats to this port, spending twenty to thirty ounces of gold each—about 300 dollars. I am confident that this town (San Francisco) has one-half of its tenements empty, locked up with the furniture. The owners—storekeepers, lawyers, mechanics, and labourers—all gone to the Sacramento with their families. Small parties, of five to fifteen men, have sent to this town and offered cooks ten to fifteen dollars per day for a few weeks. Mechanics and teamsters, earning the year past five to eight dollars per day, have struck and gone. Several U.S. volunteers have deserted. U.S. barque Anita, belonging to the Army, now at anchor here, has but six men. One Sandwich Island vessel in port lost all her men; and was obliged to engaged another crew at 50 dollars for the run of fifteen days to the Islands.

"One American captain having his men shipped on this coast in such a manner that they could leave at any time, had them all on the eve of quitting, when he agreed to continue their pay and food; leaving one on board, he took a boat and carried them to the gold regions—furnishing tools and giving his men one-third. They have been gone a week. Common spades and shovels, one month ago worth 1 dollar, will now bring 10 dollars, at the gold regions. I am informed 50 dollars has been offered for one. Should this gold continue as represented, this town and others would be depopulated. Clerks' wages have risen from 600 dollars to 1000 per annum, and board; cooks, 25 dollars to 30 dollars per month. This sum will not be any inducement a month longer, unless the fever and ague appears among the washers. The Californian, printed here, stopped this week. The Star newspaper office, where the new laws of Governor Mason, for this country, are printing, has but one man left. A merchant, lately from China, has even lost his China servants. Should the excitement continue through the year, and the whale-ships visit San Francisco, I think they will lose most all their crews. How Col. Mason can retain his men, unless he puts a force on the spot, I know not.

"I have seen several pounds of this gold, and consider it very pure, worth in New York 17 dollars to 18 dollars per ounce; 14 dollars to 16 dollars, in merchandise, is paid for it here. What good or bad effect this gold mania will have on California, I cannot foretell. It may end this year; but I am informed that it will continue many years. Mechanics now in this town are only wailing to finish some rude machinery, to enable them to obtain the gold more expeditiously, and free from working in the river. Up to this time, but few Californians have gone to the mines, being afraid the Americans will soon have trouble among themselves, and cause disturbance to all around. I have seen some of the black sand, as taken from the bottom of the river (I should think in the States it would bring 25 to 50 cents per pound), containing many pieces of gold; they are from the size of the head of a pin to the weight of the eighth of an ounce. I have seen some weighing one-quarter of an ounce (4 dollars). Although my statements are almost incredible, I believe I am within the statements believed by every one here. Ten days back, the excitement had not reached Monterey. I shall, within a few days, visit this gold mine, and will make another report to you. Inclosed you will have a specimen.

"I have the honour to be, very respectfully,

"THOMAS O. LARKIN.

"P.S. This placer, or gold region, is situated on public land."

"Mr. Larkin to Mr. Buchanan.

"Monterey, California, June 28, 1848.

"SIR: My last dispatch to the State Department was written in San Francisco, the 1st of this month. In that I had the honour to give some information respecting the new 'placer,' or gold regions lately discovered on the branches of the Sacramento River. Since the writing of that dispatch I have visited a part of the gold region, and found it all I had heard, and much more than I anticipated. The part that I visited was upon a fork of the American River, a branch of the Sacramento, joining the main river at Sutter's Fort. The place in which I found the people digging was about twenty-five miles from the fort by land.

"I have reason to believe that gold will be found on many branches of the Sacramento and the Joaquin rivers. People are already scattered over one hundred miles of land, and it is supposed that the 'placer' extends from river to river. At present the workmen are employed within ten or twenty yards of the river, that they may be convenient to water. On Feather river there are several branches upon which the people are digging for gold. This is two or three days' ride from the place I visited.

"At my camping place I found, on a surface of two or three miles on the banks of the river, some fifty tents, mostly owned by Americans. These had their families. There are no Californians who have taken their families as yet to the gold regions; but few or none will ever do it; some from New Mexico may do so next year, but no Californians.

"I was two nights at a tent occupied by eight Americans, viz., two sailors, one clerk, two carpenters, and three daily workmen. These men were in company; had two machines, each made from one hundred feet of boards (worth there 150 dollars, in Monterey 15 dollars—being one day's work), made similar to a child's cradle, ten feet long, without the ends.

"The two evenings I saw these eight men bring to their tents the labour of the day. I suppose they made each 50 dollars per day; their own calculation was two pounds of gold a-day—four ounces to a man—64 dollars. I saw two brothers that worked together, and only worked by washing the dirt in a tin pan, weigh the gold they obtained in one day; the result was 7 dollars to one, 82 dollars to the other. There were two reasons for this difference; one man worked less hours than the other, and by chance had ground less impregnated with gold. I give this statement as an extreme case. During my visit I was an interpreter for a native of Monterey, who was purchasing a machine or canoe. I first tried to purchase boards and hire a carpenter for him. There were but a few hundred feet of boards to be had; for these the owner asked me 50 dollars per hundred (500 dollars per thousand), and a carpenter washing gold dust demanded 50 dollars per day for working. I at last purchased a log dug out, with a riddle and sieve made of willow boughs on it, for 120 dollars, payable in gold dust at 14 dollars per ounce. The owner excused himself for the price, by saying he was two days making it, and even then demanded the use of it until sunset. My Californian has told me since, that himself, partner, and two Indians, obtained with this canoe eight ounces the first and five ounces the second day.

"I am of the opinion that on the American fork, Feather River, and Copimes River, there are near two thousand people, nine-tenths of them foreigners. Perhaps there are one hundred families, who have their teams, wagons, and tents. Many persons are waiting to see whether the months of July and August will be sickly, before they leave their present business to go to the 'Placer.' The discovery of this gold was made by some Mormons, in January or February, who for a time kept it a secret; the majority of those who are working there began in May. In most every instance the men, after digging a few days, have been compelled to leave for the purpose of returning home to see their families, arrange their business, and purchase provisions. I feel confident in saying there are fifty men in this 'Placer' who have on an average 1,000 dollars each, obtained in May and June. I have not met with any person who had been fully employed in washing gold one month; most, however, appear to have averaged an ounce per day. I think there must, by this time, be over 1,000 men at work upon the different branches of the Sacramento; putting their gains at 10,000 dollars per day, for six days in the week, appears to me not overrated.

"Should this news reach the emigration of California and Oregon, now on the road, connected with the Indian wars, now impoverishing the latter country, we should have a large addition to our population; and should the richness of the gold region continue, our emigration in 1849 will be many thousands, and in 1850 still more. If our countrymen in California, as clerks, mechanics, and work-men, will forsake employment at from 2 dollars to 6 dollars per day, how many more of the same class in the Atlantic States, earning much less, will leave for this country under such prospects? It is the opinion of many who have visited the gold regions the past and present months, that the ground will afford gold for many years, perhaps for a century. From my own examination of the rivers and their banks, I am of opinion that, at least for a few years, the golden products will equal the present year. However, as neither men of science, nor the labourers now at work, have made any explorations of consequence, it is a matter of impossibility to give any opinion as to the extent and richness of this part of California. Every Mexican who has seen the place says throughout their Republic there has never been any 'placer like this one.'

"Could Mr. Polk and yourself see California as we now see it, you would think that a few thousand people, on 100 miles square of the Sacramento valley, would yearly turn out of this river the whole price our country pays for the acquired ter-ritory. When I finished my first letter I doubted my own writing, and, to be bet-ter satisfied, showed it to one of the principal merchants of San Francisco, and to Captain Fulsom, of the Quartermaster's Department, who decided at once I was far below the reality. You certainly will suppose, from my two letters, that I am, like others, led away by the excitement of the day. I think I am not. In my last I inclosed a small sample of the gold dust, and I find my only error was in putting a value to the sand. At that time I was not aware how the gold was found; I now can describe the mode of collecting it.

"A person without a machine, after digging off one or two feet of the upper ground, near the water (in some cases they take the top earth), throws into a tin pan or wooden bowl a shovel full of loose dirt and stones; then placing the basin an inch or two under water, continues to stir up the dirt with his hand in such a manner that the running water will carry off the light earths, occasionally, with his hand, throwing out the stones; after an operation of this kind for twenty or thirty minutes, a spoonful of small black sand remains; this is on a handkerchief or cloth dried in the sun, the emerge is blown off, leaving the pure gold. I have the pleasure of inclosing a paper of this sand and gold, which I from a bucket of dirt and stones, in half-an-hour, standing at the edge of the water, washed out myself. The value of it may be 2 dollars or 3 dollars.

"The size of the gold depends in some measure upon the river from which it is taken; the banks of one river having larger grains of gold than another. I presume more than one half of the gold put into pans or machines is washed out and goes down the stream; this is of no consequence to the washers, who care only for the present time. Some have formed companies of four or five men, and have a rough-made machine put together in a day, which worked to much advantage, yet many prefer to work alone, with a wooden bowl or tin pan, worth fifteen or twenty cents in the States, but eight to sixteen dollars at the gold region. As the workmen continue, and materials can be obtained, improvements will take place in the mode of obtaining gold; at present it is obtained by standing in the water, and with much severe labour, or such as is called here severe labour.

"How long this gathering of gold by the handful will continue here, or the future effect it will have on California, I cannot say. Three-fourths of the houses in the town on the bay of San Francisco are deserted. Houses are sold at the price of the ground lots. The effects are this week showing themselves in Monterey. Almost every house I had hired out is given up. Every blacksmith, carpenter, and lawyer is leaving; brick-yards, saw-mills and ranches are left perfectly alone. A large number of the volunteers at San Francisco and Sonoma have deserted; some have been retaken and brought back; public and private vessels are losing their crews; my clerks have had 100 per cent. advance offered them on their wages to accept employment. A complete revolution in the ordinary state of affairs is taking place; both of our newspapers are discontinued from want of workmen and the loss of their agencies; the Alcaldes have left San Francisco, and I believe Sonoma likewise; the former place has not a Justice of the Peace left.

"The second Alcalde of Monterey to-day joins the keepers of our principal hotel, who have closed their office and house, and will leave to-morrow for the golden rivers. I saw on the ground a lawyer who was last year Attorney-General of the King of the Sandwich Islands, digging and washing out his ounce and a half per day; near him can be found most all his brethren of the long robe, working in the same occupation.

"To conclude; my letter is long, but I could not well describe what I have seen in less words, and I now can believe that my account may be doubted. If the affair proves a bubble, a mere excitement, I know not how we can all be deceived, as we are situated. Governor Mason and his staff have left Monterey to visit the place in question, and will, I suppose, soon forward to his department his views and opinions on this subject. Most of the land, where gold has been discovered, is public land; there are on different rivers some private grants. I have three such purchased in 1846 and 1847, but have not learned that any private lands have produced gold, though they may hereafter do so. I have the honour, dear sir, to be, very respectfully, your obedient servant,

"THOMAS O. LARKIN."

DESERTION FROM THE SHIPS.—We collate from other sources several other interesting letters and documents, and which will be found well worth perusal.

"Monterey, Sept. 15, 1848.

"Messrs. Grinnell, Minturn, and Co.:

"Sirs—I embrace this opportunity to inform you of my new situation, which is bad enough. All hands have left me but two, they will stay till the cargo is land ed and ballast in, then they will go. Both mates will leave in a few days, and then I will have only the two boys, and I am fearful that they will run. I have got all landed but 900 barrels; on Monday I shall get off ballast if the weather is good. There's no help to be got at any price. The store-ship that sailed from here ten days ago took three of my men at 100 dollars per month; there is nothing that anchors here but what loses their men. I have had a hard time in landing the cargo; I go in the boat every load. If I can get it on shore I shall save the freight. As for the ship she will lay here for a long time, for there's not the least chance of getting a crew. The coasters are giving 100 dollars per month. All the ships at San Francisco have stripped and laid up. The Flora, of New London, is at San Francisco; all left. You probably have heard of the situation of things here. A sailor will be up at the mines for two months, work on his own account, and come down with from two to three thousand dollars, and those that go in parties do much better. I have been offered 20 dollars per day to go, by one of the first men here, and work one year. It is impossible for me to give you any idea of the gold that is got here. Yours respectfully,

"CHRISTOPHER ALLEN, Captain of the ship Isaac Walton."

Another letter dated St. Francisco, September 1st, contains the following:—

"A day or two ago the Flora, Captain Potter, of New London, anchored in Whaleman's Harbour, on the opposite side of the Bay. Yesterday the captain, fearing he would lose all his men, weighed anchor, intending to go to sea. After getting under weigh, the crew, finding the ship was heading out, refused to do duty, and the captain was forced to return and anchor here. Last night nine of the crew gagged the watch, lowered one of the boats, and rowed off. They have not been heard of since, and are now probably half way to the gold region. The Flora is twenty-six months out, with only 750 bbls. of oil. Every vessel that comes in here now is sure to lose her crew, and this state of things must continue until the squadron arrives, when, if the men-o'-war-men do not run off too, merchant-men may retain their crews.

"The whale-ship Euphrates, of New Bedford, left here a few weeks since, for the United States, to touch on the coast of Chili to recruit. The Minerva, Captain Perry, of New Bedford, has abandoned the whaling business, and is now on his way hence to Valparaiso for a cargo of merchandise. Although two large ships, four barks, and eight or ten brigs and schooners have arrived here since my return from the mineral country, about four weeks since, with large cargoes of merchandise, their entire invoices have been sold. Vessels are daily arriving from the islands and ports upon the coast, laden with goods and passengers, the latter destined for the gold-washings.

"Much sickness prevails among the gold-diggers; many have left the ground sick, and many more have discontinued their labours for the present, and gone into more healthy portions of the country, intending to return after the sickly season has passed. From the best information I can obtain, there are from two to three thousand persons at work at the gold-washings with the same success as heretofore."

THE DIGGINGS.—Extract of a letter from Monterey, Aug. 29.

"At present the people are running over the country and picking it out of the earth here and there, just as a thousand hogs, let loose in a forest, would root up ground-nuts. Some get eight or ten ounces a-day, and the least active one or two. They make the most who employ the wild Indians to hunt it for them. There is one man who has sixty Indians in his employ; his profits are a dollar a-minute. The wild Indians know nothing of its value, and wonder what the pale-faces want to do with it; they will give an ounce of it for the same weight of coined silver, or a thimbleful of glass beads, or a glass of grog. And white men themselves often give an ounce of it, which is worth at our mint 18 dollars, or more, for a bottle of brandy, a bottle of soda-powders, or a plug of tobacco.

"As to the quantity which the diggers get, take a few facts as evidence. I know seven men who worked seven weeks and two days, Sundays excepted, on Feather River; they employed on an average fifty Indians, and got out in these seven weeks and two days 275 pounds of pure gold. I know the men, and have seen the gold, and know what they state to be a fact—so stick a pin there. I know ten other men who worked ten days in company, employed no Indians, and averaged in these ten days 1500 dollars each; so stick another pin there. I know another man who got out of a basin in a rock, not larger than a wash-bowl, two pounds and a half of gold in fifteen minutes; so stick another pin there! Not one of these statements would I believe, did I not know the men personally, and know them to be plain matter-of-fact men—men who open a vein of gold just as coolly as you would a potato-hill."

ASSAY OF THE GOLD.—Lieutenant Loeser having arrived at Washington with specimens of the gold from the diggings, the following account of its quality appeared in the "Washington Union," the government organ:—

"Understanding last evening that the lieutenant had arrived in this city, and had deposited in the War Office the precious specimens he had brought with him, we called to see them, and to free our mind from all hesitation as to the genuineness of the metal. We had seen doubts expressed in some of our exchange papers; and we readily admit that the accounts so nearly approached the miraculous, that we were relieved by the evidence of our own senses on the subject. The specimens have all the appearance of the native gold we had seen from the mines of North Carolina and Virginia, and we are informed that the Secretary would send the small chest, called a caddy, containing about 3,000 dollars' worth of gold, in lumps and scales, to the mint, to be melted into coins and bars. The specimens have come to Washington as they were extracted from the materials of the placer. The heaviest piece brought by Lieutenant Loeser weighs a little more than two ounces; but the varied contents of the casket (as described in Colonel Mason's schedule) will be sent off to-day, by special messenger, to the mint at Philadelphia for assay, and early next week we hope to have the pleasure of laying the result before our readers." The assay was subsequently made, and the result officially announced. The gold is declared to be from 3 to 8 per cent. purer than American standard gold coin.

ANOTHER ASSAY.—The following is the report of an assay of Californian gold dust, received by Mr. T.O. Larkin, United States consul at Monterey.

"New York, Dec. 8, 1848.

"Sir,—I have assayed the portion of gold dust, or metal, from California, which you sent me, and the result shows that it is fully equal to any found in our Southern gold mines. I return you 10-3/4 grains out of the 12 which I have tested, the value of which is 45 cents. It is 21-1/2 carats fine—within half a carat of the quality of English sovereigns or American eagles—and is almost ready to go to the mint. The finest gold metal we get is from Africa, which is 22-1/2 to 23 carats fine. In Virginia we have mines where the quality of the gold is much inferior—some of it so low as 19 carats—and in Georgia the mines produce it nearly 22 carats fine. The gold of California, which I have now assayed, is fully equal to that of any, and much superior to some produced from the mines in our Southern States.

"JOHN WARWICK, Smelter and refiner, 17, John-Street."

INCONVENIENCES OF TOO MUCH GOLD.—The following letter (January 12) from Captain Fulsom, of the United States Service, writing from San Francisco, confirms the fact of the difficulty of procuring servants, or indeed manual assistance of any description:—

"All sorts of labour is got at enormous rates of compensation. Common clerks and salesmen in the stores about town often receive as high as 2500 dollars and their board. The principal waiter in the hotel where I board is paid 1700 dollars per year, and several others from 1200 to 1500 dollars! I fortunately have an Indian boy, or I should be forced to clean my own boots, for I could not employ a good body servant for the full amount of my salary as a government officer. I believe every army officer in California, with one or two exceptions, would have resigned last summer could they have done it, and been free at once to commence for themselves. But the war was not then terminated, and no one could hope to communicate with Washington correspondents, to get an answer in less than six, and perhaps ten, months. For some time last summer (August and July) the officers at Monterey were entirely without servants; and the governor (Colonel Mason) actually took his turn in cooking for his mess."

EFFECTS OF THIS DISCOVERY ON THE UNITED STATES.—The following remarks upon the influence of this immense discovery, which appeared in a popular New York journal on the 23rd January, proves the extent of impression produced upon society in the States by the intelligence of this new source of natural wealth:—

"The news (February 12) from California will attract the observation of the whole community, A spirit is generated from those discoveries, which is more active, more intense, and more widely spread, than that which agitated Europe in the time of Columbus, Cortez, and Pizarro. There seems to be no doubt that, in a short time—probably less than two years—those mines can be made to produce 100,000,000 dollars per year. The region is the most extensive of the kind in the world, being 800 miles in length, and 100 in width, with every indication that gold exists in large native masses, in the rocks and mountains of the Sierra Nevada. But these vast gold mines are not the only mineral discoveries that have been made. The quicksilver in the same region seems to be as abundant as the gold, so that there are approximated to each other two metals, which will have a most important effect and utility in making the gold mines more valuable. Heretofore the gold and silver mines of Mexico and Peru have been valuable to Spain, because she possessed a monopoly of the quicksilver mines at Almaden in the Peninsula. This is surpassed by California. According to the last accounts now given to the public, emigrants were crowding in from every port in the Pacific to California—from Mexico, Peru, the Sandwich Islands, Oregon; and we have no doubt by this time the British possessions in the East, China, and everywhere else in that region, are furnishing emigrants to the wonderful regions of California. In less than a year there will probably be a population of 100,000 to 200,000 souls, all digging for gold, and capable of producing from 100,000,000 dollars to 300,000,000 dollars worth per annum of pure gold, to be thrown on the commerce of the world at one fell swoop.

"What is to be the effect of such vast discoveries on the commerce of the world—on old communities, on New York, London, and other great commercial cities? Such a vast addition to the gold currency of the world will at once disturb the prices and value of all productions and merchandise to a similar extent to that which we see in Monterey and San Francisco. The prices of every commodity will therefore rise extravagantly during the next few years, according to the produce of gold from that region. Now, in a rising market everything prospers; every one gets rich, civilisation expands, industry increases, and all orders of society are benefited. As soon as the first crop of gold from California reaches New York, the impulse which it will give to commercial enterprise, and the advance in the price of everything which it will cause, will be tremendous. The bank currency will be expanded, for the basis will be abundant; real estate will increase in value, agricultural productions and agricultural labour will advance at once 10, 15, 20, 30, or 40 per cent., even to as great an extent, perhaps, as was witnessed when the demand came from Ireland for the food of this country to feed the starving Irish. New York and her sister cities will be the centre of all those revolutionary movements which are certain to spring from the gold productions of California, on the commerce of the whole civilized world. Ship-building will increase in value, steam-boats will be wanted, the railroads projected across the Isthmus in various places, in Mexico and Central America will be pushed to completion, and we should not be surprised to see an active attempt made, under the auspices of the Federal Government, to construct a railroad across the continent, through the South Pass, from St. Louis, or some other point on the Mississippi, to San Francisco. The discovery of these great gold mines will no doubt form the agent of the greatest revolution in the commercial centres of the world and on the civilisation of the human race that has ever taken place since the first dawn of history. New York will henceforth, from its position to the Pacific and Atlantic Oceans, probably in less than a quarter of a century, present a population greater than that of Paris, and display evidences of wealth, grandeur, magnificence, and industry, in an equal if not greater degree than what we see in London at this day. We expect that, in the next twenty-five years, we shall make as rapid a march in this metropolis, and in the neighbouring cities, as any city has done during the last twenty-five centuries. There is no necessity for all going to California. Those who remain, and will raise produce, manufacture goods, build ships, construct steam-engines, and advance the Fine Arts, will enjoy the benefits of those discoveries to as great an extent as those who go to the Sacramento to dig for gold. All the results of the labours of those diggers must come to this metropolis, swell its magnificence, and increase the intensity of its action in commercial affairs. Even in a political point of view the discovery of these wonderful gold mines in California, under the Government of the United States, will have a wonderful and astounding effect. We should not be surprised to see, in a short time, all the old provinces of Mexico, as far as the Isthmus of Darien, knocking for admission into this union; while, on the other side, the British provinces of Canada, and even the Spanish island of Cuba, may be begging and praying to be let in at the same time, and be permitted to enjoy some of the vast advantages, and participate a little in the energy, which this vast confederacy will exhibit to the astonished world."

DISORDERS IN THE GOLD DISTRICT.—Up to the close of the year the accounts were with few exceptions favourable to the morals and habits of the masses of adventurers congregated on the banks of the San Francisco and the vicinity; subsequently the statements on these points began to change, and every letter noticed some robbery or murder, generally both, as of frequent occurrence, and at length they became so common that there was neither protection for life nor property. The following ominous intelligence, which appeared in the Washington Union (the organ of government), created an immense sensation. It was the substance of a letter from San Francisco, dated the end of December, addressed to Commodore Jones. "This letter (according to the Union) presents a desperate state of affairs as existing in California. Everything is getting worse as regards order and government. Murders and robberies were not only daily events, but occurring hourly. Within six days more than twenty murders had been perpetrated. The people were preparing to organise a provisional government in order to put a stop to these outrages. Within five days three men have been hung by Lynch Law. The United States revenue laws are now in force, and will yield 400,000 dollars the first year. The inhabitants are opposed to paying taxes."

LATEST ACCOUNTS (from the New York Press.)—The desperate state of affairs in California is fully confirmed. Murders and robberies were occurring daily. The following are particulars supplied by Lieutenant Lanman, of the United States navy, who had returned to New York, after having acted for a year past as collector at Monterey:—

"Only about an hour before he left, he saw a man on board the flag-ship, just arrived from the mines, who confirmed the previous reports in regard to the discoveries on the river Staneslow, where he had seen a single lump of gold weighing nine pounds, and heard of one that weighed twenty pounds. The gold excitement in Monterey had entirely abated, the immense mineral wealth of the country being looked upon as an established fact. There was no disposition (except among the landholders) to exaggerate. For a year past Lieutenant Lanman has been performing the duties of collector at the port of Monterey; and, having seen every man who had returned from a visit to the mines, his opportunities for obtaining authentic information were better than if he had visited the mines in person. He informs us that no large amounts of gold dust or ore were selling at a sacrifice; he does not believe that one hundred ounces of the gold dust could have been purchased at the reported rate of eight dollars, the ordinary prices ranging from ten to twelve dollars per ounce. The weekly receipts of gold at San Francisco were estimated at from thirty to fifty thousand dollars, and Lieutenant Lanman knew of one individual who had in his possession thirty thousand dollars' worth of pure ore and dust. The current value of gold in trade was sixteen dollars per ounce. There was a scarcity of coin throughout the country; but when Lieutenant Lanman arrived at Panama, he was informed that 600,000 dollars had just been shipped for California by certain Mexican gentlemen, and that the American consul at Paita (Mr. Ruden) had in charge coin of the value of 118,000 dollars, which he intends to exchange for ore and dust. Peru and Chili are not behind the United States in regard to the gold excitement, no less than twenty vessels having sailed from these two countries within a short time bound to San Francisco. They were all well laden with provisions and other necessaries of life, and their arrival would probably reduce the prices, which have heretofore been so exorbitant. The whole amount of gold collected at the washings since the excitement first broke out is variously estimated—some put it down as high as 4,000,000 of dollars, but this I think is a little too high."

A private letter says the produce of a vineyard of 1,000 vines brought 1,200 dollars; the vegetables of a garden of one acre, near San Francisco, 1,500 dollars. A snow-storm had covered the gold-diggings, and the people were leaving, on account of sickness, intending to return in the spring, which is said to be the best season for the gold harvest. Labourers, according to one letter-writer, demanded a dollar an hour! Adventurers continued to arrive at San Francisco from all parts of the world; and several persons, who were reported to be laden down with gold, were anxious to return to the United States, but could not very readily find a conveyance, as the sailors deserted the ships immediately on their arrival in port.

CALIFORNIAN GOLD 250 YEARS AGO.—Pinkerton, in an account of Drake's discovery of a part of California, to which he gave the name of New Albion, states:—"The country, too, if we can depend upon what Sir Francis Drake or his chaplain say, may appear worth the seeking and the keeping, since they assert that the land is so rich in gold and silver, that upon the slightest turning it up with a spade or pick-axe, these rich metals plainly appear mixed with the mould. It may be objected that this looks a little fabulous; but to this two satisfactory answers may be given: the first is, that later discoveries on the same coast confirm the truth of it, which for anything I can see ought to put the fact out of question; but if any doubts should remain, my second answer should overturn these. For I say next, that the country of New Mexico lies directly behind New Albion, on the other side of a narrow bay, and in that country are the mines of Santa Fe, which are allowed to be the richest in the world; here, then, is a valuable country, to which we have a very fair title."

EFFECTS OF THE CALIFORNIAN NEWS IN ENGLAND.—A glance at the advertisements in the daily papers (says the Examiner) will show that the public appetite for California is likely to be promptly met. The burden of the various vessels already announced as ready for immediate departure amounts to about 5,000 tons, distributed in ships ranging from 190 to 700 tons, to say nothing of the West India mail-steamer, which leaves on the 17th, carrying goods and passengers to Chagres, or of a "short and pleasant passage" advertised to Galveston, in Texas, as a cheap route to the Pacific. The rates range from L25 upwards to suit all classes. Thus far, however, we have only the arrangements for those who are able to move. The opportunities provided for those who wish to share the advantages of the new region without its dangers are still more ample. Indeed, so imposing are the plans for an extensive investment of capital for carrying on the trade in shares of L5 each, that it would seem as if the first effect of the affair would be to cause a scarcity of money rather than an abundance. About a million and a quarter sterling is already wanted, and the promoters stipulate for the power of doubling the proposed amounts as occasion may offer. There is a "California Gold-Coast Trading Association;" a "California Gold Mining, Streaming, and Washing Company;" a "California Steam Trading Company," a "California Gold and Trading Company;" and a "California Gold Mining, etc., Trading Company." The last of these alone will require L600,000 for its objects, but as half the shares are "to be reserved for the United States of America," the drain upon our resources will be lessened to that extent. Some of the concerns propose to limit their operations to trading on the coast, sending out at the same time "collecting and exploring parties" whenever the prospect may be tempting. Others intend at once to get a grant from the legislature at Washington of such lands "as they may deem necessary," while others intend to trust to chance, simply sending out a "practical" manager, accompanied by an adequate number of men "accustomed to the extraction of gold in all its forms." Along with these advertisements are some of a modified nature, to suit parties who may neither wish to go out with a batch of emigrants, nor to stay at home and wait the results of a public company. One "well-educated gentleman" seeks two others "to share expenses with him." Another wishes for a companion who would advance L200, "one half to leave his wife, and the other half for outfit;" a third tells where "any respectable individuals with small capital" may find persons willing to join them; a fourth states that respectable persons having not less than L100 are wanted to complete a party; and a fifth, that a "seafaring man is ready to go equal shares in purchasing a schooner to sail on speculation." What number may be found to answer those appeals it is impossible to conjecture. Common sense would say not one, but experience of what has been practised over and over again reminds us that the active parties on the present occasion are not calculating too largely upon the credulity of their countrymen. That the country will be a pandemonium long before any one can reach it from this side is hardly to be doubted, unless, indeed, the United States government shall have been able to establish a blockade and cordon, in which case the new arrivals will have to get back as well as they can.

PROBABLE EFFECT ON THE CURRENCY IN EUROPE.—In the description of gold mines, and rivers flowing over golden sands, we must be prepared for a little over-colouring. Such discoveries have always excited sanguine hopes, and dreams of exhaustless wealth; but if the accounts—and they really appear well authenticated—of the golden treasures of California be true, quantities of the most precious of all metals are found—not buried in mines, but scattered on the surface of the earth, and the fortunate adventurer may enrich himself beyond the dreams of avarice, almost without labour, without capital, and with no care but that which cupidity generates. The principle that the value of the precious metals, like other products of industry, is determined primarily by the cost of production, and then by scarcity, ideas of utility, and convenience, seems to be neutralized by this new discovery; and it becomes a curious question, how far it may affect the value of gold and silver in Europe. If the abundance of gold flowing from America be such as to exceed the demand, the value of gold will fall, and the price of all other commodities relatively rise, and the relative proportion between gold and silver be disturbed so as to affect the standards of value in each country and the par of exchange between one and another. The productiveness of the silver mines, there is no doubt, is greater and more regular than those of gold; but the enormous increase of the silver currency on the Continent, in the United States, and even in India, and our own colonies, has kept the price of silver a little below five shillings an ounce. On the other hand the English standard of value being gold only, the drain of gold is generally towards England, while that of silver is towards the Continent. We do not doubt that the English Mint price of gold, L3 17s. 10-1/2d. an ounce, and the price at which the Bank of England are compelled to purchase, L3 17s. 9d. an ounce, are causes which not only regulate, but, within certain limits, determine, the price of gold throughout the world. Suppose, for a moment, the circulation of England, exceeding thirty millions and the Bank store of fifteen millions, to be thrown on the markets of Europe, by an alteration of the standard of value—how material would be the fall in price! It is equally obvious that England would be first and most materially affected by any large and sudden production of her standard of value; for though America would be enriched by the discovery of the precious metals within her own territories, it is only because she would possess a larger fund to exchange for more useful and necessary products of labour. The value of silver would not fall, assuming the supply and demand to be equalised, but gold would fall in relation to silver, and the existing proportion (about 15 to 1) could no longer be maintained. Then prices would rise of all articles now estimated in our currency—i.e. an ounce of gold would exchange for less than at present. And, assuming the price of silver to keep up as heretofore, about 5s. an ounce, our sovereign would be valued less in other countries, and all exchange operations would be sensibly affected. The only countervailing influence in the reduction of gold to, say, only double the price of silver, would be an increased consumption in articles of taste and manufacture, which, however, can only be speculative and uncertain. It is said by accounts from California that five hundred miles lie open to the avarice of gold-hunters, and that some adventurers have collected from 1,200 to 1,800 dollars a-day; the probable average of each man's earnings being from 8 to 10 dollars a-day, or, let us say, L2. The same authority avers there is room and verge enough for the profitable working, to that extent, of a hundred thousand persons. And it is likely enough before long that such a number may be tempted to seek their easily acquired fortune in the golden sands of El Sacramento and elsewhere. Now two pounds a-day for each man would amount to L200,000, which, multiplied by 300 working days, will give L60,000,000 a-year! That is, L600,000,000 in ten years! A fearful amount of gold dust, and far more than enough to disturb the equanimity of ten thousand political economists. The gold utensils found among the simple-minded and philosophic Peruvians (who wondered at the eager desire of Christians for what they scarcely valued), will be esteemed trifles with our golden palaces, and halls paved with gold, when California shall have poured this vast treasure into Europe. Assuming in round numbers each 2,000 lbs., or troy ton, to be equivalent to L100,000 sterling, the above amount in one year would represent six hundred tons, and in ten years six thousand tons of gold! The imagination of all-plodding industrious England is incapable of grasping so great an idea! Can there be any doubt, then, of a revolution in the value of the precious metals?

PROHIBITION FROM THE GOVERNMENT.—It would seem that the government have at length taken measures to preserve the gold districts from the bands of foreign adventurers who are daily pouring in from every quarter. Towards the end of January we learn that General Smith had been sent out by the United States government, with orders to enforce the laws against all persons, not citizens of the States, who should be found trespassing on the public lands. Official notice to this effect was issued to the American consul at Panama and other places, in order that emigrants on their way to California might be made aware of the determination of the government previous to their arrival. The punishment for illegal trespassing is fine and imprisonment. It was not known, at the date of the last intelligence from California how this notification, which makes such an important change in the prospects of the numerous bodies now on their way thither, has been received by the population assembled at the land of promise.

JOURNEY FROM ARKANSAS TO CALIFORNIA.

The following general view of the nature of the country which divides the United States from California is taken from a narrative, published by Lieutenant Emory, of a journey from the Arkansas to the newly annexed territory of the United States.

"The country," says the lieutenant, "from the Arkansas to the Colorado, a distance of over 1200 miles, in its adaptation to agriculture, has peculiarities which must for ever stamp itself upon the population which inhabits it. All North Mexico, embracing New Mexico, Chihuahua, Sonora, and the Californias, as far north as the Sacramento, is, as far as the best information goes, the same in the physical character of its surface, and differs but little in climate and products. In no part of this vast tract can the rains from heaven be relied upon, to any extent, for the cultivation of the soil. The earth is destitute of trees, and in great part also of any vegetation whatever. A few feeble streams flow in different directions from the great mountains, which in many places traverse this region. These streams are separated, sometimes by plains, and sometimes by mountains, without water and without vegetation, and may be called deserts, so far as they perform any useful part in the sustenance of animal life.

"The whole extent of country, except on the margin of streams, is destitute of forest trees. The Apaches, a very numerous race, and the Navajoes, are the chief occupants, but there are many minor bands, who, unlike the Apaches and Navajoes, are not nomadic, but have fixed habitations. Amongst the most remarkable of these are the Soones, most of whom are said to be Albinoes. The latter cultivate the soil, and live in peace with their more numerous and savage neighbours. Departing from the ford of the Colorado in the direction of Sonora, there is a fearful desert to encounter. Alter, a small town, with a Mexican garrison, is the nearest settlement. All accounts concur in representing the journey as one of extreme hardship, and even peril. The distance is not exactly known, but it is variously represented at from four to seven days' journey. Persons bound for Sonora from California, who do not mind a circuitous route, should ascend the Gila as far as the Pimos village, and thence penetrate the province by way of Tucson. At the ford, the Colorado is 1,500 feet wide, and flows at the rate of a mile and a half per hour. Its greatest depth in the channel, at the ford where we crossed, is four feet. The banks are low, not more than four feet high, and, judging from indications, sometimes, though not frequently, overflowed. Its general appearance at this point is much like that of the Arkansas, with its turbid waters and shifting sand islands."

The narrative of Lieut. Emory, of his journey from this point across the Desert of California, becomes highly interesting and characteristic.

"November 26.—The dawn of day found every man on horseback, and a bunch of grass from the Colorado tied behind him on the cantle of his saddle. After getting well under way, the keen air at 26 deg. Fahrenheit made it most comfortable to walk. We travelled four miles along the sand butte, in a southern direction; we mounted the buttes and found a firmer footing covered with fragments of lava, rounded by water, and many agates. We were now fairly on the desert.

"Our course now inclined a few degrees more to the north, and at 10, A.M., we found a large patch of grama, where we halted for an hour, and then pursued our way over the plains covered with fragments of lava, traversed at intervals by sand buttes, until 4, P.M., when, after travelling 24 miles, we reached the Alamo or cotton-wood. At this point, the Spaniards informed us, that, failing to find water, they had gone a league to the west, in pursuit of their horses, where they found a running stream. We accordingly sent parties to search, but neither the water nor their trail could be found. Neither was there any cotton-wood at the Alamo, as its name would signify; but it was nevertheless the place, the tree having probably been covered by the encroachments of the sand, which here terminates in a bluff 40 feet high, making the arc of a great circle convexing to the north. Descending this bluff, we found in what had been the channel of a stream, now overgrown with a few ill-conditioned mesquite, a large hole where persons had evidently dug for water. It was necessary to halt to rest our animals, and the time was occupied in deepening this hole, which, after a strong struggle, showed signs of water. An old champagne basket, used by one of the officers as a pannier, was lowered in the hole, to prevent the crumbling of the sand. After many efforts to keep out the caving sand, a basket-work of willow twigs effected the object, and, much to the joy of all, the basket, which was now 15 or 20 feet below the surface, filled with water. The order was given for each mess to draw a kettle of water, and Captain Turner was placed in charge of the spring, to see fair distribution.

"When the messes were supplied, the firmness of the banks gave hopes that the animals might be watered, and each party was notified to have their animals in waiting; the important business of watering then commenced, upon the success of which depended the possibility of their advancing with us a foot further. Two buckets for each animal were allowed. At 10, A.M., when my turn came, Captain Moore had succeeded, by great exertions, in opening another well, and the one already opened began to flow more freely, in consequence of which, we could afford to give each animal as much as it could drink. The poor brutes, none of which had tasted water in forty-eight hours, and some not for the last sixty, clustered round the well and scrambled for precedence. At 12 o'clock I had watered all my animals, thirty-seven in number, and turned over the well to Captain Moore. The animals still had an aching void to fill, and all night was heard the munching of sticks, and their piteous cries for more congenial food.

"November 27 and 28.—To-day we started a few minutes after sunrise. Our course was a winding one, to avoid the sand-drifts. The Mexicans had informed us that the waters of the salt lake, some thirty or forty miles distant, were too salt to use, but other information led us to think the intelligence was wrong. We accordingly tried to reach it; about 3, P.M., we disengaged ourselves from the sand, and went due (magnetic) west, over an immense level of clay detritus, hard and smooth as a bowling-green. The desert was almost destitute of vegetation;

now and then an Ephedra, Oenothera, or bunches of Aristida were seen, and occasionally the level was covered with a growth of Obione canescens, and a low bush with small oval plaited leaves, unknown. The heavy sand had proved too much for many horses and some mules, and all the efforts of their drivers could bring them no further than the middle of this desert. About 8 o'clock, as we approached the lake, the stench of dead animals confirmed the reports of the Mexicans, and put to flight all hopes of being able to use the water.

"The basin of the lake, as well as I could judge at night, is about three-quarters of a mile long and half a mile wide. The water had receded to a pool, diminished to one half its size, and the approach to it, was through a thick soapy quagmire. It was wholly unfit for man or brute, and we studiously kept the latter from it, thinking that the use of it would but aggravate their thirst. One or two of the men came in late, and, rushing to the lake, threw themselves down and took many swallows before discovering their mistake; but the effect was not injurious except that it increased their thirst. A few mezquite trees and a chenopodiaceous shrub bordered the lake, and on these our mules munched till they had sufficiently refreshed themselves, when the call to saddle was sounded, and we groped silently our way in the dark. The stoutest animals now began to stagger, and when day dawned scarcely a man was seen mounted.

"With the sun rose a heavy fog from the south-west, no doubt from the gulf, and, sweeping towards us, enveloped us for two or three hours, wetting our blankets and giving relief to the animals. Before it had disappeared we came to a patch of sun-burned grass. When the fog had entirely dispersed we found ourselves entering a gap in the mountains, which had been before us for four days. The plain was crossed, but we had not yet found water. The first valley we reached was dry, and it was not till 12 o'clock, M., that we struck the Cariso (cane) creek, within half a mile of one of its sources, and although so close to the source, the sands had already absorbed much of its water, and left but little running. A mile or two below, the creek entirely disappears. We halted, having made fifty-four miles in the two days, at the source, a magnificent spring, twenty or thirty feet in diameter, highly impregnated with sulphur, and medicinal in its properties.

"The desert over which we had passed, ninety miles from water to water, is an immense triangular plain, bounded on one side by the Colorado, on the west by the Cordilleras of California, the coast chain of mountains which now encircles us, extending from the Sacramento river to the southern extremity of Lower California, and on the north-east by a chain of mountains, running southeast and northwest. It is chiefly covered with floating sand, the surface of which in various places is white, with diminutive spinelas, and everywhere over the whole surface is found the large and soft muscle shell. I have noted the only two patches of grass found during the 'jornada.' There were scattered, at wide intervals, the Palafoxia linearis, Atriplex, Encelia farinosa, Daleas, Euphorbias, and a Simsia, described by Dr. Torrey as a new species.

"The southern termination of this desert is bounded by the Tecate chain of mountains and the Colorado; but its northern and eastern boundaries are undefined, and I should suppose from the accounts of trappers, and others, who have attempted the passage from California to the Gila by a more northern route, that it extends many days' travel beyond the chain of barren mountains which bound the horizon in that direction. The portal to the mountains through which we passed was formed by immense buttes of yellow clay and sand, with large flakes of mica and seams of gypsum. Nothing could be more forlorn and desolate in appearance. The gypsum had given some consistency to the sand buttes, which were washed into fantastic figures. One ridge formed apparently a complete circle, giving it the appearance of a crater; and although some miles to the left, I should have gone to visit it, supposing it to be a crater, but my mule was sinking with thirst, and water was yet at some distance. Many animals were left on the road to die of thirst and hunger, in spite of the generous efforts of the men to bring them to the spring. More than one was brought up, by one man tugging at the halter and another pushing up the brute, by placing his shoulder against its buttocks. Our most serious loss, perhaps, was that of one or two fat mares and colts brought with us for food; for, before leaving camp, Major Swords found in a concealed place one of the best pack mules slaughtered, and the choice bits cut from his shoulders and flanks, stealthily done by some mess less provident than others.

"Nov. 29.—The grass at the spring was anything but desirable for our horses, and there was scarcely a ration left for the men. This last consideration would not prevent our giving the horses a day's rest wherever grass could be found. We followed the dry sandy bed of the Cariso nearly all day, at a snail's pace, and at length reached the 'little pools' where the grass was luxuriant but very salt. The water strongly resembled that at the head of the Cariso creek, and the earth, which was very tremulous for many acres about the pools, was covered with salt. This valley is not more than half a mile wide, and on each side are mountains of grey granite and pure quartz, rising from 1,000 to 3,000 feet above it.

"We rode for miles through thickets of the centennial plant, Agave Americana, and found one in full bloom. The sharp thorns terminating every leaf of this plant were a great annoyance to our dismounted and wearied men, whose legs were now almost bare. A number of these plants were cut by the soldiers, and the body of them used as food. The day was intensely hot, and the sand deep; the animals, inflated with water and rushes, gave way by scores; and although we advanced only sixteen miles, many did not arrive at camp until 10 o'clock at night. It was a feast day for the wolves, which followed in packs close on our track, seizing our deserted brutes, and making the air resound with their howls as they battled for the carcases.

"December 12.—We followed the Solidad through a deep fertile valley in the shape of a cross. Here we ascended to the left a steep hill to the table lands, which, keeping for a few miles, we descended into a waterless valley, leading into False Bay at a point distant two or three miles from San Diego. At this place we were in view of the fort overlooking the town of San Diego and the barren waste which surrounds it.

"The town consists of a few adobe houses, two or three of which only have plank floors. It is situated at the foot of a high hill on a sand flat, two miles wide, reaching from the head of San Diego Bay to False Bay. A high promontory, of nearly the same width, runs into the sea four or five miles, and is connected by the flat with the main land. The road to the hide-houses leads on the east side of this promontory, and abreast of them the frigate Congress and the sloop Portsmouth are at anchor. The hide-houses are a collection of store-houses where the hides of cattle are packed before being shipped, this article forming the only trade of the little town.

"The bay is a narrow arm of the sea indenting the land some four or five miles, easily defended, and having twenty feet of water at the lowest tide. The rise is five feet, making the greatest water twenty-five feet.

"Standing on the hill which overlooks the town, and looking to the north-east, I saw the mission of San Diego, a fine large building now deserted. The Rio San Diego runs under ground in a direct course from the mission to the town, and, sweeping around the hill, discharges itself into the bay. Its original debouche was into False bay, where, meeting the waters rolling in from the seaward, a bar was formed by the deposit of sand, making the entrance of False Bay impracticable.

"January 2.—Six and a half miles' march brought us to the deserted mission of San Luis Rey. The keys of this mission were in charge of the alcalde of the Indian village, a mile distant. He was at the door to receive us and deliver up possession. There we halted for the day, to let the sailors, who suffered dreadfully from sore feet, recruit a little. This building is one which, for magnitude, convenience, and durability of architecture, would do honour to any country.

"The walls are adobe, and the roofs of well-made tile. It was built about sixty years since by the Indians of the country, under the guidance of a zealous priest. At that time the Indians were very numerous, and under the absolute sway of the missionaries. These missionaries at one time bid fair to christianize the Indians of California. Under grants from the Mexican government, they collected them into missions, built immense houses, and began successfully to till the soil by the hands of the Indians for the benefit of the Indians.

"The habits of the priests, and the avarice of the military rulers of the territory, however, soon converted these missions into instruments of oppression and slavery of the Indian race.

"The revolution of 1836 saw the downfall of the priests, and most of these missions passed by fraud into the hands of private individuals, and with them the Indians were transferred as serfs of the land.

"This race, which, in our country, has never been reduced to slavery, is in that degraded condition throughout California, and does the only labour performed in the country. Nothing can exceed their present degradation."

The general closing remarks of Lieutenant Emory are as follow:

"The region extending from the head of the Gulf of California to the parallel of the Pueblo, or Ciudad de los Angeles, is the only portion not heretofore covered by my own notes and journal, or by the notes and journals of other scientific expeditions fitted out by the United States. The journals and published accounts of these several expeditions combined will give definite ideas of all those portions of California susceptible of cultivation or settlement. From this remark is to be excepted the vast basin watered by the Colorado, and the country lying between that river and the range of Cordilleras, represented as running east of the Tulare lakes, and south of the parallel of 36 deg., and the country between the Colorado and Gila rivers.

"Of these regions nothing is known except from the reports of trappers, and the speculations of geologists. As far as these accounts go, all concur in representing it as a waste of sand and rock, unadorned with vegetation, poorly watered, and unfit, it is believed, for any of the useful purposes of life. A glance at the map will show what an immense area is embraced in these boundaries; and, notwithstanding the oral accounts in regard to it, it is difficult to bring the mind to the belief in the existence of such a sea of waste and desert; when every other grand division of the earth presents some prominent feature in the economy of nature, administering to the wants of man. Possibly this unexplored region may be filled with valuable minerals.

"Where irrigation can be had in this country, the produce of the soil is abundant beyond description. All the grains and fruits of the temperate zones, and many of those of the tropical, flourish luxuriantly. Descending from the heights of San Barnardo to the Pacific one meets every degree of temperature. Near the coast, the winds prevailing from the south-west in winter, and from the north-west in summer, produce a great uniformity of temperature, and the climate is perhaps unsurpassed in salubrity. With the exception of a very few cases of ague and fever of a mild type, sickness is unknown.

"The season of the year at which we visited the country was unfavourable to obtaining a knowledge of its botany. The vegetation, mostly deciduous, had gone to decay, and no flowers nor seeds were collected. The country generally is entirely destitute of trees. Along the principal range of the mountains are a few live oaks, sycamore and pine; now and then, but very rarely, the sycamore and cottonwood occur in the champaign country, immediately on the margins of the streams. Wild oats everywhere cover the surface of the hills, and these, with the wild mustard and carrots, furnish good pasturage to the immense herds of cattle which form the staple of California. Of the many fruits capable of being produced with success, by culture and irrigation, the grape is perhaps that which is brought nearest to perfection. Experienced wine-growers and Europeans, pronounce this portion of California unequalled for the quality of its wines."